The Smiling Dog Café
2 Novellas

Neil S. Plakcy

Copyright 2025 Neil S. Plakcy

This book is a work of fiction. Names, characters, places, and incidents either are products of the author's imagination or are used fictitiously. Any resemblance to actual events or locales or persons, living or dead, is entirely coincidental. All rights reserved, including the right of reproduction in whole or in part in any form.

NO AI TRAINING: Without in any way limiting the author's [and publisher's] exclusive rights under copyright, any use of this publication to "train" generative artificial intelligence (AI) technologies to generate text is expressly prohibited. The author reserves all rights to license uses of this work for generative AI training and development of machine learning language models.

Code of Silence
a Smiling Dog Café Story

Chapter 1
A Carefully Constructed Life

"I can't keep waiting for you to be ready," Jeff's girlfriend Anna said, zipping her overnight bag. Late afternoon light slanted through the living room's west-facing window, catching dust motes disturbed by her packing. The radiator clanked and hissed, fighting November's early chill, but the old apartment never quite got warm enough - one of the many small imperfections Jeff had learned to live with.

He watched her pack the few items she'd gradually brought over: her toothbrush still wet from morning use, the chipped coffee mug with its faint lipstick stains, the dog-eared copy of *The Hours* by Michael Cunningham that had lived on her side of the bed. Each object disappeared into her bag with quiet finality, leaving empty spaces - a bathroom counter too clean, a kitchen shelf too bare, a bedside table collecting dust where her book should be.

"I can change," he said, but even he could hear the hollowness in his voice.

"No, you can't. Or won't." She paused at the door, adjusting her scarf against the draft that always crept under it. "That's the thing about you, Jeff. You're so afraid of making a wrong move that you never make a move at all." She reached up as if to touch his face, then let her hand fall. "I hope someday you figure out what you're so afraid of."

The door closed behind her with a soft click. Jeff stood in the living room, all the words he should have said settling around him like dust.

He retreated to his computer desk, the familiar glow of multiple monitors offering their cold comfort. Here, at least, things made sense. For months he'd been working on a side project in his free time - a program to help small non-profits match volunteers with opportunities. He'd started it after Anna mentioned her mother's struggles coordinating volunteers at the local food bank. With Anna gone, would her mother welcome a call from Jeff if he finished it?

It didn't matter. What was important was the code, which welcomed him back like an old friend. Variables behaved according to clear rules, functions returned predictable results, algorithms either worked or they didn't. No messy emotions, no complicated expectations, no disappointment. Just pure logic, clean and safe.

Hours slipped by as he lost himself in the work. Only when his stomach growled did he realize he'd missed dinner. The apartment had grown dark around him, city lights casting familiar shadows. He'd been automatically adjusting his code to account for different time zones, making sure volunteers and organizations could connect across geographic boundaries. Something about that tickled the back of his mind - a pattern he'd seen somewhere else, recently, at work maybe.

He nuked a TV dinner, though the food tasted like ash. Then he stripped and slid into his bed, which felt too big that night, Anna's side already cold. He reached automatically for her, finding only empty sheets. The radiator knocked once, twice, a syncopated rhythm that usually lulled him to sleep but tonight just emphasized his solitude. That pattern in the code kept nagging at him as he drifted off - something about connections, about systems talking to each other across boundaries.

He bolted awake at 3 AM, the realization hitting him like a surge of electricity. The volunteer matching system used the same type of cross-boundary protocols as Incredible Solutions' client database. And if his security measures for the volunteer system were necessary, then surely the same vulnerabilities must exist in the work system.

Sleep eluded him after that. He spent the pre-dawn hours documenting his thoughts, the rising sun finding him surrounded by notebooks filled with diagrams and calculations. By the time he headed to the office, stubble-faced and over-caffeinated, he knew exactly what he was looking for.

The fluorescent lights of the cube farm where Jeff worked buzzed overhead as he hurried to his desk. His cubicle, wedged between the break room and the emergency exit, was filled with the competing scents of burnt coffee and printer toner. The drone of office life surrounded him: keyboards clicking, phones ringing, the soft whir of the ancient HVAC system that never quite managed to regulate the temperature. Phil the Third, his long-suffering philodendron, drooped on the filing cabinet, its leaves edged with brown despite Jeff's careful watering schedule.

His hands trembled as he traced the pattern on his monitor for the third time. Taped-up documentation and network diagrams covered his cubicle walls, their overlapping patterns now seeming to scream of vulnerability. The morning's coffee sat cold and forgotten beside his keyboard as he spread printouts across his desk.

When he was sure beyond a doubt that he'd figured out where the code broke down, he gathered his diagrams and walked over to his supervisor's office. He spread them out and pointed to the pattern he'd discovered. "Dave, we have a problem. See these dependencies? The entire codebase is compromised. If someone found this, they could access any client's data."

Dave barely glanced up from his phone, the blue light reflecting off his glasses. "Write up a patch."

"That's just it - we can't patch this. The whole system needs to be restructured. I've documented everything here."

"Look," Dave cut him off, "the quarterly review is next week. Just keep it running until then, okay? We can deal with infrastructure issues later."

That evening, bone-tired from arguing with Dave, and struggling to find a patch that would hold, Jeff trudged home through the early darkness. Red and yellow warning tape fluttered in the wind around his building's entrance, a harsh splash of color against grimy brick. Construction dust from the high-rise site next door coated everything - the sidewalk, the stunted street trees, the line of trash cans waiting forlornly for pickup. Each gust carried the metallic taste of approaching winter, mixed with diesel fumes from the idling police cruiser.

Two officers stood by the entrance, next to a yellow notice taped to the door.

"Sorry, sir, this building has been condemned," the taller officer said. His nametag read 'Baptiste.' "Structural damage from the construction next door."

"But I live here. Apartment 3B."

Baptiste checked his clipboard and handed over an envelope. Inside: a notice from his landlord, a voucher for a week at a local hotel, instructions to call about finding a new apartment.

"You can take one supervised trip inside to collect essentials," Baptiste said. "That's all we can allow."

Officer Baptiste's boots left gray footprints on the worn carpet as they climbed to 3B. The hallway's familiar scents - Mrs. Kumar's curry from 3A, the super's cigarette smoke, the lingering mustiness of old radiator heat - felt suddenly precious, soon to be lost forever. Jeff's key stuck in the lock one last time, the familiar sideways jiggle required to open it now a farewell gesture.

A stack of flattened moving boxes leaned against the hallway wall - the landlord's one concession to his displacement. Inside, his apartment felt both intimate and strange. Early evening shadows stretched across the scratched hardwood floors where his furniture had left permanent impressions. The kitchen still smelled faintly of last night's microwave dinner, dishes left unwashed in his numbness after Anna's departure.

Jeff began with his computers, wrapping each monitor in blankets before placing them in boxes. The machines represented thousands of hours of careful collection: salvaged parts, upgraded components, each one rescued and restored. Like the gaming rig he and his college girlfriend Madeline had built, staying up all night to get the cooling system just right, her laughter when they'd finally powered it up and the fans had sounded like a jet engine.

He shook off the memory and moved to his books. Computer science textbooks from Columbia, programming manuals, tech magazines - each one marking a different phase of his career. The box grew heavy with knowledge that hadn't prevented this moment. His clothes took less time - he'd never been one for excess, even after Madeline tried to expand his wardrobe beyond hoodies and jeans.

Officer Baptiste helped him carry the boxes downstairs. Six boxes, two suitcases, and three garbage bags - his entire life Tetris-ed into the back of an Uber XL. The driver looked annoyed at the number of boxes but helped load them anyway.

"The Newton Hotel," Jeff said, sliding into the back seat. Through the window, he watched his building shrink in the twilight. Four years of careful routine, of building a space that felt safe, all reduced to what could fit in the back of a stranger's SUV.

The Newton Hotel had seen better days. The red brick Victorian mansion still wore traces of its 1890s grandeur: elaborate cornices, tall bay windows, and an imposing front door flanked by grimy stained-glass panels. Decades of neglect had turned it shabby - paint peeling from the ornate trim, concrete steps crumbling, iron security gates installed over the once-elegant windows. A neon "VACANCY" sign buzzed and flickered in a second-floor window, casting intermittent pink light over the building's worn facade.

Jeff's first-floor room faced the busy street, every passing truck making the thin windows rattle in their frames. The bedspread, a faded floral pattern in browns and oranges, held decades of other people's misfortune. A water stain on the ceiling resembled a map of Florida, and the mini-fridge hummed off-key, competing with the wheeze of the ancient wall unit that pumped in air that smelled of mildew and resignation.

He laid his suit - the good one, the one he'd worn to his last three job interviews - across the room's single chair, trying not to notice the cigarette burn on the armrest. At least he still had his job. He set up a single computer and fiddled with his charity project for a few hours. It calmed his mind, so he was able to push away his losses and try to sleep on sheets that smelled of industrial bleach and strangers.

The next morning, there was a note on his desk asking him to report to Sharon, the director of HR, before he got started on his day. He left his coat on the chair and walked down to her office, which felt too warm after the cold outside. The heat made Jeff's shirt stick to his back as he sat across from her.

"Jeff." Her voice carried practiced sympathy. "Last night the executive team sat down with the work you passed on to Dave about system vulnerabilities. They made a decision based on your findings."

Hope flickered briefly. Maybe they'd finally listened.

"We're outsourcing the entire development team. Starting fresh with an overseas contractor." She slid a packet across her desk, 'Termination' stamped across the top. "Your position has been eliminated, effective immediately."

Jeff's mouth opened, then closed. The words he should say pressed against his throat: about the system's vulnerabilities, about how an overseas team wouldn't understand its quirks, about how they were putting people's data at risk. For once in his life, he had every right to speak up, to fight back. But Sharon's practiced sympathy, so much like his mother's careful silences, drained the fight from him before it could begin.

He walked back to his cubicle in a daze. Boris's posters advertising Russian punk bands were already gone, while a white envelopes sat on Claire's desk like a tombstone.

Dave's office door stood open, his desk cleared except for a company-issued monitor. How many people had his discovery affected? Five? Ten? All those lives upended because he couldn't keep his mouth shut about the system's flaws.

His own cubicle felt suddenly foreign. He pulled down his diagrams with trembling hands, each one a testament to his obsession with perfection that had somehow led to this moment. The small Columbia lion that Madeline had given him their senior year still guarded his monitor, its blue ribbon faded but intact. Into the cardboard box it went, along with a picture frame from the Metropolitan Museum of Art holding a photo of the two of them mugging for the camera.

A coffee mug with the Aether logo followed. It was the first piece of swag his friend Shaheer had commissioned to promote his new business. His collection of jump drives, each one holding information from past projects that he might need to refer to. He carefully placed Phil the Third on the top. Somehow the bedraggled plant had somehow survived three office moves.

At the bottom drawer, he paused. The group photo from last year's holiday party caught his eye - everyone smiling, unaware their jobs would disappear because of his need to fix what was broken. He closed the drawer without taking the photo. Some memories were better left behind.

The elevator's mirrored walls reflected his face from four angles as he descended - pale, shocked, clutching his cardboard box. The security guard who had greeted him every morning for two years now watched him walk out, just another casualty of corporate restructuring.

Wind whipped between the buildings as he started his walk back to the hotel, carrying the salt-tang of the Brooklyn Marine Terminal mixed with diesel exhaust and decay. His shoe caught a crack in the sidewalk - the same one he'd stepped over every day, now registering for the first time. The cardboard box grew heavier with each block, Phil the Third's remaining leaves brushing against his chin.

His mother's voice echoed in his head: "Bad news always comes in threes, Jeffrey. Best to get them all at once and be done with it."

Anna leaving. The building condemned. Now this.

That's when he saw the dog - golden fur catching weak sunlight, eyes watching him with impossible understanding. But more striking was the scent that followed it: warm cinnamon and fresh bread, so real he could almost taste it, so out of place in this industrial wasteland that he stopped walking. The dog tilted its head, then turned and padded away, glancing back as if expecting Jeff to follow.

Without thinking, Jeff did. Through narrow streets and past shuttered warehouses, following that incongruous scent of warmth and comfort. The dog led him to a weathered brick building, where a hand-painted sign hung above a door: "The Smiling Dog Café." Light spilled from its windows, golden and inviting, and the cinnamon scent grew stronger.

The dog slipped through the open door, but Jeff stood frozen on the sidewalk. The wind picked up and he clutched his box tighter, feeling the weight of his carefully constructed life crumbling around him. Twelve years since he'd let Madeline board that plane to California without speaking the words that might have changed everything. Twelve years of playing it safe, of keeping his head down, of avoiding any risk that might lead to pain.

And where had it gotten him? Standing in the cold Brooklyn wind, staring at a café door that promised warmth he didn't deserve. Thunder rumbled overhead as the approaching storm gathered strength, but Jeff remained rooted to the spot, caught between the safety of his silence and whatever waited behind that door.

Chapter 2
Mason City

The scent of cinnamon grew stronger, and something inside Jeff - something that had been sleeping for a very long time - began to stir. With it came memories he'd spent years trying to forget, flooding back with sudden clarity: his father's thundering voice, his mother's careful silences, and one small dog who had taught him both the safety and danger of unconditional love.

Jeff's mother cleaned the houses of rich people, and every now and then she'd bring home something for Jeff. It was never perfect or new, always something used that her employers had wanted to throw away. T-shirts from rock concerts someone had attended, and then lost interest in the band. Leftovers from meals his family couldn't afford to eat at expensive restaurants, the meat and vegetables smashed together in Styrofoam containers. Always reminders of the life that existed just beyond their reach.

Even Toby had been someone else's discard, marked for euthanasia because of a limp. Jeff had spent hours massaging the dog's bad leg, applying stolen pain-relief cream, whispering promises that everything would be okay. Toby had given him four years of unconditional love—the only kind Jeff had ever known how to accept.

He remembered the afternoon he'd led the Toby to the vet.

Twelve-year-old Jeff had saved up quarters from returning bottles, but it wasn't nearly enough for treatment for the dog's limp. The receptionist had taken one look at the scared boy and his trembling dog and called the vet anyway. His father's rage upon discovering the bill had been volcanic, but Toby had pressed against Jeff's leg all through the shouting, steady as a heartbeat, teaching him that some things were worth the risk of breaking silence.

Standing there in the Brooklyn cold, Jeff felt the weight of memory press against him. As he became more confident as a software developer, he wrote detailed reports about vulnerabilities, argued technical points with his bosses, documented every flaw in a system. But when it came to matters of the heart - to fighting for someone he loved, to admitting his own needs, to asking for what he truly wanted - the words died in his throat. That paralysis, that terror of emotional truth, had its roots in Mason City, Iowa, in the past he'd tried so hard to escape.

He could see it all so clearly now: the peeling paint of the houses on Cherry Street, the battered sedans in driveways, the sound of his father's anger echoing through poorly insulated walls. Every silence he'd learned, every word he'd swallowed, could be traced back to those quiet streets where he'd first learned that safety meant keeping your head down and your mouth shut. When he'd finally spoken up, he'd lost his job and hurt his coworkers. Had his father been right all along?

The houses in his neighborhood all looked the same: modest two-story structures with peeling paint and chain-link fences, each yard containing someone's faded version of the American dream. The Hodges house was distinguished only by the Ford pickup in the driveway, up on blocks more often than not.

Hank Hodges was a big man who'd once played defensive tackle for the Mason City High Mohawks, back when Friday night lights had promised him more than a future of dead-end jobs and mounting bills. Now he carried his former glory like a wound, nursing it with beer and whatever cheap whiskey was on sale at Murphy's Liquor Store.

Jeff learned early that silence was safety in the Hodges house. The lesson came one autumn evening when he tried telling his fourth-grade teacher, Mrs. Reynolds, about the bruises on his mother's wrists. The next day, his father attended the parent conference wearing his Sunday shirt and his car-salesman smile.

"Kids and their imaginations," his father had said, voice honey-smooth. "Jeff's always been creative. Maybe too creative—telling stories, making things up." He'd squeezed Jeff's shoulder, fingers digging in just enough to make the meaning clear.

That night, after his mother had gone to bed, his father cornered him in the kitchen. "Think you're smart, boy?" The empty whiskey bottle caught the light as it flew past Jeff's head, missing him by inches before shattering against the wall. "Nobody likes a tattletale."

The moment between the whiskey bottle shattering and Jeff's next breath seemed to contain entire worlds. Not empty time, but space charged with meaning—like the pause between lightning and thunder, when you know something powerful is coming but haven't yet felt its force. In that interval, he learned that words were dangerous things, better kept in that silent space between thought and voice.

The next morning, Jeff helped his mother clean up the glass while his father slept it off. They worked without speaking, mother and son, in the early morning quiet. But it wasn't a barren silence. Like the space between shards of glass, it held meaning—shared understanding, shared fear, shared survival. Each careful movement, each piece collected, spoke volumes in their wordless language of endurance.

The only sound was the soft clink of broken pieces being swept into the dustpan. His mother's movements were gentle, practiced—she'd done this so many times before.

"Just stay quiet," she whispered finally, her eyes never meeting his. "It's safer that way."

The Iowa summer pressed against the windows like a living thing, humid air making the curtains stick to the screens. On nights when his father's anger filled the house, the heat seemed to magnify everything—the sharp crack of a slammed door, the muffled sound of his mother's crying, even the silence that followed. Thunder would roll across the prairie, nature's own version of his father's rage, while Jeff huddled in his room, counting seconds between lightning flashes like counting breaths between explosions.

Jeff learned his lessons well. At school, he sat in the middle row—not front, not back—and turned in perfect assignments without ever raising his hand. At home, he became expert at reading his father's moods, at making himself invisible when the front door slammed and the heavy footsteps stumbled in the hall. Words became dangerous things, better kept locked inside where they couldn't spark explosions.

There were good days—rare moments when Hank would teach Jeff how to change spark plugs or adjust timing belts, his huge hands surprisingly gentle with machinery. "Cars make sense," he'd say, grease blackening his fingers. "Not like people. People will always let you down, but if a car ain't working right, there's a reason. You just gotta find it."

But those moments never lasted. The garage door would slam, the TV would blare, and the nightly ritual would begin: Hank raging about his latest job, his wife Margaret's silence a counterpoint to his thunder. Jeff would retreat to his room, where Toby would already be waiting, somehow knowing when he was needed.

The old collie mix had appeared on their porch one rainy night, limping and hungry. Hank had wanted to call the pound, but for once Margaret stood firm. "The boy needs something of his own," she'd said, her quiet voice carrying unusual steel. Perhaps she recognized in the dog's careful movements something of her own survival instincts.

Jeff would bury his face in Toby's fur, whispering his dreams and fears while downstairs glasses shattered against walls. Toby listened with infinite patience, his warm presence a shield against the chaos below. Together, they created their own silent language of comfort and understanding.

School became Jeff's other sanctuary. Numbers made sense to him the way cars did to his father—each problem had a solution if you knew the right steps to take. His third-grade teacher, Mrs. Arbuthnot, noticed how quickly he finished the math worksheets, how he'd help other students when he thought no one was watching.

"You have a gift," she told him one day, after discovering he'd solved all the problems in the back of the textbook just for fun. But when she sent a note home suggesting advanced classes, Hank had laughed bitterly.

"Advanced classes won't put food on the table," he'd said, crumpling the note into a ball. "Boy needs to learn practical skills, not waste time with fancy book learning."

That night, Jeff heard his mother's voice through the heating vent, unusually fierce: "He's not going to end up like you, Hank. He's got a chance to be different."

The sound of breaking glass ended the conversation.

By junior year of high school, Jeff had perfected the art of invisibility. But Diane Reeves, who taught AP Computer Science, didn't believe in letting students hide. She'd come to Mason City High from Austin, Texas, bringing with her stories of startups and innovation that seemed as distant as fairy tales to her Iowa students.

The day she changed Jeff's life started ordinarily enough. She'd assigned the class to create a simple program to calculate baseball statistics. Jeff finished early, as usual, then quietly added features: a graphic interface, player comparison tools, historical data integration.

Ms. Reeves walked past his desk, then stopped. She leaned over his shoulder, her wire-rimmed glasses reflecting the screen. "This is not the assignment I gave, Mr. Hodges."

Jeff's shoulders hunched. "Sorry. I can do the regular version—"

"This is better." She pulled up a chair. "Where did you learn to code like this?"

He shrugged. "Just... figured it out."

"Just figured it out," she repeated softly. Then, louder: "Stay after class, please."

Those fifteen minutes after the final bell changed everything. Ms. Reeves pulled up the Columbia University website on her computer. "They have one of the best computer science programs in the country," she said. "And a strong financial aid program."

"I'm not—" Jeff started, but she cut him off.

"You are. You're exactly what they're looking for." She turned to face him fully. "Jeff, I've worked with professional programmers who couldn't do what you do instinctively. This gift you have? It's your ticket out."

She helped him with the application after school, editing his essays, gathering recommendations. When he worried about the application fee, an envelope appeared stuffed in a textbook containing exactly the right amount. He never knew if it came from Ms. Reeves or his mother.

The night the acceptance letter came, Hank Hodges stood in their small living room, his face flushed with more than just whiskey. "New York City?" he spat the words like poison. "You think you're better than us now?"

"Full scholarship," Margaret said quietly, smoothing the creased letter with trembling hands. "Everything's covered."

"Everything except his pride." Hank snatched the letter. "You'll fail. End up crawling back here with your tail between your legs."

Jeff stood frozen, the familiar paralysis gripping him. But upstairs, Toby started barking—sharp, insistent. The sound broke through Jeff's fear.

"I'm going," he said, his voice barely a whisper.

"What was that?"

"I'm going." Louder this time.

Hank stepped closer, his bulk casting a shadow over his son. But Jeff didn't move. He thought of Ms. Reeves saying, "You are exactly what they're looking for." Thought of all the nights he'd spent coding while the rest of the house slept, creating worlds where everything followed logical rules, where chaos could be contained in elegant loops and functions.

"I'm going," he said one final time.

Later that night, his mother slipped into his room. She sat on the edge of his bed like she used to when he was small, before silence became their shared language.

"Your father," she said slowly, "is afraid you'll succeed. Because then he'll have to face all his failures." She touched his hand briefly. "Go to New York. Learn everything you can. Just..." she paused. "Don't forget how to come back."

But he did forget. Or maybe he never learned how in the first place. The day he left for Columbia, Toby pressed against his legs, whining softly. Jeff knelt and hugged him fiercely, whispering promises to return. Two months later, his mother called to say Toby had died—heart failure, probably from that old injury that had never fully healed.

Jeff didn't go home for Christmas that year, or any year after. He told himself he had too much schoolwork, that he couldn't afford the ticket. But really, he was afraid that if he went back, the gravity of Cherry Street would pull him down, trap him in its orbit of quiet desperation.

He stared at the door of the café, but the box holding his past weighed him down too much. Instead, he turned back to the hotel, as behind him the wind from the harbor carried the promise of approaching rain.

Chapter 3
Regular Business Hours

Betty Martinez hadn't planned on becoming the keeper of a café. Truth be told, she hadn't planned on much of anything after losing her wife Maria to cancer in 2001. Their dream had been simple: retire together, open a coffee shop where Maria could bake and Betty could mother lost souls, just as she had during her thirty years as a grief counselor. Instead, Betty found herself alone in their Brooklyn brownstone, surrounded by Maria's collection of dog paintings and the lingering scent of her famous chocolate-cinnamon coffee.

The house felt wrong with only one person in it. Too quiet, too empty, too full of spaces where Maria should be. Betty would catch herself turning to share a thought, only to find empty air where her wife's smile should have been. She stopped cooking—what was the point of Maria's recipes without Maria there to taste them? She ignored the ringing phone, let mail pile up. Grief was a familiar companion after decades of counseling others through it, but experiencing it herself was different. Like knowing the anatomy of drowning versus actually being underwater.

The German Shepherd arrived three months after Maria's passing.

It was raining that November night, the kind of rain that turned Brooklyn into a film noir set. Betty sat in Maria's favorite armchair, watching water stream down windows they'd planned to replace "someday." The knock at the door was so faint, she thought it was the wind.

But when she opened the door, a dog sat on her stoop. Rain plastered its fur into dark rivulets, and one leg was held carefully off the ground. Something in its eyes—a depth of understanding, a gentle wisdom—reminded Betty of the way Maria used to look at her patients.

"You're hurt," Betty said, surprised to hear her own voice. She hadn't spoken aloud in days.

The dog stood, shook itself, then began limping down the steps. At the bottom, it turned to look at her expectantly.

Betty Martinez, who had never understood her wife's love of dogs, who had spent twenty years negotiating their home into a cats-only zone, found herself following this stranger into the rain. She didn't even grab an umbrella.

The dog led her six blocks to McGolrick Park. There, on a bench near the central pavilion, a young woman sat crying, a manila envelope clutched to her chest. Even through the rain, Betty recognized the particular curve of those shoulders, the specific weight of that grief. She'd seen it hundreds of times in her office.

"You'll catch your death out here," Betty heard herself say, channeling Maria's practical kindness.

The woman looked up, startled. Mascara traced dark rivers down her cheeks. "I... I didn't know where else to go."

When Betty looked around for the German Shepherd, it was gone.

She brought Sarah—that was the woman's name—home for coffee. Maria's coffee, the special blend she'd perfected over decades of serving comfort to Betty's clients. Betty hadn't touched the beans since Maria died, but something about this moment demanded them.

As Sarah sipped from one of Maria's hand-painted mugs, the

story spilled out. Her husband's affair. The divorce papers in the manila envelope. The shame of failing at marriage, of not being enough.

"I used to be a grief counselor," Betty said, surprising herself again. "Want to talk about it?"

They did. For hours. Somewhere between the second and third cup of coffee, Sarah's tears turned to memories, then to laughter, then to hope. When she left near midnight, her steps were lighter, her spine straighter.

That night, Betty dreamed of Maria painting. In the dream, Maria worked on her last canvas—the one that still sat unfinished in her studio. But instead of the lighthouse she'd been planning, she was painting a dog. The German Shepherd.

"They always know who needs help," dream-Maria said, adding highlights to the dog's knowing eyes. "You just have to follow them."

Betty woke to sunlight and possibility. For the first time since Maria's death, she made coffee for herself. The familiar ritual of grinding beans and heating water felt like a prayer, like conversation with a loved one, like coming home.

When Sarah returned a week later with a tin of butter cookies and eyes that could see future happiness again, Betty asked about the German Shepherd.

"What German Shepherd?" Sarah asked.

Betty looked at Maria's dog paintings on the walls. One was a German shepherd, with his paw lifted like the dog in the rain.

"Never mind," she said, pouring them both another cup of coffee. "Tell me more about that job interview you mentioned."

That night, she dreamed of Maria again. This time, her wife was hanging a new painting—one Betty had never seen before. In it, a golden retriever sat smiling, waiting.

"That one's for later," dream-Maria said. "He's got someone special to find. But not yet. First, you need to help the others. Build them a safe place. When it's time, Cooper will know."

Betty woke knowing two things: she was going to open a café, and somewhere out there, someone was going to need that smiling dog someday.

More dogs came after that. A spotted pit bull led her to Marcus, a veteran who thought his PTSD made him unlovable. A crop-eared pug brought Frances, who had stopped painting after her mother's cruel words. Each dog appeared, led Betty to someone in need, then vanished as mysteriously as the German Shepherd.

Her living room became an unofficial sanctuary. People started dropping by "just for coffee," which really meant just for healing. Betty learned to keep Maria's special blend ready, to stock the kinds of cookies that encouraged conversation, to create the same safe space she'd once maintained in her office.

The café itself came later, born of necessity—her living room simply couldn't hold them all anymore. But that first night, following a limping German Shepherd through the rain, was when Betty realized that grief and love and healing don't keep regular business hours.

And neither do dogs with missions.

Chapter 4
Chemical Bonds

On his way back to the hotel, Jeff noticed a sign on one of the close warehouses, a manufacturer of industrial glass.

The first time Jeff saw Madeline, she was laughing at a failed experiment in the chemistry lab. He'd been walking past the open door, head down as usual, when the sound caught him—bright and fearless and utterly without shame. He looked up to see foam spilling over the sides of a beaker while other students backed away in alarm. But Madeline stood her ground, dark hair escaping its ponytail as she calmly documented the reaction in her lab notebook.

"Well, that wasn't supposed to happen," she said, and something in her voice—the way it held both humor and scientific curiosity—made Jeff stop in the doorway. She looked up and caught his eye. "Hey, you! Don't suppose you know the chemical composition of whatever's currently eating through my lab manual?"

Before his usual shyness kicked in, Jeff found himself stepping into the lab. "I'm pretty sure lab manuals are mostly cellulose," he heard himself say. "Though the binding might be polyethylene."

She grinned. "A man who knows his polymers. Must be my lucky day." She gestured at the still-bubbling mess. "Want to help me clean up this spectacular failure?"

Together they mopped up the foam, Jeff carefully following her lead on proper chemical disposal procedures. He kept stealing glances at her as they worked—the way her hands moved with precise efficiency despite her earlier chaos, how she hummed softly to herself, some tune he didn't recognize.

"I'm Madeline, by the way," she said as they finished. "Mad scientist in training, clearly."

"Jeff," he managed. "Computer science."

"Ah, that explains the polymer knowledge. You must have taken Henderson's Materials Science elective."

He blinked in surprise. "How did you—"

"Only Henderson makes CS majors learn about polymers. He's convinced the future is all about bio-compatible computing." She started peeling off her latex gloves. "I'm getting coffee. Want to come with me and help me analyze what went wrong?"

Jeff's first instinct was to retreat. Coffee meant conversation, and conversation meant the possibility of saying the wrong thing, of revealing too much or too little. But Madeline was already hanging up her lab coat, her movements containing an energy that seemed to pull him into her orbit.

"I know this great place on Amsterdam," she continued, either not noticing or choosing to ignore his hesitation. "Unless you're one of those people who thinks bean temperature doesn't affect extraction quality?"

"I... don't actually know much about coffee," Jeff admitted.

"Perfect! A blank slate. Come on, I'll corrupt you with coffee snobbery."

The café was tiny, wedged between a laundromat and a cell phone repair shop. Madeline greeted the barista by name and launched into a detailed discussion about their latest Ethiopian roast. Jeff hung back, watching in amazement as she drew others into her enthusiasm, making the simple act of ordering coffee feel like a scientific expedition.

"Jeff needs the full experience," she told the barista. "What do you recommend for a coffee virgin?"

He felt his face heat up at the phrase, but before he could retreat into his usual silence, Madeline touched his arm lightly. "Trust me," she said, and somehow he did.

They found a small table by the window. Outside, students hurried past in the October chill, but inside it was warm and smelled of vanilla. The barista brought them two ceramic cups, the coffee in Jeff's topped with an intricate leaf design.

"Try it without any extra sugar first," Madeline instructed. "Really smell it before you taste it. Coffee has over 800 aromatic compounds—more complexity than wine."

Jeff lifted the cup, feeling oddly ceremonial. The aroma was nothing like the bitter break room coffee he was used to. He took a careful sip.

"Well?" Madeline leaned forward, her eyes bright with anticipation.

"It tastes like... blueberries?" He surprised himself by trying to find the right words. "And something else. Almost like chocolate, but not quite."

"Yes!" Her smile could have lit up Manhattan. "That's the natural processing. See? You have an excellent palate. Now, about that explosion..."

She launched into a detailed explanation of her experiment, her hands dancing as she described molecular structures and unexpected reactions. Jeff found himself drawn into the puzzle of it, offering suggestions about potential variables she might not have considered.

"That's it!" She slapped the table, making their cups rattle. "The ambient temperature in the lab must have been affected by the maintenance work on the heating system. Of course the reaction would be different!" She pulled out her lab notebook and started scribbling. "You're brilliant!"

"I just thought about how our code compiles differently when the processor heats up," Jeff said quietly, but he felt a warm glow at her praise.

"See? This is why we need interdisciplinary perspectives." She looked up from her notes. "We should do this again. I mean, if you want to. No pressure. But I'm usually here between classes on Wednesdays, and I've got about fifty more reactions that could use an outside perspective."

Jeff thought about his carefully structured schedule, his habit of eating lunch alone in the computer lab, his practice of keeping his head down and just getting through each day. Then he looked at Madeline, with her escaped curls and her infectious enthusiasm and her complete lack of fear about taking up space in the world.

"I'm free on Wednesdays," he heard himself say.

Her smile was like a chemical reaction itself, catalyzing something new and unexpected inside him. For the first time since leaving Mason City, Jeff felt himself wanting to be seen rather than hidden.

"Fair warning," she said, gathering her things. "I'm going to teach you about single-origin beans next time. They'll change your life."

That autumn seemed designed specifically for their love story. Leaves spiraled down around them in perfect choreography as they walked to class, red and gold like nature's confetti celebrating their connection. Even the notorious wind that swept through the center of Columbia's campus behaved differently, gentling itself to ruffle Madeline's hair in ways that made Jeff's heart skip.

Looking back years later, Jeff would realize she'd been right. But it wasn't the coffee that changed his life—it was the way Madeline treated every moment as an experiment worth trying, every failure as data worth collecting, every person as a story worth knowing. In her presence, he began to imagine a version of himself who might be worth knowing too.

Their relationship grew like a chemical reaction—gradual at first, then all at once. At first, they'd study together in Butler Library, claiming the same table tucked away in the stacks. Jeff would watch Madeline's face as she concentrated, the way she'd absently twist a strand of hair around her pencil, how she'd mouth chemical equations to herself as she worked. Sometimes she'd catch him looking and smile, and he'd quickly return to his coding problems, his cheeks warm.

They developed their own rituals. Every Wednesday, they'd meet at the café and Madeline tutored him on the terroir of different coffee growing locations, the flavor profiles of beans. "Have you heard of kopi luwak?" she asked one day.

"Is he a rapper?"

She laughed. "No, it's a kind of coffee that consists of partially digested coffee cherries, which have been eaten and defecated by the Asian palm civet. The cherries are fermented as they pass through the civet's intestines, and after being defecated with other fecal matter, they are collected and processed into coffee."

Jeff made a face. "Coffee made from civet poop?"

"Don't knock it until you've tried it. I keep asking Abebe to order a bag of it and try it out."

Their first real date wasn't meant to be a date at all. They'd stayed late at the computer lab, debugging one of Jeff's projects, and suddenly it was midnight and they were starving. The only place open was Tom's Restaurant, its neon sign a beacon in the November darkness.

Over greasy eggs and endless cups of coffee, Madeline told him about growing up in Vermont, about the telescope her grandfather had given her when she was eight, about how she'd mapped the night sky from her bedroom window. Jeff found himself sharing things he'd never told anyone—about Toby, about his father, about the silence in his childhood home. Madeline reached across the table and took his hand, and neither of them mentioned how their fingers stayed intertwined long after the check came.

On Friday evenings they'd get dollar pizza slices from a place on Amsterdam Avenue and eat them at a window table, watching other students rush past. Madeline would share random facts about the chemistry of pizza dough fermentation, and Jeff would nod, fascinated less by the science than by the way her eyes lit up when she talked about it.

Later, Jeff would remember these Friday nights with a particular kind of pain - not just for their loss, but for his blindness to their importance at the time. How he'd focused on the pizza's price rather than the wealth of having someone to share it with. How he'd never told her that he loved watching her talk more than he cared about what she was saying. How he'd assumed there would always be another Friday, another chance to say the things that mattered.

The restaurant's neon sign would burn long after they were gone, illuminating other couples sharing dollar slices and dreams, while somewhere in California, Madeline would explain molecular structures to someone else. But that was still ahead of them. For now, they sat in their window seat, warm and safe in their pocket of time, while outside the city spun through space at hundreds of miles per hour, carrying them all toward changes they couldn't yet imagine.

Chapter 5
Winter's Warmth

Madeline's tiny apartment became his sanctuary. It was a fourth-floor walkup in a crumbling brownstone on 112th Street, barely bigger than a closet, but she'd transformed it into a wonderland. She filled it with plants—rescued from garden center clearance sales and nursed back to health—and interesting rocks she'd collected on geological field trips. Star charts papered the walls, and her windowsill hosted a growing collection of crystals that threw rainbow patterns across the room on sunny mornings.

On clear nights, they'd climb to the roof with blankets and thermoses of hot chocolate (always with a dash of cayenne pepper—" Trust me," she'd said, and he did). The city spread out below them like its own constellation, streetlights and car headlights creating patterns as complex as any star system. She'd point out real constellations hidden behind the city's glow, telling him the stories behind their names.

"See that W-shape? That's Cassiopeia," she'd say, tracing the pattern with her finger. "She was a queen who bragged about her beauty until the gods punished her by tying her to a chair in the stars, forcing her to spend half the year upside down."

"Harsh," Jeff would say, but he was really thinking about how her hair smelled like lavender and how perfectly she fit against his side.

On weekends, they explored the city together, finding pockets of magic in its chaos. They discovered a tiny bookstore in the East Village where the owner let them read for hours without buying anything, though they always did eventually. They found a hidden garden tucked between buildings in Morningside Heights, where an elderly Chinese man grew vegetables and offered them fresh snap peas. They kissed in Riverside Park, under a pine tree perfectly shaped for holiday decoration, while a street musician played "What a Wonderful World" on a battered saxophone.

Sometimes they'd take the subway to random stops and explore, making up stories about the people they saw. Madeline had a gift for it. "See that woman with the red umbrella?" she'd whisper. "She's actually a time traveler from 2257, studying twenty-first century fashion mistakes." Jeff would add to the tales, surprising himself with his imagination. With Madeline, everything felt possible.

As Christmas break approached, Jeff prepared his excuse for his parents carefully: a non-existent winter coding project that required him to stay near campus. He delivered it during his once-a-month phone call to Mason City, his mother's silence on the other end saying more than words could. She knew he was lying. She also understood why.

What he hadn't prepared for was Madeline's response when he told her he'd be spending Christmas in his dorm.

"Absolutely not," she said, looking up from her quantum mechanics textbook. They were in their usual spot in Butler Library, the winter sunset casting long shadows through the Gothic windows. "You're coming home with me."

"Madeline, I can't—"

"You can and you will." She closed her book with unusual force, earning a glare from a nearby student. "My dad's already planning the menu. He stress-bakes during the holidays, and he needs someone new to experiment on. My regular taste buds are too jaded."

Which was how Jeff found himself on an Amtrak train heading north through a December snowstorm, watching the Hudson River disappear and reappear through breaks in the white curtain of snow. Madeline sat beside him, reading a scientific paper about crystal formation in zero gravity, occasionally sharing interesting facts that somehow connected to the patterns of frost on the train windows.

"Do you think your parents will mind?" he asked for the third time. "I mean, Christmas is for family."

Madeline lowered her paper. "Jeff. You're family." She said it so simply, as if it were an obvious scientific truth, like the atomic weight of carbon or the speed of light in a vacuum.

The Montpelier station was small but warmly lit, holiday decorations twinkling in every window. As they stepped onto the platform, their breath clouding in the Vermont cold, Jeff saw a tall man in a wool cardigan waving enthusiastically.

"Dad!" Madeline broke into a run, somehow managing not to slip on the snowy platform, and launched herself into her father's arms.

Maury Hinckley caught his daughter with practiced ease, his laugh as warm as his sweater looked. He was a big man, but there was nothing intimidating about him. Maybe it was the flour still dusting his sleeve, or the way his eyes crinkled at the corners just like Madeline's.

"And you must be Jeff," he said, extending his hand. "Welcome to Vermont. Hope you like snickerdoodles. I may have gotten carried away this morning."

The drive to their house took them through downtown Montpelier, past the gold-domed state capitol draped in fresh snow. Maury's old Subaru smelled of gingerbread and yeast—he'd been stress-baking all morning, he explained, a habit that intensified during the holidays.

Through the foggy windows, Jeff watched rows of historic homes pass by, each one decorated for Christmas. Warm light spilled from bay windows, and he glimpsed scenes that looked like living Christmas cards: families decorating trees, children hanging stockings, parents carrying wrapped presents.

"Your mother's at her studio," Maury explained as they turned onto a quiet street where every pine tree wore a coat of twinkling lights. "She's finishing a commission. But she'll be home for dinner." He glanced at Jeff in the rearview mirror. "Madeline tells us you're a computer scientist. Any interest in helping me debug my bread recipe spreadsheet? I can't get the hydration calculations right."

The Hinckley house sat on a hill overlooking the city, a rambling Victorian painted deep blue with white trim. Smoke curled from the brick chimney, carrying the scent of burning applewood. Holiday candles glowed in every window, and a wreath of fresh pine hung on the red front door. The porch steps creaked under their feet, the wood worn smooth by generations of footsteps.

Inside, the air was warm and heavy with the scent of butter and sugar. Christmas music played softly—not the usual carols, but jazz interpretations that made familiar tunes feel new. A massive tree dominated one corner of the living room, still undecorated except for lights. Boxes of ornaments waited nearby, each one labeled in an artistic hand: "Madeline's First Christmas," "Wedding Ornaments," "School Projects."

"I hope you're hungry," Maury said, leading them into a kitchen that looked like a happy explosion had occurred in a flour mill. Every surface was covered with cooling racks of cookies, and a ball of dough was rising in a bowl by the window, covered with a tea towel embroidered with molecular structures—a gift from Madeline, Jeff learned later. "The snickerdoodles are just the beginning. Wait until you try my cardamom star bread."

"Dad stress-bakes," Madeline explained, already reaching for a cookie. "Mom stress-paints. Between them, the holidays are very productive."

"Better than your grandmother's stress-caroling," Maury added, dusting flour from his beard. "The neighbors still talk about the Great O Holy Night Incident of 1987."

Jeff watched them move around the kitchen together, their comfortable banter punctuated by gentle teasing and shared memories. No one was watching their words, measuring their reactions, bracing for sudden storms. A timer dinged, and Maury grabbed potholders decorated with dancing molecules—another of Madeline's gifts, marking her presence even in the smallest details.

Through the kitchen window, Jeff saw a bird feeder where cardinals flashed like Christmas ornaments against the snow. Inside, the refrigerator was covered with Madeline's childhood drawings, science fair ribbons, and recent photos: Madeline in her lab coat, Madeline and her mother painting together, Madeline and Maury covered in flour from some past baking adventure. A whole life documented with pride and love.

Later that evening, Madeline's mother Gaye arrived home in a swirl of cold air and paint-stained clothes, her silver-streaked hair escaping from a messy bun. Without ceremony, she hugged Jeff as if she'd known him forever, and he caught the scent of oil paints and turpentine.

"You must be frozen," she said, her artist's eyes taking in every detail of him. "Maury, did you make hot chocolate? The real kind, not that powder stuff?"

Soon they were all in the living room, decorating the tree while drinking hot chocolate spiced with cinnamon and cayenne—Madeline's special recipe, Jeff realized with a start. Each ornament came with a story: the twisted glass icicle Madeline had bought with her first allowance, the ceramic star she'd made in third grade, the tiny artist's palette Maury had given Gaye the year they met.

"Here," Gaye said softly, pressing something into Jeff's hand. It was a small painting of a winter night sky, stars glowing against deep blue. "Every family member gets their own ornament. Welcome to the collection."

Jeff's throat tightened as he hung it on the tree, watching it catch the light. Here was proof that he existed in this space, that he belonged in this warm circle of love and laughter. When Madeline slipped her hand into his, he squeezed it tight, anchoring himself in this moment of perfect belonging.

"Tell me about your coding projects," Maury said to Jeff. "Madeline says you're brilliant with patterns."

So Jeff found himself explaining his latest algorithm ideas, surprised at how easily the words came. Maury asked intelligent questions, clearly interested rather than just being polite. Gaye sketched absently in a notebook as she listened, and when she showed Jeff the drawing—a visual interpretation of his coding concept—he was struck by how perfectly she'd captured it.

Oh no," Madeline groaned. "Now you've done it. They're going to drag you into their weird art-science collaboration thing."

Indeed, Maury and Gaye had already begun discussing how to represent programming concepts through painting, with Maury suggesting various mathematical color theories while Gaye argued for a more intuitive approach.

That night, in Madeline's childhood bedroom—Jeff was staying in the guest room down the hall, a fact that Maury had mentioned casually without any of the loaded significance it would have carried in Mason City—Madeline found him looking at her old science fair ribbons, each carefully preserved.

The room was a timeline of her growth: posters of the periodic table gave way to advanced chemistry diagrams, stuffed animals shared space with molecular models, and everywhere there were books—evidence of parents who encouraged their child's passions instead of fearing them.

"You okay?" Madeline asked softly.

He turned to her, this wonderful girl who had brought him into her world of light and warmth and possibility. "Your parents are amazing," he said.

"They're a bit much sometimes," she admitted. "But they mean well. And they already love you, you know."

Jeff thought about his own parents, about the silence in their house that grew deeper every year. He thought about his father's bitter dismissal of "college boys" and his mother's quiet resignation. Then he looked at Madeline's walls, covered in star charts and scientific posters and family photos showing a childhood full of laughter and experiments and love.

"Thank you," he said, "for sharing them with me."

She kissed him then, soft and sweet as her father's snickerdoodles. "Merry Christmas, Jeff."

The next morning, he woke to the smell of fresh bread and coffee, and the sound of Maury and Gaye singing off-key carols in the kitchen while they made breakfast. Madeline was still asleep down the hall, but Jeff headed downstairs, drawn by the warmth and light.

"Ah, perfect timing!" Maury handed him an apron. "I need someone to help me laminate this croissant dough. Madeline says you're good with precise measurements."

As Jeff helped fold butter into dough in the early morning light, listening to Gaye and Maury's gentle bickering about the proper egg-wash ratio, he realized something: this was what a home could feel like. This was what he wanted to build with Madeline—a place where love smelled like fresh bread and creativity flowed as naturally as conversation.

He should have told her then. Should have found the words to express how she'd opened up his world, how she made him believe in possibilities he'd never dared to imagine. But the words felt too big, too dangerous still. He thought they had time.

Chapter 6
Artistic Theory

He was wrong about that, but he was right about one thing: years later, trying to find his way back to himself in a Brooklyn hotel room, he would remember that Christmas morning as a glimpse of what life could be—warm and safe and full of light.

When they returned from Vermont, the January wind howled outside Madeline's apartment, rattling the single-pane windows in their frames. Inside, they'd transformed her tiny living room into a fortress of creativity. The pillow fort had started modestly—just a few couch cushions and her spare blanket—but had grown more elaborate as the afternoon wore on. Now it incorporated her shower curtain as a roof, all her kitchen chairs as support columns, and Christmas lights rescued from a dumpster for illumination.

In the spring semester, her apartment became their laboratory for culinary experiments. They'd try to recreate dishes from ethnic restaurants they couldn't afford, filling the tiny space with exotic smells and laughter when things went wrong. The time they attempted pad Thai and set off the smoke detector became known as "The Great Noodle Disaster of Junior Year." Even their failures felt like successes because they were failing together.

Sitting in the hotel room, he pulled out his wallet to check how much cash he had to carry him until he got to the bank, and he noticed the student ID card he still carried - not because he needed it, but because he couldn't bring himself to throw it away. The plastic was worn smooth at the corners, and his younger self smiled up at him with an optimism he barely recognized. Their IDs had gotten them into the Metropolitan Museum of Art on a Saturday in February, during one of its pay-what-you-wish periods. He remembered Madeline flashing her card with a theatrical flourish, declaring them "poor but culturally sophisticated students."

They'd started in the modern art wing, where Madeline had stared at a completely white canvas for a long moment before declaring it "an obvious representation of entropy in closed systems."

Not to be outdone, Jeff had gestured to a twisted metal sculpture and solemnly announced: "Note how the artist has clearly incorporated principles of recursive algorithms, using dynamic programming to optimize the spatial relationships."

They'd continued through the gallery, inventing increasingly elaborate technical descriptions for each piece. A splash of red paint became "an exploration of heterogeneous catalyst degradation in non-Newtonian fluids." A pile of wooden boxes was obviously "a physical manifestation of blockchain architecture vis-à-vis distributed computing paradigms."

They'd gathered quite a following—other visitors trailing behind them, stifling laughter—before the security guard caught on. Even then, Madeline had managed to keep a straight face while explaining that they were "doctoral candidates in avant-garde techno-artistic theory" before they finally ran away giggling.

Now, twelve years later, Jeff ran his thumb over the ID's scratched surface. The Metropolitan still did pay-what-you-wish days, but he hadn't been back since. Some memories were better left sealed away, like artifacts in a museum case.

The day after their museum visit, they nestled in the fort together, each working on class assignments. Hers was on quantum entanglement, while his focused on neural networks. "I'm getting lost in my own brain," she said, from her nest of pillows. She wore fuzzy socks with periodic table elements on them and one of Jeff's tattered Columbia sweatshirts from freshman year.

"I'll trade you," Jeff said. He was sprawled on his stomach, laptop balanced on a textbook, his sock feet sticking out the fort's entrance. "I think I'm starting to go cross-eyed myself."

"Deal." She reached for his paper, then stopped. "Wait. Fort protocol." She cleared her throat. "Chief Science Officer Madeline, requesting permission for classified documents from Fort Laboratory's Head of Computing."

"Permission granted." He smiled as he handed her his paper and took hers.

She grabbed it and flopped back onto her pillow pile. "God, I love pillow forts. Everything feels more possible inside them, you know?"

Jeff did know. Something about their cozy shelter made the outside world—with all its expectations and anxieties—feel far away. Here, under their canopy of blankets and Christmas lights, he could be braver, sillier, more himself.

"We should write a paper together," Madeline said now, rolling onto her back and holding Jeff's paper above her head. "Based on our experience at the museum. The Application of Computational Models to Post-Modern Artistic Expression: A Quantitative Analysis."

"With a subsection on using mass spectrometry to date coffee stains on canvases?"

"Obviously. And don't forget the statistical analysis of viewer head-tilting angles as a function of artistic abstraction."

Jeff pushed his laptop aside and shifted to face her. The multicolored lights cast soft patterns across her face, reminding him of the way she looked on their rooftop stargazing nights. "You know what I appreciate about you?"

She lowered her notes. "My extensive knowledge of quantum mechanics? My excellent fort-building skills? My remarkably symmetric electron orbitals?"

"How you make everything an adventure." He reached out and tucked a stray curl behind her ear. "Even these research papers. Even museum visits. Even just... existing."

"Jeff Hodges, are you getting sentimental in our Laboratory Fortress of Science?"

"Maybe." He pulled back slightly, feeling suddenly vulnerable. But Madeline caught his hand.

"Hey," she said softly. "I love that about you. How you notice things. How you're always paying attention in that quiet way of yours. Like how you remembered exactly how I take my coffee after seeing me order it once. Or how you started carrying extra hair ties after that time I lost mine in the lab."

The moment between her "I love that about you" and his response expanded like the cityscape before them. In that pause lived everything he wanted to say—how she'd changed his world, how she made him believe in magic, how terrified he was of losing her. But like the spaces between buildings defining the city's shape, sometimes what wasn't said gave form to what was. He just pulled her closer, staring at streetlights until they blurred before his eyes.

Outside their fort, the wind rattled the windows harder, and someone's car alarm started wailing. But inside, time seemed to slow down, measured in heartbeats and the soft glow of those twinkling lights.

"We should present our art theory paper at a conference," Jeff said finally, because it was easier than saying all the other things swelling in his chest.

"Definitely. We'll need proper titles, of course. I'll be Dr. Madeline Hinckley-Schrodinger, Head of Quantum Artistic Probability."

"And I'll be Professor Jeffrey von Neuralnetwork, Chair of Computational Aesthetics."

"Perfect." She sat up suddenly, nearly taking out one of their support chairs. "Oh! We need snacks for our research. Proper brain fuel. I think I have some Oreos left..."

She scrambled out of the fort, her sock feet silent on the worn hardwood floor. Jeff watched her go, marveling at how she could switch from profound to playful in an instant, how she made every moment feel worth documenting, worth remembering.

When she returned with cookies and two mugs of hot chocolate (with a dash of cayenne, of course), they spread their papers out like an academic picnic. They worked on their actual research between bits of elaborate fort protocol and increasingly ridiculous art theories, their laughter a shield against the winter wind and the world beyond their blanket walls.

Later, Jeff would remember this as one of their perfect moments —the kind that feels eternal while you're in it but becomes achingly precious in retrospect. He should have known that anything that burned so brightly couldn't last forever. But in that moment, in their fort of pillows and possibilities, forever felt not just possible but inevitable.

Chapter 7
Regular Visitors

Betty knew which kind of day it would be at the Smiling Dog Café when Gigi appeared in the alley. The black miniature poodle only showed up when someone was grieving lost love, and she had a particular way of sitting—head slightly tilted, eyes full of ancient wisdom—that meant the visitor would be a difficult case.

"Another broken heart?" Betty asked, pausing on her way to the dumpster with the morning's coffee grounds. Gigi's tail wagged, a gentle affirmative.

Inside, the café was preparing itself, as it always did. The Brazilian jazz that Maria had loved began playing softly through hidden speakers, though Betty hadn't turned the sound system on. The mirrors along the back wall took on that peculiar depth they sometimes had, as if they might reflect more than just the present moment. Even the sunlight seemed intentional, creating pools of warmth at certain tables while leaving others in comfortable shadow.

Sarah arrived first, as she had every Thursday morning for the past three years. She didn't need Duke anymore—hadn't since that rainy night when the German Shepherd first led Betty to her—but she kept coming back. Betty suspected it wasn't just for the coffee.

"Morning, Betty!" Sarah's smile had long since lost its brittleness.

She carried a cardboard box that smelled of fresh bread. "Mom's newest experiment. She's trying to recreate your cinnamon rolls."

Betty accepted the box with a knowing look. Sarah's mother had been attempting to reverse-engineer Betty's recipes for months, ever since Sarah had brought her to the café. What neither of them knew was that the secret ingredient wasn't in the recipe—it was in the way Maria had taught Betty to bake with love worked into every fold of the dough.

The morning regulars filtered in: Thomas, who now ran a scholarship fund in his brother's memory; Frances, paint under her fingernails from her latest gallery preparation; Marcus, who had finally learned to sleep through the night and now helped other veterans do the same. Each carried their own story of healing, their own memory of the dog that had led them here.

But Betty's attention kept drifting to the empty table in the corner, the one the morning light never quite reached. Something about its shadows felt expectant, waiting.

She scrubbed the tables, removing the fine dust of cinnamon that gathered on each wooden top, even though when she turned around the cinnamon was there again.

The bell above the door chimed, and Gigi's prediction walked in. The woman was young, maybe twenty-five, with red-rimmed eyes and a crumpled envelope clutched in one hand. Betty recognized the envelope type—wedding invitations. Not her own, given the grief in her bearing.

"Welcome to the Smiling Dog," Betty said softly. The woman startled, as if she hadn't meant to come in, hadn't even seen where her feet were carrying her. That happened sometimes; the café had its own way of collecting lost souls.

"I'm sorry," the woman said, "I don't know why I—" She stopped, her eyes fixing on something behind Betty. "That painting..."

Betty turned to follow her gaze. Gigi's portrait hung there, the Dark Lady of Lost Love, as Maria had titled it. In the painting, Gigi sat in falling snow, her fur catching moonlight, her eyes holding all the world's broken hearts.

"She's beautiful," the woman whispered. "She looks like... but that's impossible. I just saw a dog like that outside, and I followed... but that's crazy, right?"

"Not crazy," Betty said, already reaching for a specific mug—the one Maria had painted with silver swirls that looked like falling snow. "Sometimes we follow things we don't understand to places we didn't know we needed to be. Coffee?"

The woman sank into a chair—at exactly the table Betty would have chosen for her, where the light and shadow met in a gentle mingling. "I don't even like coffee."

Betty smiled. "You haven't tried mine."

The music seemed to know what each hour needed. Morning brought gentle bossa nova, the soft Portuguese lyrics floating like mist above the early customers' quiet conversations. By mid-morning, it would shift to instrumental jazz, the kind that made people tap their feet without realizing it. Each song flowed into the next like cream swirling into coffee, never jarring, never interrupting.

As she prepared the coffee—Maria's special blend, with a hint of vanilla and the secret ingredient that wasn't on any recipe card—Betty watched the café work its subtle magic. The jazz shifted to something softer, a melody that spoke of endings and beginnings. The mirrors caught the woman's reflection at just the right angle, showing her a glimpse of her stronger self. Even the other customers played their parts, their quiet conversations creating a cocoon of normality around this fragile moment.

The café's chairs seemed to arrange themselves according to some invisible choreography. A deep leather armchair would mysteriously migrate to catch the best reading light just as an elderly man with a well-worn novel arrived. A pair of comfortable seats would find themselves angled toward each other moments before old friends arrived for their weekly catch-up. Even the smooth wooden chairs at the counter knew to turn slightly inward when someone needed to talk, creating little pockets of privacy in the public space.

The woman cradled the coffee mug Betty set before her. "My best friend," she said suddenly. "She's marrying my ex. They want me to be maid of honor. Said it's been two years, shouldn't I be over it by now?" A tear splashed into the coffee, creating ripples that caught the light like lunar circles.

"Grief doesn't wear a watch," Betty said, sitting down across from her. It was one of Maria's sayings, one of many that had become part of the café's wisdom. "Neither does healing."

The woman took a sip of coffee, then blinked in surprise. "This tastes like... like Christmas morning. Like the first snow. Like..." She struggled for words.

"Like possibility?" Betty suggested.

The door chimed again. Frances was leaving for her gallery, but she paused at their table. "That's exactly what I thought, my first time here," she said. "Betty's coffee tastes like starting over." She smiled at the woman. "I'm having an opening next week, by the way. All new works. You should come. Sometimes the best way past an ending is to witness someone else's beginning."

After Frances left, the woman stared into her coffee. "I used to paint too," she said quietly. "Before them. Before everything."

"The art supply store on Atlantic Avenue has a sale on watercolors," Betty mentioned casually. "Just until Tuesday."

By the time the woman left, she had Frances' gallery invitation, a list of art supply sales Betty had "happened" to notice, and something new in her eyes—a glimmer of the self she'd buried under betrayal. Gigi was gone from the alley, her work complete for now.

The day continued, each hour bringing its own visitors, its own small miracles of healing. Betty served coffee, listened, and watched the café work in its mysterious ways. But her eyes kept drifting to that corner table, the one still waiting in shadow.

That evening, as she was closing up, she noticed something odd about Cooper's portrait. The golden retriever's eternal smile seemed different somehow—more anticipatory than usual. In the painting's background, a storm was brewing over Brooklyn, dark clouds gathering above shadowy buildings.

"Not yet," Betty told the painting, thinking of Maria's words in that long-ago dream. "But soon, I think."

She cleaned the coffee machines, restocked the beans, wiped down the tables. Regular closing tasks, preparing for tomorrow's regular visitors.

But as she turned out the lights, Betty smiled at Cooper's portrait. Sometimes the regulars weren't the only ones who needed the café's magic. Sometimes, very occasionally, the café itself needed someone —someone who could remind it, and her, what they were really waiting for.

The Brooklyn night settled around the café like a soft blanket, and somewhere in the distance, a storm was building.

Chapter 8
Up on the Roof

Ever since they met at freshman orientation, Madeline's best friend had been a Pakistani immigrant in the engineering school. Shaheer Ali had arrived at the university on a scholarship, carrying his mother's prayers and his father's expectations in a single worn duffel bag. The day Madeline introduced him to Jeff, Shaheer was sitting cross-legged on the floor of the computer lab, surrounded by disassembled hard drives, his fingers flying over a keyboard while three monitors displayed scrolling code.

"He's brilliant," Madeline had whispered to Jeff. "But he's also kind. Watch this."

Sure enough, every time a freshman wandered in looking lost, Shaheer would pause his work, turn down his Bollywood music, and patiently explain whatever concept the student was struggling with. He had a way of making complex ideas sound simple, sketching diagrams on scraps of paper or using candy from his bottomless supply of Werther's Originals to demonstrate algorithms.

Jeff and Shaheer bonded over late-night coding sessions, sharing cups of chai that Shaheer made in an electric kettle he kept under his desk. "My mother would be horrified at this American version," he'd laugh, but he made it anyway, the spicy-sweet aroma filling the lab while they debugged each other's projects.

When Madeline joined them, she'd curl up in the lab's single comfortable chair, working on her chemistry papers while the two men argued good-naturedly about optimal database structures. Sometimes she'd look up and catch Jeff's eye, her smile saying she was happy her two favorite people had found each other.

Jeff and Madeline spent much of their free time during the spring in Central Park, where Madeline identified plants and explained their chemical properties while Jeff watched a side of New York he'd never noticed before come alive. She taught him to see beauty in the city's smallest details: the way sunlight hit puddles after rain, the unexpected flowers pushing through sidewalk cracks, the perfect geometry of spider webs between fire escapes.

All the while, Jeff felt himself opening up like one of Madeline's rescued plants, turning toward her light. He'd never known love could be like this—not a storm to weather, but a garden to tend. When she'd fall asleep during their late-night study sessions, her head on his shoulder and her chemistry notes scattered around them, he'd think about his parents' cold silences and marvel at how different love was when it grew in fertile soil.

The hotel room's ancient air conditioning unit wheezed and sputtered, reminding Jeff of another summer when the heat had been unbearable. He got up to adjust the temperature, but the knob came off in his hand - cheap plastic, worn out by countless other temporary residents.

The useless piece of plastic reminded him of the solar calculator he'd used that summer between junior and senior year, its display flickering in the brutal New York heat. He didn't need to invent a reason why he couldn't go back to Mason City during that break. He was offered an internship with one of his professors, a chance to create his own coding project for a non-profit in sub-Saharan Africa that calculated the best places to place solar collectors to provide reliable electricity to remote communities.

During July, he came to understand what those African communities were experiencing, when New York City was hit by one of the worst heat waves in city history.

Their regular study spots had become unbearable—Butler Library's air conditioning was struggling, their favorite café had fans that only pushed the hot air around, and Madeline's tiny apartment felt like a convection oven.

"The roof," she said one evening, as they sat on her floor sharing a bag of frozen peas as an improvised cooling device. "It'll be cooler up there, and the Perseids are starting."

"Who are the Perseids?"

"Not a who, but a what. Meteor showers."

The building superintendent, Mr. Guzman, caught them hauling blankets and pillows up the narrow stairwell. Jeff froze, but Madeline smiled. "Testing some theories about atmospheric cooling patterns," she said. "For science."

Mr. Guzman sighed the sigh of a man who had learned not to ask too many questions, especially of the college student who'd spent three weekends helping his daughter build a working model of the solar system for her science fair. "Just don't fall off," he said, then added, "And tell Carolina if the meteor shower is good. She's doing a summer astronomy project."

They created their sanctuary behind the mechanical room, where the air conditioning units provided both cover and a constant white noise that muffled the city sounds below. Madeline had thought of everything: fairy lights strung across their makeshift shelter, her grandfather's old telescope carefully positioned, a cooler stocked with fruit and bottles of water, and even a small fan that stirred the heavy air.

The first night, they lay on their backs watching heat lightning play across the distant clouds. The city spread out around them like a galaxy of human-made stars, each light representing someone else's story. A siren wailed somewhere in the distance, and a car alarm briefly joined the urban symphony before falling silent.

"Tell me about the stars," Jeff said, because he loved the way her voice changed when she talked about the cosmos.

Madeline pointed upward. "See that bright one? That's not a star but a planet. Venus. And over there—that's Vega. It's part of the constellation Lyra, the harp. The Greeks believed it belonged to Orpheus, the musician who tried to rescue his love from the underworld."

"How'd that work out for him?"

"Terribly. He looked back when he wasn't supposed to, and lost her forever." She rolled onto her side to face him. "But I prefer the Chinese story about Vega. They say it's the Weaving Princess, separated from her love the Cowherd Star by the Silver River—what we call the Milky Way. They can only meet once a year, when magpies form a bridge between them."

Jeff thought about that—love strong enough to bridge the space between stars. He reached for Madeline's hand in the darkness.

The heat made sleep impossible until well past midnight, so they talked. About everything, about nothing. Madeline described her latest research project, her words painting pictures of molecules dancing at the quantum level. Jeff shared his ideas about adaptive algorithms, and she asked questions that made him see his own work in new ways.

"What if," she said during their third night on the roof, her voice dreamy in the darkness, "We could really make an impact on the world? You through coding, like you're doing for the solar panel project. Me through chemistry."

A shooting star traced a bright line across the sky, and Madeline grabbed his arm. "Make a wish!"

Jeff closed his eyes, but he couldn't think of anything to wish for. He already had everything he wanted, right here on this rooftop.

On the fourth night, they saw the first real meteor of the shower. Madeline had been explaining her thesis ideas, her hands gesturing in the darkness as she described complex chemical reactions. The streak of light cut across her words, and they both gasped.

"Did you see that?" She sat up, her hair wild in the fairy lights. "It was probably a small one, maybe the size of a grain of sand, but the speed—can you imagine? Kilometers per second, all that kinetic energy converted to light in one brilliant moment!"

Jeff watched her face, more captivating than any celestial show. "Tell me more about your research," he said. "The bio-compatible materials you're working on."

She launched into an explanation of her latest breakthrough, about polymers that interfaced directly with neural tissue. "The applications for medical technology would be revolutionary," she said. "And there's this lab in San Francisco that's doing amazing work with similar materials."

A slight breeze stirred the hot air, carrying the scent of someone's rooftop garden from the building next door. In the distance, the Empire State Building's lights shifted from white to blue. Jeff should have noticed then—the way her voice lifted when she mentioned San Francisco, how her dreams were already reaching beyond their shared horizon. But he was lost in the moment, in the magic of their private universe six stories above the city.

On the fifth night, they brought up ice cream, which melted faster than they could eat it. Madeline had chocolate dripping down her chin, and when Jeff kissed her, she tasted like summer and sweetness and infinite possibility.

"What do you want?" she asked him later, her head on his chest as they watched the stars wheel slowly overhead. "After graduation, I mean. What's your dream?"

The space between her question and his answer stretched like the city below them—vast and full of unspoken possibilities. It wasn't an empty silence; it was heavy with all the dreams he'd never dared to voice, all the futures he couldn't let himself imagine. The traffic sounds from below faded, as if the night itself was waiting to hear what he would say.

The question caught him off guard. In Mason City, dreams had been dangerous things, better left unspoken. "I don't know," he said finally. "Something... stable. A good job, maybe at one of the big tech firms. Regular hours, decent benefits."

He felt rather than saw her frown. "But what do you want to create? What problems do you want to solve?"

The truth was, he'd never let himself think that far ahead. Every time he'd shown enthusiasm for something as a child, it had become ammunition for his father's mockery. Safer to keep your head down, to aim for adequate rather than exceptional.

"I just want..." He struggled to find the words. "I want to build something that lasts."

She lifted her head to look at him. "Then build it with me. With Shaheer. We could do something amazing together, something that matters."

A police helicopter passed overhead, its searchlight briefly illuminating their nest of blankets. In that flash of artificial daylight, Jeff saw something in Madeline's eyes that scared him—a hunger for more, for bigger, for brighter. A hunger he wasn't sure he could match.

Their last night on the roof, as the heat wave was breaking and it was time to head back to classes, the meteor shower peaked. They lay tangled together, counting shooting stars and sharing the last popsicle from their cooler. The city had finally cooled somewhat, and a gentle breeze carried the first hint of autumn.

"One day," Madeline said sleepily, "we'll go somewhere where we can see all the stars. Maybe the desert, or the top of a mountain. Somewhere where the sky goes on forever."

Jeff tightened his arm around her. "One day," he echoed, but already something was shifting, like clouds across the moon. Their perfect week was ending, and with it, something else was beginning—though neither of them knew it yet.

When dawn came, they packed up their makeshift camp. Mr. Guzman was sweeping the lobby as they carried their blankets downstairs.

"Carolina saw six meteors," he told them. "She says thank you for the tip about the best viewing times."

Madeline beamed. "Tell her to keep watching the sky. There's always something wonderful up there, if you know where to look."

Years later, alone in his Brooklyn hotel room, Jeff would remember that week on the roof—how close the stars had seemed, how infinite the possibilities. He would remember Madeline's voice describing celestial mechanics and molecular bonds, the way she made the universe seem simultaneously vast and intimate. Most of all, he would remember how he'd had everything he ever wanted within his grasp, and still somehow let it slip away, like a meteor burning bright and fast before fading into darkness.

Chapter 9
Impending Change

Senior year started with a sense of impending change that made Jeff uneasy. The campus hummed with nervous energy as his classmates talked about job interviews and graduate school applications. Even the coffee cart outside Butler Library had been replaced by a sleek new kiosk—progress, everyone said, but Jeff missed the old cart's familiar dents and the way its owner had known everyone's orders by heart.

He and Madeline still had their routines—Wednesday coffee dates, Sunday morning challah from Mrs. Kowalski's bakery—but something felt different. Madeline spent more time in the lab, working late into the night on research for her honors thesis. Her excitement was infectious when she talked about it, her hands dancing as she described molecular structures and potential applications.

"The interface between organic and synthetic materials," she explained one October evening in their usual study spot in Butler. Yellow leaves drifted past the Gothic windows, and someone's abandoned coffee cup had left a ring on their table. "That's where the real breakthroughs are happening. And the lab at Berkeley—"

Jeff's fingers froze on his keyboard. "Berkeley?"

"Oh." She tucked a strand of hair behind her ear, a gesture he recognized as nervousness. "I was going to tell you. Dr. Harrison thinks I should apply to their Ph.D. program. They're doing amazing work there with bio-compatible computing materials."

"California," Jeff said, the word feeling like glass in his mouth.

"It's just an application," she said quickly. "Nothing's decided. And anyway, Shaheer says the tech industry out there is incredible. His contact at the incubator—"

"Shaheer too?"

She reached across the table and took his hand. "Jeff. These are just possibilities right now. But we should talk about them, about what we both want for the future."

He nodded, but the future suddenly felt like a dark room he wasn't ready to enter. That night, he lay awake in his dorm room, listening to his roommate's steady breathing and thinking about distance—how far California was from New York, how many miles could fit between two hearts before they stopped beating in sync.

Shaheer's latest obsession was the Business School's Entrepreneurship Club. He'd started attending their meetings, coming back full of terms like "market penetration" and "seed funding" that made Jeff's head spin. The whole thing felt like playing dress-up to Jeff—all these computer science students suddenly wearing blazers and carrying leather portfolios, pretending they knew how to run companies.

"You have to come to the next meeting," Shaheer insisted one afternoon in the computer lab. He was wearing a tie—an actual tie—with his usual jeans and sneakers. The incongruity made Jeff uncomfortable. "I'm presenting my debugging algorithm concept. They have venture capitalists sometimes, real ones!"

Jeff tried to focus on the code in front of him. "I don't know, man. That's not really my thing."

"What's not your thing? Success?" Shaheer's voice held an edge of frustration. "Jeff, you're brilliant with patterns. You see things in code that nobody else catches. But you can't just hide in a cubicle forever."

"I'm not hiding," Jeff protested, but his voice sounded weak even to himself.

The meeting was the following Thursday. Jeff borrowed a blazer from his roommate and spent ten minutes fighting with a tie before giving up. The Business School building felt alien—all glass and chrome, nothing like the comfortable shabbiness of the computer science department. Students in suits moved through the hallways with purposeful strides, carrying coffee cups like shields.

Shaheer was waiting outside the lecture hall, practically vibrating with excitement. "They're going to love it," he said, straightening Jeff's collar. "Just watch."

Jeff watched. He watched his friend transform into someone else entirely—confident, articulate, throwing around terms like "scalable solution" and "market disruption" as if he'd been born speaking them. The visiting venture capitalists in the front row nodded along, making notes on expensive-looking tablets.

When it was over, people clustered around Shaheer, telling him about their own ideas, asking questions about implementation timelines. Jeff stood at the back of the room, tugging at his borrowed blazer, feeling like an imposter in a world he didn't understand.

While Madeline worked on her thesis, and Shaheer spent hours on the phone with contacts his family had in Pakistan, New York and California, Jeff kept his head down, reading, taking quizzes and writing code.

Sunday mornings he and Madeline ate breakfast in bed, letting crumbs from the Polish bakery fall between the sheets, planning impossible futures. Madeline would trace mathematical equations on his bare back with her fingertip, making him guess the formulas. He never got them right, but he never wanted her to stop.

He remembered one Sunday in particular. At the door to the apartment, he balanced the paper bag and coffee carrier as he fumbled with his key. The early morning air had been crisp, worth the three-block walk to the bakery. Mrs. Kowalski had pulled the challah from the oven just as he'd arrived, and the warm, yeasty smell clung to his jacket.

The door creaked—he really should oil those hinges—as he stepped inside. Through the bedroom doorway, he saw Madeline stirring under his rumpled sheets, sunlight catching in her dark hair through the cheap blinds.

"They had challah still warm from the oven," he called out. "Mrs. Kowalski says hello. And that you're too skinny."

"Mrs. Kowalski thinks everyone under eighty is too skinny." Madeline sat up, gathering the sheets around her shoulders in that unconsciously graceful way that always made his breath catch. "Did you get—"

"Extra poppyseeds?" He appeared in the doorway, proud of his morning's work. "When have I ever forgotten the poppyseeds?"

"There was that one time..."

"That was a Sunday morning crisis. They'd run out. I thought Mrs. Kowalski was going to fire her own grandson over it." He settled onto the bed, carefully managing the coffee cups. Madeline reached toward him, and he felt her fingers in his hair.

"You've got autumn all over you," she said, showing him a few cranberry-colored leaves she'd rescued.

"Better than pigeons." He handed her a coffee cup. "Though one did consider dive-bombing me for the challah."

She tore off a piece of the bread, releasing a curl of steam. "Smart pigeon. This is better than sex."

"Hey now."

"Almost better than sex," she amended, and kissed him. Her lips were soft, and he felt her smile against his mouth.

They ate in comfortable quiet until he felt her shifting under the sheets. "What are you doing down there?"

"Preparing you for your math quiz." She poked his side with her toe. "Ready?"

"No fair doing equations before I'm fully caffeinated."

But she was already tracing numbers on his back with her index finger. Each slow, deliberate movement sent a shiver down his spine. "Come on, genius. What am I writing?"

"Is it... your phone number?"

She snorted. "It's the Fibonacci sequence, you fraud. How did you even pass calculus?"

"I cheated off you."

"We didn't have Calculus together!"

"I was very sneaky about it." He twisted around and caught her hand, pulling her close. Challah crumbs scattered across the sheets. "Very, very sneaky."

He was in the computer lab on a Tuesday in November, helping Shaheer debug a particularly tricky piece of code for his thesis project. His phone buzzed with his mother's number, unusual for the middle of the day.

"Jeff?" Her voice sounded strange, distant. "You need to come home. Your father... there was an accident at work. He's gone."

The fluorescent lights buzzed overhead. Shaheer was saying something, but the words didn't make sense. Jeff felt Madeline's hand on his shoulder—when had she arrived?—and then somehow he was sitting in a chair, his mother's voice still in his ear, explaining about the cardiac arrest, about how quick it had been.

The next hours passed in a blur. Madeline helped him book a flight while Shaheer packed his bag, neither of them commenting on how few personal items he kept in his dorm room. His mother's words kept echoing: "He asked about you, last week. Wanted to know if you were still doing well in school."

He flew to Chicago, then transferred to propeller plane for the last leg. The Mason City airport was smaller than he remembered, or maybe he had grown larger in his time away. His mother waited by baggage claim, gray hair escaping her usual tight bun. When had she gotten so small? She hugged him briefly, her arms thin but strong.

"The funeral's tomorrow," she said as they walked to her car—the same ancient Chevy she'd had since his childhood. "Pastor Mike will do the service. Your father... he'd started going to church again, these past few months."

The house on Cherry Street looked exactly the same, down to the Ford pickup still up on blocks in the driveway. But the silence inside felt different—empty rather than threatening. Jeff's old room remained unchanged, like a museum exhibit of his teenage years: programming books stacked neatly on the desk, a faded poster of the first Mars rover on the wall.

He sat on his bed, his suitcase on the floor beside him. Who had he been when he lived in this room? Who had he become?

When he went downstairs for dinner, he found his mother sitting at the kitchen table, a bottle of his father's whiskey unopened before her.

"He poured all the others out," she said quietly. "Three months ago. Said he was done with it. Kept this one, though. Said he'd open it when you came home for Christmas."

Jeff sat across from her, the familiar vinyl chair creaking under his weight. "Mom..."

"He was trying," she said. "At the end. Got a steady job at the recycling plant. Started going to AA meetings. He wanted..." she traced the whiskey bottle's label with one finger. "He wanted to be someone you could be proud of."

The words hit Jeff like a physical blow. He thought of all the unanswered calls, the holiday visits avoided, the carefully constructed excuses. He thought of his father, sitting in church pews and AA meetings, fighting battles his son hadn't stayed to witness.

"There are letters," his mother continued. "In his dresser drawer. He wrote to you every week, this past year. Never mailed them. Said he had to earn the right first."

His mother made his childhood favorite for dinner, boiled elbow macaroni with butter and grated cheese from a green shaker can. As they sat at the scratched kitchen table where he'd done his homework and eaten countless silent meals, Jeff found himself telling her about Madeline - about the way she turned everything into an experiment, including love. About her parents in Vermont who baked their feelings into bread and painted them onto canvas. His voice grew thick when he described their Christmas, full of family warmth he'd never known existed.

Then he told her about Shaheer, whose dreams were big enough to change the world, who saw possibilities where others saw only problems. As he spoke about his friend's courage to chase those dreams to California, his mother's hands trembled slightly on her coffee cup.

"They sound like wonderful people," she said softly. "I wish..." She didn't finish, but Jeff heard the rest anyway: I wish we could have given you that. I wish you hadn't needed to find family elsewhere. I wish we'd known how.

Jeff reached across the table and covered her hand with his - their first real touch since he'd arrived. Her fingers were rough from years of cleaning other people's houses, but they gripped his with surprising strength. In that moment, he understood something about love and forgiveness that all his father's letters had tried to say: sometimes the bravest thing you can do is acknowledge what was broken without demanding it be fixed.

"I know, Mom," he said. "I know."

After dinner, he retrieved the letters his father had left, and carried them to his room, where he sat at his old desk, feeling their weight. The space between picking them up and beginning to read stretched like the years of silence they contained—not an empty space, but one filled with everything they'd never said to each other. Even the sound of the paper unfolding seemed loud in that pregnant pause, as if the very act of breaking their silence had physical form.

He read the letters by the light of his old desk lamp. His father's handwriting was surprisingly neat, each page dated and carefully preserved. They started formally—"Dear Son"—but gradually became more personal.

He read about a day when Jeff was six, playing catch in the backyard. "You were so determined," his father wrote. "The ball kept sailing over your head, but you never got frustrated. Just kept running after it, trying different ways to catch it. I should have told you how proud that made me." Jeff had forgotten that afternoon, but reading about it brought back the smell of fresh-cut grass, the weight of the baseball in his small hands, the way his father had smiled—a rare, unguarded expression.

Another letter mentioned the science fair in seventh grade. "Found your old ribbon cleaning out the garage," his father wrote. "First place. Your mother told me you built a computer from spare parts. I acted like it was nothing special, but truth is, I didn't understand how you'd done it. Made me feel stupid, and I handled that wrong. Should have asked you to explain it to me. Should have let you teach me."

The words blurred as Jeff read about the night he got his Columbia acceptance letter. "You looked so tall standing there in the kitchen. Not my little boy anymore. I wanted to hug you, tell you I was wrong about college being a waste. But all I could think about was how you were going to leave, going to find out how small your old man really was. So I got angry instead. Been regretting that night ever since."

There were smaller memories too. Helping his father change spark plugs when he was ten, the two of them working in comfortable silence. The time Jeff had tried to make pancakes and nearly burned down the kitchen, and his father had quietly cleaned up the mess without a word of reproach.

A morning when eight-year-old Jeff had found his father crying at the kitchen table and wordlessly brought him a glass of water, the way Toby would nose at their hands when they were sad.

"Maybe that's where you learned it," his father wrote. "Being quiet when things hurt. Watched me do it your whole life. Difference is, you had good things to say. I just had anger and shame."

The last letter was shorter than the others, as if his father had sensed time running out. "Been sober 90 days now. They tell us in AA to make amends, but they also say not to do it if it'll cause more harm. Wasn't sure which one telling you would do. Just want you to know I see you, son. Always did, even when I couldn't show it. You're nothing like me, and that's the best thing I ever did in my life."

It ended with "I hope someday you'll let me tell you I'm sorry in person."

Jeff sat for a long time after reading that last page, holding it carefully as if it might dissolve like sugar in rain. Outside his window, the Mason City streets were quiet, the same streets where he'd learned that love and silence went hand in hand. But in these letters, his father had finally found his voice, even if only on paper. Maybe, Jeff thought, it wasn't too late for him to find his own.

Jeff wept then, for the first time since hearing the news. He cried for the father he'd never really known, for the man who'd died trying to bridge the silence between them, for all the words they'd left unspoken.

The funeral was small—a handful of AA members, some guys from the plant, a few neighbors. Pastor Mike spoke about redemption and second chances, and Jeff wondered if everyone could hear the irony. His father had found his second chance, but Jeff hadn't been there to see it.

After, at the house, his mother handed him a small box. Inside was his father's sobriety chip—90 days clean—and a folded piece of paper with Jeff's name on it.

"He was proud of you," she said softly. "Even if he never learned how to say it right."

He held the chip in his palm, feeling its weight. The space between who his father had been and who he was trying to become lived in this small circle of metal. Like the empty chairs at AA meetings waiting to be filled, it was a moment of potential change that death had frozen in place forever.

Madeline met him at La Guardia, and she held him as a city bus carried them back to Manhattan, her quiet presence more comforting than any words. The campus felt simultaneously familiar and strange, like a photograph slightly out of focus.

That night, in her tiny apartment with its star charts and rescued plants, she asked him what he needed.

"Time," he said, thinking of his father's letters, of all the chances they'd missed. "I just need some time."

She nodded, but something in her expression made him think of Berkeley, of California, of all the miles that could fit between two people before it was too late. He should have told her then that he loved her, that he was scared of losing her like he'd lost his father, with too many things left unsaid.

Instead, he let her hold him while he cried, the stars watching silently through her window, bearing witness to another chance at love slipping quietly away.

Outside her window, the December sky hung low and colorless, like a blank canvas waiting for someone brave enough to paint dreams on it. The weather forecasters had predicted snow, but instead a thin, mean drizzle fell, turning everything to gray slush—not quite rain, not quite ice, caught between states just like Jeff's words caught in his throat.

Chapter 10
Self-Sabotage

Spring came reluctantly to Columbia's campus that year, winter stubbornly holding on like Jeff's lingering grief. The cherry trees finally bloomed along College Walk, their petals carpeting the ground in white and pink, but Jeff barely noticed. He was too busy cycling through a series of increasingly dispiriting job interviews.

"Tell us where you see yourself in five years," the interviewer at Microsoft asked.

Jeff's carefully prepared answer stuck in his throat. The truth—that he couldn't imagine tomorrow, let alone five years from now—must have shown in his eyes. The rejection email came within an hour.

Google was worse. He froze during the technical interview, his mind blank before a problem he'd solved dozens of times in class. The interviewer's patience felt like pity, and Jeff knew before he left the building that he'd failed.

After his sixth rejection, he sat with Madeline in their usual spot in Butler Library. Spring sunshine streamed through the windows, catching the dust motes in golden light that reminded him of her family home in Vermont.

"You're sabotaging yourself," she said, pushing aside her own work—letters from Berkeley's graduate program that she hadn't opened yet. "I've seen you solve harder problems than these interview questions in your sleep."

"I just get... stuck," he said. "When they start asking about leadership and initiative and where I want to be in five years."

"Then practice with me." She closed her laptop decisively. "Right now. I'm the interviewer."

"Madeline..."

"Ms. Hinckley," she corrected, putting on an exaggerated serious expression. "Now, Mr. Hodges, tell me about a time you demonstrated leadership in a challenging situation."

Despite himself, Jeff smiled. She'd pulled her hair back into a severe bun and was peering at him over imaginary glasses.

"I... uh..."

"Remember that group project in Data Structures?" she prompted. "When Jamie's laptop crashed the night before the presentation?"

"That wasn't really—"

"You stayed up all night reconstructing his part from the backup files. Organized the whole team to rewrite sections. Got everyone coffee and kept them motivated. The project was better than the original version."

"I was just solving a problem."

"That's leadership, Jeff. It's not about being the loudest voice in the room. It's about seeing what needs to be done and doing it."

They practiced for hours, Madeline helping him reshape his experiences into stories that showcased his strengths. She made him articulate things he'd never thought about—how his quiet attention to detail made systems more reliable, how his careful documentation helped other developers build on his work.

"You see yourself as someone who maintains things," she said, finally dropping her interviewer persona. "But I see someone who makes things better, who cares about quality and consistency. That has value, Jeff. Real value."

The next day, she helped him revise his resume, highlighting achievements he'd dismissed as routine. When Allied Insurance called to schedule an interview, she ran him through practice questions until his answers felt natural.

"Remember," she said as he knotted his tie the morning of the interview, "they're not just evaluating you. You're evaluating them. Look for a place where you can grow."

The interview went surprisingly well. The company needed someone to maintain and improve their legacy systems—work that required patience, attention to detail, and a deep understanding of how complex systems interacted. For the first time, Jeff felt his careful nature might be an asset rather than a liability.

The offer came two days later. The salary was decent, the benefits good. Not Google money, but enough to start a life in New York. He could imagine himself there, building something stable, something that would last.

That evening, they celebrated with takeout from their favorite Vietnamese place, eating on the roof of Madeline's building. The spring air was warm, carrying the scent of newly awakened things.

"Berkeley sent their acceptance," she said carefully, setting down her chopsticks. "Full funding for the Ph.D. program."

Jeff's heart stumbled. "Oh."

"But I'm going to stay at Columbia for a year before I leave," she continued quickly. "Dr. Harrison has that grant for the biocomputing research. She says I can lead one of the project teams."

"You'd turn down Berkeley?" The words felt thick in his mouth. "That's your dream program."

Madeline shrugged, too casually. "Columbia's just as good. And this way we can be together. Figure things out. The Harrison project is just for a year, so I'll have flexibility if... if other opportunities come up."

She didn't mention Shaheer's excitement about the growing buzz about his ideas for self-debugging code. She didn't have to. Jeff saw it in the way she'd hesitate sometimes, mid-sentence, as if catching herself before saying too much.

"You should take Berkeley," he said, the words feeling like stones in his mouth.

"Jeff—"

"It's your dream. You shouldn't compromise that. Not for..." He couldn't finish.

She moved closer, fitting herself against his side like she had so many nights on this roof. "Some dreams are worth adjusting," she said softly. "We have time to figure it out. Shaheer's ideas are still in the early stages, the incubator's just a possibility. Let's just... see what happens."

Jeff nodded, pulling her closer. Below them, the city was coming alive with spring, trees budding in Riverside Park, students sprawling on the lawn with textbooks and frisbees. Everything changing, everything growing. He should have recognized it for what it was—not an ending averted, but merely postponed. Should have known that dreams deferred don't die immediately, they wait for that final death knell.

But in that moment, with Madeline warm against him and their whole future seemingly ahead of them, he let himself believe in the possibility of a life where love was enough, where dreams could be reshaped without being abandoned, where staying still didn't mean being left behind.

Later, much later, he would remember this night and recognize it as their last perfect moment—the last time both of their dreams seemed to point in the same direction. But for now, he held her, watching the spring stars emerge above the city lights, each one a possible future they hadn't yet chosen or lost.

Chapter 11
Between Past and Present

Betty's morning routine hadn't changed in twenty-three years. She still made coffee for two, though now she never poured Maria's cup. She still played the Brazilian jazz station that Maria had loved, still traced her fingers along the café's walls as she opened up each morning, checking its pulse like a doctor with a patient.

The café had been Maria's dream first. "Everyone needs a place to heal," she'd say, planning it all out in her sketchbooks - the wall of mirrors to "reflect people's true selves," the perfect arrangement of tables and chairs to create intimate spaces within the public room. But Maria hadn't lived to see it become real. Cancer took her quickly, leaving Betty alone with a collection of dog paintings and a dream she didn't know how to fulfill.

That first year after losing Maria had taught Betty about different kinds of silence. There was the silence of their brownstone, too big now for one person. The silence of meals eaten alone. The silence of questions that would never have answers. But most of all, there was the silence within herself, where grief had carved out spaces she thought would never fill again.

Then came Duke the German Shepherd that first rainy night, leading her to Sarah. Betty hadn't wanted to follow - what could she possibly offer anyone when she was so broken herself? But something in the dog's eyes reminded her of how Maria used to look, and Betty found herself stepping into the rain.

The café's magic had grown slowly, like trust between strangers. First it was just the dogs appearing, leading people who needed help. Then the mirrors began showing more than reflections, and the jazz music would change to match each visitor's mood. Betty learned to read the signs: when the scent of cinnamon grew stronger, someone was about to make a breakthrough. When she put the beans in the grinder, but an unexpected aroma rose in the air. When the light shifted to create a spotlight on a particular table, that's where the next healing would begin.

"You're learning," Maria's voice sometimes seemed to whisper in the quiet moments between customers. Betty would find herself reaching for cups she didn't remember buying, brewing coffee blends she'd never stocked, yet somehow they were always exactly what someone needed.

The wall of paintings grew as Betty learned to see what each visitor required. Gigi for the broken-hearted, Duke for the lost, Vinnie the one-eared Staffordshire Terrier for those who needed courage. And Cooper... Cooper's portrait was special. Maria had painted him last, working on it days before she passed. "He's waiting," she'd said, adding final touches to his gentle smile. "When the right person needs him, he'll know."

Betty learned to trust the café's rhythms. Some days it wanted to be busy, filling with people who needed to witness each other's healing. Other days it would empty out entirely, preparing itself for a single visitor who needed absolute privacy. The coffee machine might suddenly produce the exact blend someone's grandmother used to make, or the sound system would play a song that held a particular memory.

"I'm not a counselor anymore," Betty had protested that first year, when the café began drawing more and more lost souls. But Maria's voice seemed to answer in the steam from the espresso machine: "You're exactly what they need you to be."

Over time, Betty discovered that tending to others' wounds was its own kind of healing. Each person who found their way to the café brought something new - Sarah's determination, Ray's music, Frances' rediscovered creativity. The empty spaces grief had carved in Betty began to fill with their stories, their courage, their gradual journeys back to wholeness.

She noticed the café changed subtly for each visitor. For Ray, the acoustics shifted, making every note he played on the old piano resonate perfectly. For Sarah, the light had been gentle, soft as forgiveness. For Frances, the mirrors had shown not just reflections but possibilities.

Now, watching Cooper's portrait, Betty recognized the signs of imminent change. The café was preparing itself for someone special, someone who needed more than just comfort or guidance. Someone who needed to learn the same lesson Betty had: that healing isn't about filling the empty spaces left by loss, but about learning to hold both the absence and the presence, the grief and the joy, the endings and the beginnings.

"We're ready," she told Cooper's portrait each morning, though she wasn't sure if she meant the café or herself. The silence that followed wasn't empty anymore - it was the kind that comes just before dawn, full of possibility and anticipation.

After all, Betty had learned from Maria that the most important ingredient in any cup of coffee wasn't the beans or the brewing temperature. It was the intention behind it, the willingness to sit with someone in their pain and help them find their way back to light. She'd learned that from Maria, and now she could teach it to others. That was its own kind of magic, its own kind of love.

The café hummed around her in agreement, and somewhere in the distance, a dog barked - once, twice, three times. Betty smiled, recognizing the signal. Cooper had found someone at last.

Chapter 12
Guardian of Lost Hearts

Betty always knew when a dog's portrait was about to wake up. The café would grow quieter, more contemplative, as if gathering itself for something important.

Sarah sat in her usual corner, grading papers from her literature class. She'd been there when Archie the crop-eared pug woke up for Ray the musician, had watched the café's gentle magic at work.

"I love the dogs who work with artists," Sarah said. "Tell me about Archie again."

Sometimes stories needed retelling, like bread needed kneading, to reach their proper shape. "It was about six months after I opened. I was still figuring out how this place worked, wondering what I was going to do with that old piano. Ray came in following a little pug with one ear folded over. Archie led him straight to the piano."

"That old upright that never quite stayed in tune," Sarah smiled. "You told me you loved it because its imperfections made the music more human. Ray sat down and stared at the keys. Didn't touch them, didn't speak. Just sat there like he was looking at something that might bite him."

"Three hours," Betty recalled. "He sat there for three hours before he played a single note."

"But when he did…" Sarah's voice softened with the memory. "I'd never heard 'Yesterday' sound so much like healing."

The café seemed to sigh around them, remembering. That piano was gone now, donated to a music school after Ray started playing regular gigs again. But sometimes, on quiet afternoons, Betty still heard its slightly off-key notes through the hidden speakers.

The textures of the café had become as familiar as a well-worn sweater - the smooth edges of the counter where thousands of hands had rested, the soft give of leather seats that seemed to remember every person who'd sat in them, the delicate roughness of handmade ceramic mugs that Betty somehow matched to each customer's needs. Even the air had texture - thick with steam from the espresso machine, soft with flour dust from the morning's baking, warm with the breath of conversations and confidences shared over countless cups of coffee.

"Archie stayed visible the whole time," Sarah continued. "Sat right next to the piano bench, head on Ray's knee. That's never happened before or since. Usually the dogs vanish once they've led someone here."

"He knew Ray needed an anchor," Betty said. "Someone to feel with him until he could feel on his own again."

After Sarah left, Betty went through her closing routine. She thought about all the people the dogs had helped over the years, appearing to guide them to the café when their hearts needed healing. The teacher who'd lost her hope. The writer who'd lost his words. But something told her this time was different. This wasn't just about healing—it was about awakening something that had never been allowed to fully live.

Betty smiled at Cooper's portrait, understanding finally what Maria had meant about him being special. Some dogs led people to healing. But Cooper? Cooper led them to themselves.

Chapter 13
The Next Chapter

The May sunshine turned Columbia's campus into a postcard version of itself, with light glinting off Alma Mater and Butler Library's windows. Jeff sat beside Madeline among the engineering graduates, sweating under his light blue gown, the same color as Tiffany boxes. The air smelled of fresh-cut grass and possibility, though the latter made his stomach churn.

His mother sat with the Hinckleys in the crowd of parents and well-wishers spread across the South Lawn. She looked small and out of place in her best church dress, the one she saved for weddings and funerals. But Maury and Gaye had immediately drawn her into their orbit, Maury sharing his contraband snacks while Gaye sketched quick portraits of the surrounding families in her ever-present notebook.

Madeline's graduation cap was decorated with a model of a caffeine molecule. She'd tried to convince Jeff to add something to his —"Come on, at least a USB!"—but he'd left his unadorned. Now, watching the sun catch the glitter on her molecule, he wished he'd let her personalize his too.

The ceremony seemed designed to last forever. Speakers droned about bright futures and changing worlds, their words carried away by the spring breeze. Jeff barely heard them, too aware of his mother sitting there among all these successful families, too conscious of the weight of expectations—hers, his own, the Hinckleys'.

Each school had its tradition for the moment degrees were conferred. The business school graduates threw fake hundred-dollar bills into the air, drawing laughs from the crowd. The dental school's rainbow of toothbrushes created a surprising arc of color against the blue sky. When it was the engineering school's turn, Jeff and Madeline joined their classmates in launching plastic slide rules skyward. He watched them spiral up and away, carried by the wind toward Butler Library before falling somewhere in the crowd.

The ceremony was a mass one; each of the schools had their own smaller event where students walked across the stage and received an empty diploma cover, the real thing to be mailed out once final grades had been processed.

The last speaker seemed to take forever, bloviating about 'the next chapter' in graduates' lives. Representatives of the college a cappella groups sang the alma mater, "Stand, Columbia," followed by a rendition of Frank Sinatra's "New York, New York."

When the graduates were dismissed, Jeff and Madeline met their parents at a pre-arranged spot in front of Havemeyer Hall. Maury insisted on taking dozens of photos. "For posterity!" he boomed, arranging and rearranging them in different ways. Jeff's mother stood slightly apart until Gaye gently pulled her into the frame, keeping a warm hand on her shoulder.

"Now just the lovebirds," Maury directed, and Jeff and Madeline posed by the building's front door. Jeff remembered how much time the two of them had spent in that building and other iconic locations on campus. Everything was about to change.

Madeline's caffeine molecule kept tilting precariously, and Jeff reached up to steady it, his fingers brushing her hair. The touch felt electric, significant. They were graduates now, adults supposedly. The thought terrified him.

Dinner was at an Italian restaurant Maury had somehow gotten reservations for despite graduation day chaos. The table was crowded with wine glasses (except for Jeff's mother, who ordered iced tea) and plates of pasta that Maury insisted everyone share.

"To the graduates," Gaye proposed, raising her glass. "May you change the world in exactly the ways it needs changing."

Jeff watched Madeline beam at her parents, her face flushed with wine and accomplishment. She'd already accepted the research position at Columbia, deferring Berkeley's offer. He should feel relieved, he knew. They had time to figure things out. But something in Gaye's toast nagged at him—change the world? He could barely handle changing dorm rooms every year.

His mother was quiet through most of the meal, but she smiled at Maury's jokes and answered Gaye's gentle questions about life in Mason City. Watching her there, Jeff realized she'd never sat in a restaurant this nice, never had someone pull out her chair or unfold her napkin into her lap. She handled it all with quiet dignity, but he saw how her hands shook slightly when lifting her water glass.

"Your boy's got a bright future," Maury told her over dessert. "We're going to see great things from both of them."

Jeff's mother nodded, then said softly, "He always was good with computers. Fixed our old one when he was twelve. Never did understand how he learned all that."

It was more than she'd said all evening, and Jeff felt the words settle in his chest like stones. All the things they'd never talked about, all the silence between them—and here she was, trying in her own way to bridge it.

Later, saying goodbye outside the restaurant, his mother hugged him briefly. "Your father would have been proud," she whispered, then stepped quickly away, as if the words might burn her.

Jeff watched her cab disappear into the Manhattan traffic, remembering all the times he'd watched her count out exact change for groceries, how she'd worked extra cleaning jobs just to keep the lights on. She'd taught him that survival meant playing it safe, keeping your head down, never reaching too high.

He turned to find Madeline watching him with soft eyes. Behind her, Maury and Gaye were arguing good-naturedly about the best route back to their hotel, their comfortable bickering so different from the tense silences of his childhood home.

"You okay?" she asked quietly.

He nodded, not trusting his voice. The weight of the diploma cover in his hands suddenly felt like anchor chain, pulling him down into depths he wasn't ready to explore.

The May evening was settling over the city, string lights twinkling in restaurant windows, the air sweet with the promise of summer. They had graduated. They were supposed to be ready for anything. But standing there between his mother's hard-won wisdom and Madeline's fearless ambition, Jeff had never felt less ready in his life.

Now, twelve years later, Jeff realized that graduation night had been the first time he'd truly felt the weight of his choices. The diploma cover still sat in a box in his hotel room, a reminder of the moment he'd chosen his mother's path of safety over Madeline's dreams of discovery.

Chapter 14
387 Square Feet

Jeff's last day in the dorm arrived with New York's particular brand of summer heat—thick and unyielding. Jeff stood in his half-empty room, surveying what remained: three monitors, a custom-built PC tower, tangles of cables, and two boxes of computer books. His entire life fit into the trunk of Shaheer's borrowed Honda Civic, except for the few delicate electronics he carried in his backpack.

"We should have hired movers," Madeline suggested, wiping sweat from her forehead. She'd pulled her hair up into a messy bun, escaping curls plastered to her neck. "I saw an ad for College Hunks Moving Junk."

"You already have two hunks," Shaheer said. "How many more do you want?"

Jeff said, "For five boxes and some computer stuff? We can handle it."

But after the third trip up those narrow stairs, each step groaning under their feet, he was reconsidering. The monitors had to be carried one at a time, cradled like oversized babies. The tower was worse—too heavy for one person but awkward for two, leading to a complicated dance of coordination through the tight stairwell.

Madeline's apartment was exactly 387 square feet—she'd measured it herself when she first moved in, plotting out every inch on graph paper. Now, standing amid the boxes and equipment, to Jeff it felt more like 37.

"Okay," she said, hands on hips, surveying the chaos. "We can put your desk... um." She turned in a slow circle, reality setting in. Her own desk already occupied the only logical spot for computer work, beneath the room's single window.

Jeff set down the last monitor, trying not to let doubt creep in. "Maybe we could share the desk? Take shifts?"

"Or..." She brightened. "We could combine them! Make one mega-desk!"

They spent the next hour rearranging furniture like a real-life Tetris game. Madeline's desk joined with Jeff's to form an L-shape in the corner. Her chemistry journals stacked beneath his programming books. His three monitors curved around the workspace like a command center.

"Where did you get all these anyway?" she asked, helping him untangle cables.

"Built them from parts. People throw away perfectly good monitors because of minor issues." He didn't add that he'd learned this from his mother, who'd brought home discarded electronics from the houses she cleaned.

The rest of his possessions took no time to unpack. A few t-shirts and hoodies, worn jeans, the suit from his Allied interview. Some papers from school he couldn't bring himself to throw away. A single photo of himself with Toby, creased and faded.

"Is this all?" Madeline asked gently, watching him put the photo on their shared desk.

"Never needed much else." He busied himself with cable management, a task that required focus and prevented eye contact.

"Well, now you have my stuff too," she said, wrapping her arms around him from behind. "My rocks, my plants, my star charts. Our stuff."

Her collection of minerals had already colonized every available surface—chunks of rose quartz and amethyst, a piece of meteorite she'd splurged on at a science museum. Plants hung in macramé holders, their vines reaching toward each other like curious fingers. The star charts on her walls had migrated upward as they'd rearranged the furniture, now floating above their merged workstation like a paper galaxy.

That evening, they sat on her—their—double bed, sharing takeout pad Thai and watching the monitors' screensavers cast shifting patterns on the walls. The room was hot despite the ancient window unit laboring away, and the bed felt smaller than it had during his previous stays. But Madeline was explaining how they could build shelves above the desk for more storage, her hands gesturing enthusiastically with chopsticks, and Jeff felt something inside him settle.

"Welcome home," she said later, as they lay in the dark, fan whirring overhead. "To our very own shoebox in the sky."

Jeff reached for her hand in the darkness. The apartment was too small, the stairs too many, the heat too persistent. But Madeline's fingers intertwined with his, and somehow that made all the dimensions feel exactly right.

Chapter 15
The Art of Maintenance

The orientation room at Allied Insurance felt like a liminal space, neither real office nor quite school. Twenty new hires sat in uncomfortable chairs, watching PowerPoint slides about corporate culture and retirement plans. Jeff's new suit—bought on sale at Men's Wearhouse—felt stiff and foreign, like borrowed skin.

"Welcome to the Allied family!" The HR representative's enthusiasm seemed genuine, which somehow made it worse. She handed out employee handbooks thick enough to stop bullets. "You'll find everything you need to know in here, from dress code to dental benefits."

Jeff's cubicle assignment was on the third floor, in a maze of identical beige partitions. His supervisor, Rod, a skinny guy with stringy hair who needed to shower more frequently, showed him around with the distracted air of someone checking off a task list.

"Bathroom's down that way," Rod gestured vaguely. "Break room's around the corner. We've got three microwaves but the middle one's haunted—heats unevenly. You'll figure it out." He paused at an empty cube. "Home sweet home."

His cubicle felt like a metaphor for his life - beige, bounded, and barely lived in. The only splash of color came from a dying philodendron that no one else had wanted. "Been here since before my time," Rod had said. "Feel free to toss it."

But Jeff couldn't bring himself to throw away something just because it was struggling. That evening, he looked up plant care on his phone. The next morning, he brought in a small spray bottle and some plant food he'd bought at the corner store.

"Guess we're in this together," he told the plant, misting its leaves. He named it Phil, and cared for it the way he nurtured the ancient code he'd been hired to maintain.

The company's claim processing software was written in languages so old they practically qualified for social security. Each morning, Jeff would sit in his cube, adding patches to patches, watching the system grow more Byzantine with every fix.

"Just keep it running," Rod would say whenever Jeff suggested improvements. "If it ain't broke, don't fix it." But it was broke. The whole system was a digital house of cards, held together with virtual duct tape and programmer prayers. Jeff documented everything meticulously, drawing maps of the system's twisted logic, much like he used to diagram his father's moods as a child.

The worst part was that he was good at it—this careful maintenance of mediocrity. His performance reviews were consistently positive in the most depressing way possible. "Jeff excels at maintaining existing systems," they'd say. "Shows admirable caution in implementing changes."

He thought often of Shaheer during those long afternoons, imagining his friend's reaction to this digital labyrinth, this monument to patch-upon-patch programming. "At least one of us is growing," he'd whisper to Phil, whose leaves had begun to perk up under his care. The plant's silent resilience felt like both comfort and accusation.

Over the next few weeks, Jeff learned the unwritten rules of office life. Mohammed in the next cube over would share his wife's homemade samosas if you complimented his anime figurines. Debby three cubes down collected state postcards—she had thirty-seven so far and was determined to get all fifty. She recruited anyone who traveled to keep an eye out for cards for her. Fortunately she already had Iowa, so Jeff didn't need to tell her he had no intention of ever going back to Mason City. The break room fridge was cleaned out every Friday at 4pm exactly, and anything left inside disappeared forever.

Jeff's cubicle smelled perpetually of stale coffee and the lasting odor of Debby's tuna casseroles. When he needed to share information with a coworker he rolled his chair across the carpet.

He talked with Shaheer only on weekends, when his friend took a break from his obsessive desire to turn his idea of self-repairing code to a reality. He had declined all the jobs he'd been offered, from Apple to Intel to Gateway, preferring to focus on his startup, which he'd called Aether Code. He had no employees, held meetings in coffee shops, and lived on an allowance from his parents. But Jeff had never seen him happier.

The other developers at Allied had a betting pool on how long it would take before the whole system collapsed, but nobody seemed interested in preventing that collapse.

During lunch breaks, he'd sit with Phil, sharing his sandwich and explaining his latest coding challenges. The plant's leaves had begun to perk up, reaching toward the fluorescent lights like a person stretching after a long sleep.

"See that new growth?" he told Phil one day. "That's what happens when you don't give up on something."

Sometimes, in quiet moments between meetings, Jeff would think about Shaheer and his startup dreams. Whenever he and Madeline drew Shaheer away from toiling in his Brooklyn apartment he talked nonstop about neural networks and self-debugging code. The words blurred together, each one a reminder of the future Jeff had been too afraid to chase.

But here, in his beige cube with his rescued plant, Jeff had found a kind of peace. It wasn't the revolution Shaheer dreamed of or the adventure Madeline craved, but maybe there was value in being the person who kept things running, who noticed when systems—or plants—needed care.

"We're maintenance workers," he told Phil, adjusting the spray bottle's nozzle. "Nothing wrong with that. Cleaning up other people's mess. My mother has spent her whole life doing that."

He gradually noticed the way that people had decorated their areas. Rod had photos of beach vacations, with beautiful girls in bikinis holding tropical drinks. Jin-Ho hung posters of WWE wrestlers.

Because Jeff's salary was low, as was Madeline's research stipend, their date nights were creative exercises in economy. They discovered free concert nights at obscure bars, where jazz musicians practiced their craft while Jeff and Madeline danced in the back, her head fitting perfectly against his shoulder. They found a tiny Vietnamese restaurant with wobbly tables and the best pho in Manhattan, where the owner would slip them extra spring rolls because Madeline always asked about her grandchildren.

It they lured Shaheer away from his computer to join them whenever Jeff complained about his job, Shaheer would say, "This is exactly what's wrong with the software industry. Too stuck in old patterns, refusing to change with new developments."

Madeline's grant money ran unexpectedly short one month, and Jeff had to pay the rent himself. They spent two weeks eating nothing but ramen noodles, but they made it into an adventure. Each night they tried to outdo each other with creative additions—an egg stolen from the lab's break room refrigerator, vegetables rescued from the discount bin, sauces cadged from Chinese takeout packets.

One night, they sat cross-legged on the floor of Madeline's apartment, surrounded by empty ramen packets and takeout containers.

"Drum roll, please." Jeff held up a bowl with flourish.

Madeline dutifully drummed on an empty Cup Noodles container. "Presenting tonight's culinary masterpiece..."

"I call it Manhattan Midnight Ramen." He set the bowl between them. Steam rose from the noodles, carrying an odd mixture of scents.

Madeline peered in. "Is that... did you put Oreos in there?"

"And a hot dog. For protein."

"That's not food. That's a cry for help." But she was already reaching for a fork. "Does the health department know about this?"

"Try it before you judge."

She took a small bite, her face contorting. "Oh god. Oh no. This is..." She couldn't finish, dissolving into laughter so hard she had to put the fork down.

"What? What's wrong with it?"

"Everything. Everything is wrong with it." She was gasping now, tears running down her face. "We have to call Shaheer. He needs to document this atrocity."

She reached for her phone, still hiccupping with laughter, while Jeff defended his creation. "The sweet and savory combination is very trendy right now!"

"In what universe?" She had Shaheer on speaker now. "Shaheer, you have to hear what your friend has done to perfectly innocent ramen..."

Chapter 16
Unscrambling the Code

Another memory came to mind as he walked the streets around the hotel, with nothing better to do. Of a rooftop bar in midtown. It was closing, their single shared beer long empty. The bartender was stacking chairs, giving them pointed looks, but neither moved.

"Look," Madeline said softly, pointing at the city lights. "The pattern of streetlamps on Fifth Avenue. It's like a double helix."

Jeff followed her gesture. "More like a binary sequence to me."

"That's because you have no poetry in your soul." But she leaned against him, her hair tickling his neck. "What do you think all those lights represent? How many stories are happening down there right now?"

"At least seven."

"Only seven?"

"Seven important ones. The rest are just people watching Netflix."

She laughed, the sound carrying across the empty rooftop. "You're ridiculous." Then, more quietly: "I love that about you."

The words hung in the cooling air. Jeff felt them settle on his skin like dew, each one a chance to respond, to say what lived in his heart.

But he just pulled her closer, counting streetlights until they blurred before his eyes.

Though they had graduated into a recession, Shaheer seemed unfazed. He was so sure that Aether Code would be a success. On weekends, he'd invite Jeff and Madeline to his small apartment, cooking elaborate meals while telling them about his dreams.

"The problem with software," he'd say, stirring a pot of curry, "is that it doesn't learn from its mistakes. But what if it could? What if we could write code that evolved, that fixed its own bugs?" His eyes would light up, and he'd nearly forget about the cooking until Madeline rescued whatever was on the stove.

Jeff watched his friend's passion with a mixture of admiration and unease. Shaheer had such certainty about his path, such clear vision of what he wanted to create. Jeff's own career felt like a ship without a rudder in comparison. He had taken a safe job at an established company, working on stable but uninspiring projects while Shaheer's ideas grew bigger and bolder.

Some nights, they'd lie on their shared bed staring at the glow-in-the-dark star charts on the ceiling, planning trips to dark-sky locations they couldn't afford. Jeff would hold her hand in the artificial starlight, feeling like he was touching something rare and precious.

She kept odd hours at the lab, sometimes calling him at three in the morning to share a breakthrough. He'd listen to her excited voice, not understanding the chemistry but loving the way passion made her words tumble over each other. Sometimes she'd fall asleep mid-sentence, and he'd stay on the line, listening to her breathing, wondering how he'd gotten so lucky.

Even their fights were gentle. Madeline never pushed when Jeff grew quiet, seeming to understand there were doors inside him that had rusted shut long ago. Instead, she'd give him space, then leave silly notes in his jacket pockets—terrible chemistry puns or stick-figure drawings of them as superheroes. "The Adventures of Chemistry Girl and Code Boy," she called them, and each one was a reminder that she accepted him, silences and all.

When the first hints of bigger opportunities appeared—Shaheer's increasingly excited calls about investors from Silicon Valley, new opportunities developing in the PhD program at Berkeley—Jeff tried to ignore them. He wanted to preserve their small, perfect world in amber, protected from the winds of change. But Madeline's eyes grew brighter with each call from California, and he began to feel time slipping through his fingers like sand.

On their last perfect day together, just before everything changed, they played hooky from work. It was one of those brilliant autumn afternoons that made New York feel magical. They rode the Staten Island Ferry back and forth, drinking bad coffee and making up stories about their fellow passengers. Madeline's hair whipped in the wind as she pointed out chemical tanks on the Jersey shore, explaining how she could make them explode "in a purely hypothetical way, of course."

Later, they wandered through the East Village, ducking into used bookstores where Madeline would find the most obscure science books and read aloud the funniest passages. They bought one hot dog and shared it while sitting on a park bench, throwing the last piece of bun to a hopeful pigeon. As the sun set, they found another rooftop bar where they could only afford one beer between them, but the view of the city made them feel rich.

Jeff knew he should tell her then—when her eyes were bright with happiness and the city was spread out before them like a carpet of possibilities. The words were there, glowing like the sunset, but he swallowed them with the last sip of beer. It was enough, he told himself, to just have this moment. To hold it like a photograph in his memory, perfect and unchanged.

He didn't know that soon the conversations would turn serious, that Shaheer's dreams and Madeline's ambitions would grow too big for their small, safe world.

Then came the night that changed everything. Shaheer had invited them over, but this time there was no curry on the stove.

Instead, he had a whiteboard propped against his living room wall, covered in flowcharts and calculations.

"I've done it," he said, barely letting them through the door. "I've figured out the core algorithm. And I've got investors interested." He turned to Jeff, his eyes bright with excitement. "I want you on my team. You see patterns nobody else catches, Jeff. You could help make this real."

Madeline squeezed Jeff's hand, and he felt the weight of possibility pressing down on him. Shaheer wasn't just offering him a job—he was offering him a chance to be part of something revolutionary. Something that would require him to believe in more than just a steady paycheck and a safe routine.

The next few weeks were a blur of planning sessions and late-night discussions. Shaheer had already secured initial funding and was in talks with a major tech incubator in San Francisco. Berkely had offered Madeline the opportunity to begin the PhD program in January. All the pieces were falling into place.

Jeff felt himself withdrawing. The certainty he saw in Shaheer's face, the excitement in Madeline's voice—they only highlighted his own doubts, his own inability to trust in something as intangible as possibility.

The morning Shaheer signed the incubator agreement, setting Aether Code's course for California, Jeff watched his friend's hands tremble as he filled out the paperwork. "This is it," Shaheer said, looking up with a grin. "We're really doing this."

Jeff nodded, but inside, he was already building walls against the wave of change threatening to sweep him away.

Shaheer's salary offer was modest, matching what he was making at Allied Insurance, but the equity package made his hands sweat. Madeline squeezed his fingers under the table, her eyes bright with barely contained excitement.

He thought about growing up watching his mother count pennies at the grocery store, the times the electricity had been shut off because his father had drunk away the utility money. The constant gnawing fear that they were always one missed paycheck away from disaster.

Allied Insurance might not be exciting, but it was stable—a regular salary, health insurance, a 401k. Shaheer's startup was all possibilities and dreams, but dreams didn't pay rent or keep the lights on. Jeff had spent his childhood watching his father chase dreams into the bottom of a whiskey bottle. He couldn't risk ending up the same way, couldn't bear the thought of failing and having to crawl back home like his father had always predicted he would.

Later that night, she'd spread out pros and cons lists on their bed, but they both knew the only con that mattered was Jeff's paralysis in the face of change.

It was early December, and it was clear a cold winter was coming. Outside the apartment, workers were beginning to hang Christmas decorations from the streetlamps. The sound of metal striking metal echoed through the thin windows as they worked, like a clock counting down moments he couldn't get back.

Madeline sat cross-legged on the bed. A cardinal landed on the fire escape outside his window—brilliant red against the gray day—and then flew away as a worker's wrench clattered to the sidewalk below.

It all came down to this final conversation, when she begged him to open his heart, to say the words that sat like lead on his tongue, poisoning him with their weight.

"Tell me how you feel, Jeff," she pleaded, her eyes bright with unshed tears. "Why won't you come to San Francisco with me? We've been so good together, haven't we? I love you—I want to build a life with you. But this PhD program... I can't keep turning Berkeley down unless you give me a reason to stay."

The silence between them wasn't empty—it was filled with a lifetime of learning to swallow words, of believing silence meant safety. Like the space between heartbeats, between breaths, between wanting to fly and being afraid to fall. While the workers' radio played below, that pause grew until it became a chasm neither of them knew how to cross.

He stood there, paralyzed, drowning in the silence of his own making. Below, the workers called to each other as they unloaded garlands to wrap around streetlights, Santas to hang from stanchions. "Time to get moving!" one shouted. "Holidays will be here whether we're ready or not!"

"It's not like anything's keeping you here," Madeline continued, her voice cracking. "You hate your job, and Shaheer will match your salary. It could be our adventure, Jeff. Something we build together."

The words were there, pushing against his lips like prisoners against cell bars: "I love you. I want the same things. I'll follow you anywhere. We'll create a new life together." But his shoulders sagged under the weight of his own cowardice, and the silence stretched between them like an unbridgeable chasm. Outside, the workers' radio played "California Dreamin'"—someone's idea of a joke about the unseasonable cold—the Mamas and Papas singing about brown leaves and gray skies while all the leaves stopped pretendin'.

Finally, Madeline rose, her face a mask of resignation. The cardinal returned to the fire escape, watched for a moment through the window, then took flight again. "I put off Berkeley once, but I can't let this opportunity slip away," she said. "I'm sorry you won't be part of it."

The workers' truck pulled away, leaving the street decorated with false promises of a merry Christmas. Changes were coming, whether he wanted them or not. He hadn't cried then—he'd been too numb, too wrapped in the comfortable lie that this was just how life worked. People moved on. He had to do the same.

The lease had been in Madeline's name, and Jeff decided it was time to move to cheaper lodgings. She packed all her belongings and had them shipped to California, and he hired a guy to move the desk, the bed and all his computers to Brooklyn.

When Jeff couldn't commit to Madeline, when he stood there

paralyzed by his own demons, Shaheer had quietly withdrawn the offer.

Three months after Madeline and Shaheer left for California, Jeff saw Aether Code mentioned in a tech magazine. The space between his life and Shaheer's wasn't empty—it was filled with all the chances he'd never taken, all the leaps he'd been too afraid to make. Like the white space in well-written code, these pauses didn't represent nothing; they gave structure to everything around them, defining by absence what could have been.

Six months after that, Aether Code secured its first major contract. A year later, its innovative self-debugging software caught the attention of every major tech company in Silicon Valley. The day they went public, Jeff calculated what his shares would have been worth. Then he deleted his stock tracking app and spent the night staring at his ceiling, listening to the couple upstairs argue about money.

Chapter 17
Empty Space

The morning Cooper's portrait went blank, Betty wasn't surprised. She'd felt it coming for days—in the way the café's mirrors had deepened, in how the Brazilian jazz had slowed to songs about redemption, in the impossible-to-clean dusting of cinnamon that now coated every surface. Even the other dogs in Maria's paintings seemed more alert, their eternal expressions fixed on something about to happen.

Betty had opened the café that morning to find Cooper's familiar golden form missing from his frame, leaving only the stormy Brooklyn background. In all the years since Maria painted him, he'd never actually left his portrait before. Even with Ray the musician, he'd only seemed to move within the painting's confines.

"Today then," she said to the empty frame. The café hummed in response, a subtle vibration she felt more in her heart than her ears.

Sarah arrived with fresh scones and questions in her eyes. "The mirrors are doing that thing again," she said, setting down her basket. "But different this time. Look."

Betty turned to the wall of mirrors that had been salvaged from an old dance studio. Usually, they showed fragments of memory—moments of healing captured like photographs in silver. But today they reflected only darkness, as if they opened onto a night sky without stars.

"Someone's lost in the dark," Betty said softly. "Someone who's forgotten how to see their own light."

The café had been preparing itself all week. Tables had rearranged themselves overnight, clearing a path from the door to that corner table—the one that usually sat in shadow but today seemed to gather what little light made it through the storm clouds. The old armchair that normally stayed by the window had migrated to that table, its worn leather gleaming with fresh possibility.

Even the coffee machines were participating. No matter what Betty tried to make, they produced only Maria's special blend, the one with the secret ingredient that wasn't written in any recipe. The scent of it filled the café, mingling with cinnamon and rain-washed air in a way that made Betty think of new beginnings.

"Should I stay?" Sarah asked, but Betty shook her head.

"Not this time. This one needs empty space to fill."

After Sarah left, Betty stood in the center of her café, watching as years of carefully cultivated magic prepared itself for what was coming. Betty had learned to read these signs like a conductor reading a score.

The empty portrait of Cooper, the first time the dog had ever fully left his frame, meant this wasn't about simple healing. This was about transformation, about someone finally becoming who they were meant to be.

The cinnamon dust that gathered on freshly wiped surfaces wasn't just spice - it was Maria's signature, her way of marking the café's deepest magic. Every dog painting on the walls, every cup in the kitchen, every beam of light through the windows had been carefully chosen to recall Maria, creating a space where lost souls could find their way back to themselves.

Today, all of it - the mirrors, the furniture, the coffee, the paintings - was aligning for one specific person. Betty felt the café gathering its power, like a storm building over the ocean. When he arrived, the café would show him not just what he'd lost, but who he'd never allowed himself to become. That was the true magic of the Smiling Dog - not just healing what was broken, but awakening what had never been given a chance to live.

Betty touched the wall gently, feeling the café's pulse beneath her fingers. "We're ready," she whispered, and somewhere in the distance, a dog barked in response.

The regulars seemed to know to stay away. A few poked their heads in, saw the empty portrait and darkened mirrors, and quietly retreated. Even Gigi, who usually appeared like clockwork to guide the broken-hearted, was absent from her usual spot in the alley.

By afternoon, the storm in Cooper's portrait had seeped into the real Brooklyn sky. Thunder growled overhead like a warning, or maybe an announcement. The café's lights dimmed slightly, creating pools of warmth in strategic locations. The hidden speakers began playing "The Girl from Ipanema"—Maria's favorite, her way of saying pay attention.

Betty thought about all the people the dogs had helped over the years, appearing to guide them to the café when their hearts needed healing. But something told her this time was different. This wasn't just about healing—it was about awakening something that had never been allowed to fully live.

Betty had learned over the years that the café's magic lived as much in its silence as in its sounds. The spaces between customers' visits were never truly empty, just as the rests between notes in Maria's jazz weren't really quiet. They were moments of gathering, of preparation. Today those intervals felt deeper somehow, more purposeful, as if the café itself was learning to breathe differently in anticipation of what was coming.

Chapter 18
Ghosts of Almost Love

Spring in the city had its own way of punishing those who stayed behind. The sunshine, the blossoming trees, the sense of possibility that rose from every weed that pushed through cracks in sidewalks. In the unseasonable heat, his apartment's air conditioning wheezed and sputtered, mirroring his own struggles to breathe through another day of careful maintenance and quiet desperation. Even the plants Madeline had left behind drooped, their leaves curling inward as if trying to protect themselves from caring too much.

As the years passed, Jeff couldn't manage to hold onto a job for more than a year or two. He cycled through girlfriends, never finding anyone to compare to Madeline.

After Madeline, there was Rachel, who loved adventure and wanted to go skydiving. Jeff stood at the airfield watching her jump, unable to follow. "It's not about the parachute," she'd said when she landed. "It's about letting go." She left him a month later.

Then came Roxanne, who filled her apartment with paintings and asked Jeff what he felt when he looked at them. The truth was, he felt nothing—all his emotions had been color-blind since Madeline. Roxanne's goodbye note had been written in red paint across one of her canvases: "You can't love art if you can't feel it."

Nancy lasted the longest, almost a year. She was a therapist, and at first Jeff thought maybe she could fix him. But one night over dinner she'd said, "I can't be your therapist and your girlfriend, Jeff. And you need the first more than the second." Her kindness had hurt worse than rejection.

In his room at the Newton hotel, Jeff opened his browser and typed "Aether Code" into the search bar. Their latest product was all over the tech news—an AI system that could predict and prevent software failures before they happened. The promotional video showed Shaheer, older now but still with that same infectious enthusiasm, explaining how they'd revolutionized code debugging.

Jeff closed the browser. Phil the Third's leaves trembled in the air conditioning, and Jeff couldn't tell if it was judgment or pity.

He shook his head. All those failed connections. Now he sat in a cheap hotel room, surrounded by the scattered pieces of a life that had somehow slipped through his fingers. The walls seemed to close in, suffocating him with the reality of his situation: jobless, nearly homeless, savings dwindling to nothing. His body began to shake with sobs he couldn't contain, tears he'd held back for twelve years finally breaking free like a dam giving way.

He cried, his whole body shaking with pain he'd kept under wraps for so long. He didn't know how long he sat like that, but finally he wiped his eyes with trembling hands, and looked out the grimy hotel window at the desolate Brooklyn street. A golden retriever sat there, staring up at him, its mouth curved in what seemed like a gentle smile.

The sight of the dog, alone and vulnerable, stirred something in Jeff's chest—a feeling he'd thought long dead. What was it doing out here, unprotected in this urban wasteland? One distracted driver, one moment of canine curiosity, and... He pressed his palm against the cold window glass. Maybe he couldn't salvage the wreckage of his own existence, but he could prevent one more tragedy in this merciless city.

His body moved before his mind talked him out of it. He grabbed his coat and bolted from the room, his footsteps echoing through the hotel's dingy hallway like a drumbeat of desperation. The first-floor location was a small mercy—probably the only one he'd been granted lately—and he burst through the front door into the gathering gloom.

The dog waited, its gentle eyes holding his gaze. "Hey boy," Jeff called, his voice rough with disuse. When was the last time he'd spoken to anyone besides his Sharon or the hotel clerk? The dog rose to its feet and began padding away, each step deliberate, as if inviting pursuit.

"Wait," Jeff called, but the words died in his throat—just like every other important thing he'd ever tried to say. No collar, no leash. Even if he caught up, how could he hold on? The story of his life: never any way to keep the good things from slipping through his fingers.

His heart nearly stopped as the dog approached an intersection. Surely this would be it—another loss to add to his growing collection. But the animal simply sat, waiting for the light to change with infinite patience. He almost reached it before it rose again, continuing its mysterious journey.

Jeff followed, nearly colliding with a turning car that blared its horn in angry protest. The sound pierced him like an accusation: You don't belong here. You don't belong anywhere. The narrow Brooklyn streets closed in around him, a maze of asphalt and ancient cobblestones, buildings pressing close like judgmental witnesses to his failure. His calls to the dog emerged as broken whispers, each one as ineffective as his attempts to fix his shattered life.

It was Madeline all over again—the words trapped inside him like birds in a cage, beating their wings against his ribs but never finding freedom. What fundamental flaw in him made even the simplest human connections impossible?

Up ahead of him, the dog slowed near an alley entrance, and

Jeff's pulse quickened with a hope he didn't deserve. Above the doorway hung a weathered sign: "The Smiling Dog Café." He recognized it from his previous wandering. The door stood open like an invitation, and the dog trotted inside as if returning home.

Jeff followed, anger suddenly replacing his despair. If this was where the dog belonged, he'd give its owner a piece of his mind about responsibility and care and all the things he himself had failed at so miserably. The contrast between outside and in was like stepping through a portal. Behind him, Brooklyn bared its teeth in wind and grime, but here the air hung still and warm, scented with possibilities.

Even the light seemed different—softer somehow, filtered through windows that couldn't possibly be this clean in this neighborhood. The storm clouds that had chased him across the city didn't exist in here; instead, the café seemed to generate its own gentle radiance, like dawn breaking in a sheltered place.

The soft Brazilian rhythms caught him off guard - how many Sunday mornings had he and Madeline spent like this? Her swaying to similar music while measuring coffee beans, him pretending to code but really watching her dance, both of them suspended in the gentle space between night and day. The café's hidden speakers seemed to know exactly how to find these tender spots in his memory.

The café's warmth embraced him like a forgotten memory of comfort. The music's gentle rhythm mingled with the rich aroma of coffee and something sweeter—chocolate, maybe, and the indefinable scent of fresh-baked possibilities. The dog had vanished, though its twin smiled down from an oil painting above the register, captured in eternal contentment.

Chapter 19
Stars Being Born

As the day progressed, the light in the café would shift and change, moving through the space like a slow dance. By afternoon, it would soften into amber pools that gathered in corners, making even the shadows feel welcoming. The evening light brought a different magic, turning the café's windows into mirrors that reflected the warm interior back on itself, creating an intimate space that felt separated from the world outside.

The bell above the door chimed softly—not its usual bright ring, but a deeper tone that reminded Betty of church bells at twilight. And then he was there, the man Cooper had waited years to find.

His coat was rumpled and his shoulders hunched against a weight Betty recognized from her years as a counselor. But there was something more here, something that made her breath catch. In all her years of watching the café work its gentle magic, she'd never seen someone so completely walled away from their own heart. Most who came here were grieving something lost—love, hope, purpose. But this man... he was grieving something he'd never allowed himself to have in the first place.

The Brazilian jazz softened to almost a whisper, and the shadows in the corner where Cooper's special table waited grew deeper, more expectant. Even the other portraits on the walls—Gigi with her broken-hearted charges, Duke who led the lost, Baxter who guided the hopeless—seemed to turn their painted eyes toward this visitor.

Betty felt Maria's presence stir, strong as it had been that first night with Duke and Sarah. This wasn't about healing what was broken—it was about finally allowing something to exist that had been buried so deep, for so long, it had forgotten it was meant to live.

"Welcome to the Smiling Dog," Betty said softly, already reaching for Maria's special cup—the one with the silver swirls that looked like fog rolling in off an ocean. The man barely seemed to register her voice, his eyes fixed on Cooper's portrait. Betty held her breath, watching the first crack appear in those carefully constructed walls—just a hairline fracture, but enough. Enough for what needed to happen next.

"There was a dog," the man said, and Betty heard the desperation in his voice. He gestured at the painting. "Just like that one. I followed it here."

Her smile deepened with understanding. "That's Cooper. But he crossed the rainbow bridge long ago."

"I saw him," the man insisted.

"Have a seat," she said. "I'll make you a cup of coffee."

The café had chosen Maria's special blend today - the one with precisely measured spices that seemed to unlock memories in those who needed to remember.

After decades of witnessing these moments, she'd learned to read the signs of a soul beginning to thaw. It started in the eyes—a flicker of something ancient and hurt beginning to stir. Then the shoulders, usually, as tension either broke or gathered. Some fought it, their bodies going rigid against the flood of feeling. Others collapsed into it, like snow finally giving way to spring.

He did neither. Instead, he grew very still, the way a river does before the ice breaks. The air around him seemed to shimmer, the way it had with Ray the musician, with Marcus the veteran, with all the others the dogs had led here when they'd lost their way.

But this was different. Betty had seen people remember how to feel joy, how to bear grief, how to find hope. She'd watched them learn to live with loss, to forgive themselves, to trust love again. But she'd never seen someone learning to exist for the first time, not really. This wasn't about healing a wound or filling an emptiness. This was about a soul finally allowing itself to be born.

The mirrors along the back wall deepened, their darkness now shot through with tiny points of light like distant stars. The jazz shifted to a melody Betty had never heard before, though it carried echoes of Maria's favorite songs.

While the coffee brewed, neither of them spoke. The pause was a moment pregnant with possibility—like the space between lightning and thunder, between question and answer, between being lost and being found. The steam rising from his cup moved in slow spirals, as if the air understood the importance of this interval between what was and what could be.

"Oh, sweetheart," Betty whispered. "It's going to hurt. But that's how you know you're finally alive."

The cinnamon scent intensified, and Betty felt Maria's presence wrap around her like a warm shawl. Yes, this one was special. This one wasn't just about healing—it was about becoming. Cooper had waited years for him, watching from his portrait as others came and went, knowing that someday this particular lost soul would need more than just comfort or guidance. Would need to learn that feeling deeply doesn't mean drowning, that speaking truth doesn't mean destruction, that being seen doesn't mean being judged.

The light painted the café in layers of gold and shadow, transforming ordinary surfaces into something magical. The counter's marble top gleamed like morning frost, while the copper espresso machine caught and reflected a warm glow in its curved surfaces. The collection of cups behind the counter - each one hand-selected by Betty over the years - created a rainbow of subtle colors, from deep cobalt to soft cream, waiting to be matched with just the right customer and just the right brew.

The café hummed around her, a sound like hope taking root, like silence learning to sing. Betty poured the coffee, ready to wait however long the journey took.

Chapter 20
A Walk Along the Beach

Betty brought Jeff a mug of steaming coffee, on a mismatched saucer. He inhaled the aroma. "That smells delicious," he said. "Can't just be coffee, though. There must be something in it."

She smiled. "That's my secret ingredient," she said. "Of course, if I told you, I'd have to kill you." She laughed and went behind the counter again.

He looked around the café, sure the dog was somewhere. Light filtered through windows that somehow caught and held the sun's warmth despite the gray Brooklyn day outside. It pooled in honey-colored patches on the worn wooden floorboards, highlighting years of footsteps that had worn smooth paths between the mismatched tables.

Each piece of furniture seemed to have its own story - deep leather armchairs with soft, cracked surfaces that invited touch, sturdy oak tables marked with coffee rings like tiny crop circles, delicate wrought-iron café chairs whose cushions had molded themselves to welcome countless visitors.

He remembered the furniture in Madeline's parents' house in Vermont, that first Christmas he had spent there. How every chair, every table held generations of memories, yet somehow had room for new ones. Maury had told stories about each piece while they decorated the tree, weaving past and present together as naturally as breathing.

The way Betty listened reminded him of Ms. Reeves, his high school computer science teacher - that same quality of attention that made you feel like your words mattered, like you mattered. He hadn't thought of Ms. Reeves in years, but now he saw her clearly: wire-rimmed glasses, patient smile, the way she'd believed in him before he could believe in himself.

He lowered his tired body into a chair that seemed to accept his weight like an old friend. The wood was smooth beneath his fingers, worn by years of other hands seeking comfort. Only then did he notice the walls - a gallery of canine joy, every breed imaginable captured in moments of pure happiness. Their painted eyes seemed to watch him with sympathy rather than judgment.

The sight triggered memories of Toby. A beautiful mess of collie, shepherd, and probably a dozen other breeds, Toby had a particular way of pressing against his leg during thunderstorms. Even now, years later, Jeff could feel that pressure - warm, steady, unconditional. The way Toby would appear in his room before the shouting even started downstairs, as if the dog could sense approaching storms of any kind.

Betty handed him a mug of steaming coffee, and Jeff wrapped his hands around it, letting its warmth seep into his frozen fingers. The café stood empty except for him, which seemed impossible given the quality of what he was smelling. How did Betty keep the place running, tucked away in this forgotten alley? He hadn't seen a price list anywhere, and his stomach clenched at the thought of his nearly maxed-out credit card, the one he could barely make minimum payments on each month.

But for this moment, he was here, in this warm and gentle place, holding a cup of coffee that promised... something. He lifted it to his lips, inhaling once more before taking a careful sip.

The coffee's taste defied description—sweet and savory notes dancing above the rich coffee base, like a symphony he could drink. His eyes drifted closed as warmth spread through his chest, carrying with it an impossible scent of salt air and sea spray.

The moment hung suspended between one reality and the next, like the pause between movements in a symphony. It wasn't that the café was disappearing—rather, it was opening, the way a flower opens, each petal of reality slowly unfurling to reveal something new. In that interval between was and would be, Jeff felt himself opening too, as if he'd finally found the space his soul needed to unfold.

When he opened his eyes, the café's walls blurred at the edges, like watercolors left in the rain. The Brazilian jazz playing softly through hidden speakers transformed, becoming the distant cry of seabirds. The warm wood of the table beneath his fingers felt grainy, then shifted into something finer—sand, he realized, as the café's comfortable dimness gave way to a pearl-gray light that could only come from fog rolling in off an ocean.

The transition happened in waves, like tide washing over shore. With each blink, more of the café faded: the gallery of painted dogs dissolved into mist, Betty's collection of mismatched chairs became weathered pieces of driftwood, the concrete floor beneath his feet softened into damp sand. The café's warmth remained, but now it came from somewhere deep inside him rather than from the space around him.

A foghorn sounded in the distance—low and mournful, calling across hidden waters. Through the thickening mist, a shape emerged: the stark silhouette of the Golden Gate Bridge, its towers reaching up into the gray like ancient sentinels. The fog swirled around him now, cool and dense with possibility, carrying that distinctive mix of salt and seaweed that marked the Northern California coast.

A familiar figure bounded across the sand—the golden retriever, real and solid as his memories.

"Cooper?" The name came naturally to his lips, though he couldn't have said why.

The dog romped toward him across the sand, its joy as pure as sunlight. Like Toby had so many years ago, Cooper pressed close, offering unconditional affection with a warm tongue against Jeff's cheek. Jeff buried his fingers in the dog's soft fur. "Who's a good boy," he whispered, his voice thick with emotion.

Cooper barked once—a sound of happiness—then backed away and turned, beginning to trot down the beach.

"Not again," Jeff said, but this time a smile tugged at his lips. He buttoned his coat against the ocean breeze and followed, feeling lighter with each step.

The fog rolled in thick ribbons across the beach, but Cooper's golden coat glowed like a beacon. Jeff followed, his feet leaving temporary impressions in the wet sand that the tide would soon erase —just like all the temporary marks he'd left on the world these past twelve years.

As Cooper bounded ahead of him across the sand, memories of Toby flooded back with startling clarity. Both dogs had appeared when Jeff needed them most—Toby on that rainy night in Mason City, and then Cooper leading him through Brooklyn's shadows. Both golden-furred, though Toby's had been mixed with patches of black and white. Both with that same knowing look in their eyes, as if they understood more about human pain than any animal should.

"You remind me of him," Jeff said softly to Cooper's retreating form. "Toby always knew when I needed him too. When Dad was having one of his bad nights, Toby would slip into my room and press against me, let me bury my face in his fur until the storm passed."

Cooper paused and looked back, his expression so similar to Toby's that Jeff's heart clenched. That same patient wisdom, that same unconditional acceptance.

"Toby was my voice when I couldn't speak," Jeff continued, surprised by the words tumbling out. "He knew all my secrets, all the things I was too afraid to say out loud. When I left him behind, and then he died..." Jeff's throat tightened. "It was like losing my translator. Someone who understood the language of my silence. Like Madeline."

Cooper trotted back and pressed against Jeff's legs, just as Toby used to do. The gesture was so familiar that Jeff had to blink back tears. He knelt in the wet sand and buried his fingers in Cooper's fur.

"Is that why you found me?" he whispered. "Because I needed another translator? Someone to help me find my voice again?"

Cooper's tail wagged once, and he licked Jeff's cheek—exactly as Toby had done all those years ago. Then he pulled away, looking down the beach with purpose. When Jeff followed his gaze, his heart stopped.

Madeline stood at the water's edge, her dark hair lifting in the salt breeze. She wore the same cream-colored sweater she'd had on the last time he saw her, the one she'd hugged around herself as she walked away. Cooper bounded up to her, and she bent to ruffle his ears, her smile as bright as Jeff remembered.

His feet stopped moving. His heart didn't.

She straightened and turned toward him. "Jeff," she said, and her voice carried perfectly despite the sound of the waves. "You finally made it to San Francisco."

"Madeline." His throat tightened. "I—"

"It's okay," she said. "Take your time."

Those words unlocked something in his chest. How many times had anyone said that to him? His father's voice had always been sharp with impatience. "Speak up, boy!" he'd demand when Jeff tried to explain anything—a bad grade, a torn shirt, a missing toy. His mother's silence had been worse, her tired eyes avoiding his as she moved through their house like a ghost, cleaning up the mess his father left behind.

"My father," Jeff started, then had to stop. But Madeline waited, patient as the tide. "He never wanted to hear what I had to say. Unless it was 'Yes, sir' or 'No, sir.' Everything else made him angry. And Mom... she was afraid of words. Afraid they'd set him off. So she taught me to be quiet. To keep everything inside."

He took a step closer to Madeline. "The day you left... I wanted to tell you. The words were there, but they felt dangerous. Like they'd destroy everything if I let them out."

"And now?" she asked softly.

"I loved you," he said, and the truth of it broke through him like sunrise. "I loved you so much it terrified me. Because love in my house always led to pain. To broken promises and broken furniture and broken people. I thought if I didn't say it, it couldn't hurt either of us."

"Oh, Jeff." Her eyes glistened. "It hurt us both anyway."

"I know that now." He was close enough to see the light freckles across her nose, the ones he used to kiss on lazy Sunday mornings. "I loved you then, and I love you now, and I'm so sorry I couldn't say it when it mattered."

She reached out and took his hand. Her touch was warm, real. "It matters now. You're saying it now."

Cooper pressed against their legs, and Jeff felt the dog's solid warmth. "I had a dog when I was young," he said. "Toby. He was the only one I could talk to. The only one who just listened, who never got angry or afraid. I guess I never learned to talk to people the way I spoke to him."

"And now you're talking," Madeline said. "That's what matters."

The fog swirled around them, and for a moment Jeff almost believed they were in their own pocket of time, safe from the world and its sorrows. But there was something in Madeline's eyes, a depth of knowing that made his chest ache.

"You're not really here are you?" he whispered.

She squeezed his hand. "I was here," she said. "Right here on this beach. I used to walk it every morning before work, thinking about you, hoping you'd find your way here somehow."

"What happened?"

"A drunk driver," she said simply. "Two months after I moved here. I was walking home from dinner with Shaheer and his girlfriend. We were celebrating the first big contract for Aether Code." She smiled sadly. "I never got to see how successful it became."

The words hit like a physical blow to his solar plexus. A high-pitched ringing filled Jeff's ears, drowning out the sound of the waves. The fog-swept beach seemed to tilt beneath his feet, and he stumbled, Cooper quickly pressing against his legs to steady him. Somewhere far above, a foghorn sounded - three long, mournful notes that seemed to echo his internal cry of denial.

"I didn't know," he managed, his voice emerging strange and hollow, as if from very far away. His tongue felt thick, clumsy. "All these years, I thought you were out there somewhere, living your life, maybe married with kids..."

Through the ringing in his ears, he became aware of a container ship's horn answering the foghorn - a deeper, more resonant sound that vibrated in his chest where his heart should be, if it hadn't just shattered into a million pieces.

The metallic taste of shock flooded his mouth as the magnitude of his ignorance crushed him. While he'd been hiding in his safe, predictable jobs, building walls around his heart, she'd been gone. All those moments he'd imagined her thriving in California - celebrating breakthroughs in her lab, watching Pacific sunsets, falling in love again with someone braver than him - had never happened.

The realization hit him with the force of a rogue wave - Madeline, his Madeline, had been gone for years, while he'd wasted so much time living half a life, too afraid to open himself to joy or heartbreak. He thought of all the mornings she'd be up before him, humming softly as she mixed her experimental coffee concoctions, eager to share the results. The weekends they'd spend exploring the city, discovering hidden pockets of magic. The quiet nights on her rooftop, mapping the stars and dreaming of a future together.

All those small, mundane moments that had felt so infinite at the time were now gone, irretrievable. The weight of their loss crashed over him, leaving him gasping. How could he have been so blind, so paralyzed by fear that he'd traded away the chance to truly live? Madeline's laughter, her curiosity, her boundless capacity for wonder

- all silenced forever, leaving only an echoing void where a vibrant life had once been.

The foghorns sounded again, their mournful cries underscoring the transience of everything. Even the mighty bridge, its towers now shrouded in mist, was but a fragile thing, gradually crumbling with each passing year. Nothing was permanent; all that remained were these fleeting impressions, like foam on the waves, dissolving even as they formed.

This was the cruel truth at the heart of the Japanese term *"mono no aware"* - the bittersweet acceptance that beauty and joy were inherently ephemeral, that the things we loved most were doomed to pass away. And Jeff, who had guarded his heart so carefully, had lost the chance to truly cherish what he'd been given.

The fog rolled in thicker now, its cold tendrils wrapping around them like a shroud. On the rocks below, waves crashed in a rhythm that reminded Jeff of sobbing. A seabird's cry pierced the gray air - sharp and grieving, giving voice to the keening loss that was building in his chest.

"Would knowing have changed anything?" she asked gently. The familiar scent of her shampoo - lavender and something uniquely her - drifted to him on the salt breeze, so real it made his eyes burn.

"Everything," he whispered, then caught himself. The word tasted like ashes in his mouth. Sand shifted beneath his feet, unstable as his certainty. "No. Maybe not. I wasn't ready to face anything real back then. Not even grief."

The foghorns continued their mournful conversation overhead - call and response, like the words he and Madeline had never spoken. A piece of kelp had washed up nearby, its surface gleaming wet and dark like her hair had been that last morning.

Jeff could see it now, the life they might have had: a small house in Berkeley with a garden where Madeline could grow the herbs she loved to experiment with. The sharp scent of rosemary would have mingled with coffee every morning. Weekend trips to Napa Valley, where she'd explain the chemistry behind wine fermentation while he coded on his laptop. Children who would inherit her curiosity and his patience, who would grow up knowing it was safe to feel, safe to speak, safe to love.

Through the thickening fog, he made out the massive towers of the Golden Gate Bridge, their peaks lost in the gray like the future he'd forfeited. A container ship's horn sounded again - closer now, warning of hidden dangers in the fog. Jeff understood suddenly that he'd been like that ship, navigating blind, never knowing he'd already lost everything that mattered.

Salt stung his eyes - from tears or sea spray, he couldn't tell anymore. The cold fog had soaked into his clothes, but he barely felt it. All he felt was the warmth of Cooper's fur against his leg and the ghost of Madeline's touch on his hand.

"We would have had a lab in the garage," he said, his voice raw as salt wind. The foghorn sounded again, and beneath it he heard the distant clang of a buoy bell, marking hazards hidden beneath the water's surface. "You always wanted that. And I would have built you a better coffee machine than anything on the market—one that could maintain the exact right temperature for every different bean variety."

Madeline's eyes softened, and for a moment they held the same warm amber glow they'd had in their college coffee shop. "With a custom interface that analyzed optimal brewing times."

"And a predictive algorithm for when we were running low on your favorite roasts." The words tumbled out like shells being pulled back by the tide. He saw it so clearly—the life they'd planned but never lived. The fog swirled between them, and through it came the cry of another seabird, its wings cutting through the gray like years slicing past.

"Oh, Jeff." She squeezed his hand, and he felt it as clearly as the wet sand beneath his feet. Cooper whined softly, pressing closer against his leg. "You're being brave right now. That's what matters."

"But it's too late." The words tasted bitter as seawater, sharp as regret. Above them, the fog was beginning to take on a pearl-like luminescence as the hidden sun rose higher. Somewhere in the distance, a ship's bell tolled eight times—the end of a watch, the marking of time's passage.

"For us, yes," she said, and her voice carried notes of the same jazz that had played in her apartment on those long-ago Sunday mornings. "But not for you. That's why Cooper brought you here. That's why Betty's café exists. Some people need a safe place to learn how to feel again—even if what they're feeling is regret."

The fog was thickening now, becoming almost luminous, and Madeline's form grew less substantial. Her edges blurred like one of her mother's watercolor paintings left in the rain. But before she faded completely, Jeff needed her to know one more thing. The words pushed against his chest like waves against the shore.

"I looked for you once," he admitted, each word carrying the weight of years of silence. The foghorn sounded again, closer now, its cry mixing with the distant echo of ship's bells and the eternal rhythm of the waves. "About five years ago. I'd finally worked up the courage to try to find you. I searched online but couldn't find anything recent. I told myself you must have gotten married, changed your name. That you were happy somewhere, living the life you deserved." His breath came out in visible puffs in the cold air. "I should have looked harder. Should have called Shaheer, your parents. Anyone."

A gust of wind carried the scent of her—lavender and coffee and that indefinable chemistry that had always been uniquely Madeline. Cooper's fur ruffled in the same breeze, golden in the diffused light.

"The past is past," Madeline said softly, her voice beginning to blend with the sound of the waves. "What matters is what you do now, with this moment of clarity. Will you build new walls, or will you finally let yourself feel everything—the joy and the pain, the love and the loss?"

Jeff looked at Cooper, who sat watching them with that gentle doggy smile, his fur catching the strange, pearly light that seemed to be coming from everywhere and nowhere. "I think... I think I'm ready to feel it all. Even though it hurts. Especially because it hurts." He turned back to Madeline, trying to memorize her face one last time—the constellation of freckles across her nose, the curve of her smile, the light in her eyes that had always made him believe in possibility. "I'm so sorry I wasted our time together being afraid."

"You didn't waste it," she said, her voice now carrying the same ethereal quality as the fog-diffused light. "You just weren't finished becoming who you needed to be. But you are now."

The fog was almost solid now, transforming the beach into a space between worlds. The sounds of the harbor—the foghorns, the ship's bells, the crying gulls—seemed to be coming from another universe entirely. Madeline's form was barely more than a suggestion of light and shadow.

"Don't go," Jeff said, the words finally coming freely, even though he knew they couldn't change anything. His voice cracked like a wave against rocks.

"I have to," she said, and now her voice seemed to come from everywhere at once, carried on the salt breeze. "But you don't have to stop feeling. That's the gift we're giving you—Cooper, Betty, and me. Take it back to Brooklyn with you. It's not too late to start again."

"I love you," he said once more, because he could, because he finally understood that speaking truth was more important than protecting yourself from pain.

Her smile was the last thing to fade, lingering like the afterimage of sunset. "I know. I always knew."

Then she was gone, and Cooper with her. The foghorns fell silent. The seabirds stilled their crying. Jeff stood alone on the beach as the fog began to lift, showing him the bright California morning that might have been his, in another life.

He blinked, and found himself back in the Smiling Dog Café. The coffee cup was empty in his hands, but the warmth remained in his chest. The scent of lavender lingered in the air, mingling with Betty's coffee and fresh-baked possibilities. Betty stood nearby, watching him with knowing eyes.

"Was it real?" he asked her, tasting salt on his lips that might have been tears or might have been ocean spray.

She smiled that same gentle smile. "What do you think?"

Jeff reached up and touched his cheek, where the salt of grief mingled with what might have been the lingering touch of an ocean breeze. Outside, a passing truck's horn sounded—not a foghorn, but close enough to make his heart catch. "I think... I think I'm ready to live again."

"That's why Cooper brings people here," Betty said softly. "The ones who need to remember how to feel."

The café's windows had fogged over, creating a barrier between this safe space and the harsh world outside. But as Jeff sat with his empty cup, the fog began to clear in slow swirls, like curtains being drawn back from a stage. Through the gradually clearing glass, he saw the Brooklyn sky changing—not the usual dirty gray of a winter morning, but something deeper, more significant, as if the atmosphere itself was preparing for revelation. Somewhere in the distance, a dog barked once—a sound of joy, a sound of beginning.

Epilogue
Vermont Spring

The Hinckley house looked smaller than Jeff remembered, though its deep blue paint still stood out against the melting snow. Early March sunshine glinted off icicles that dripped steady tears from the eaves, and the first crocuses were pushing through patches of bare earth beside the front porch.

He'd called ahead this time - another small victory in his new effort to stop hiding from difficult moments. The job interview last month had been another. When they'd asked him where he saw himself in five years, he'd told them the truth: building systems that helped people, that made the world a little more manageable for those who struggled to navigate it. Something in his voice must have convinced them, because they'd offered him the position.

His hand shook slightly as he reached for the doorbell, but he made himself press it. The same creaky floorboards announced approaching footsteps, and then Maury Hinckley filled the doorway, his wool cardigan as memorable as ever, though his beard had gone completely white.

"Jeff?" Maury's voice cracked on the single syllable.

"I should have come sooner," Jeff said, the words he'd practiced on the five-hour drive up from New York feeling inadequate now. "I'm so sorry I didn't."

Maury's arms wrapped around him before he could say more, and Jeff caught the familiar scent of yeast and cinnamon. Some things hadn't changed - Maury still stress-baked.

"Gaye!" Maury called over his shoulder, his voice thick with emotion. "Come see who's here!"

The kitchen was exactly as Jeff remembered, though the molecular structure tea towels had faded with washing. Fresh-baked hot cross buns covered every surface - Easter was coming, and Maury had been preparing. The coffee maker was the same one that had been there twelve years ago, the one Jeff had always meant to upgrade for them.

Gaye appeared in the doorway to her studio, paint streaking her silver hair, her artist's eyes taking in every detail of him. "Oh," she said softly. "Oh, my boy."

They sat at the kitchen table, steam rising from coffee cups, while Jeff told them everything - about his years of running from feeling, about Betty's café, about seeing Madeline one last time. About finally learning to speak his truth.

"She would have loved that café," Gaye said, wiping tears with the back of her hand. "All those dogs, all that healing."

"She always said dogs were better judges of character than people," Maury added, pushing another hot cross bun toward Jeff. "Remember that mutt that used to follow her around town when she was a teenager?"

The stories flowed then, each one a piece of Madeline they could share. Jeff learned things he'd never known - how she'd written her college application essay about the chemistry of baking, how she'd once tried to build a telescope out of cardboard tubes and her grandfather's old reading glasses, how she'd kept every letter Jeff had written her whenever they'd been apart.

"We have them," Gaye said quietly. "The letters. And some of

Code of Silence

her journals, if you'd like to see them someday. Not today," she added quickly, seeing something in his face. "But when you're ready."

"I'd like that," Jeff said, and meant it. "I'd like to come back, if that's okay. Maybe help digitize some of your recipes?" he added to Maury. "Build you a proper database?"

"Only if you promise to be here for testing new variations," Maury said, his eyes twinkling despite their moisture.

As the afternoon light began to fade, Jeff helped them clean up the kitchen. Through the window, he saw Madeline's herb garden, still sleeping under patches of melting snow. Soon it would wake up, pushing new growth through the earth, just as he was learning to let new feelings grow in his heart.

"You should stay for dinner," Maury said. "We've been trying some of Madeline's old recipes. She left notes about the chemistry of everything - the way different ingredients interact, how temperature changes affect the results. It would mean a lot to share them with you."

Jeff thought about his empty apartment back in Brooklyn - nice enough, with plenty of natural light for the houseplants he'd started collecting, but still missing something essential. He thought about Madeline, about how she'd always believed in creating spaces where people could heal and grow together.

"I'd like that," he said. "I'd like that very much."

Later that evening, as they shared memories over Madeline's favorite dishes, Jeff felt something shift inside his chest. Not an ending, exactly, but maybe the beginning of a new chapter. One where he could honor what he'd lost while still being open to what might come next.

Somewhere in the darkening Vermont sky, a star winked into view. Jeff smiled, remembering Madeline's voice explaining constellations on their rooftop nights. She would have liked this moment, he thought. She would have wanted this for all of them - her parents finding a son again, Jeff learning to open his heart, old connections healing like spring soil welcoming new growth.

The snow was melting, and beneath it, things were beginning to grow.

A Mother's Heart

a Smiling Dog Café Story

Chapter 1
Stronger Than Fear

The fluorescent lights in the emergency room that Monday evening turned everyone a sickly shade of green, transforming them into sea creatures trapped in an aquarium. The air was thick with disinfectant and fear, overlaid with the metallic tang that all hospitals seemed to share. A voice crackled over the PA system -- "Dr. Lucas to Trauma One, Dr. Lucas to Trauma One" -- competing with the ping of elevator doors and the steady beep of distant monitors.

Sophia Greenwood's nine-year-old daughter Emma lay small and pale on the examination table, her dark curls -- just like Sophia's mother's -- spread across the paper-covered pillow. The same hair, the same pale skin, the same delicate wrists where the nurse was now wrapping a blood pressure cuff. In that moment, she mirrored the photographs of Sophia's mother so precisely that Sophia's chest seized up.

Even the way Emma held her pencil echoed her mother's grip - the same careful precision, the same slight tilt to the wrist. These small inheritances had felt like gifts rather than burdens, until moments such as this when the bigger, scarier legacy made itself known.

From the intake area came the sound of rising voices -- someone demanding attention, someone else trying to maintain control. "My son needs help NOW!" A crash of something being swept off the counter. The soft squeak of security guards' shoes on linoleum as they hurried to intervene.

The sharp scent of antiseptic couldn't quite mask the underlying hospital smells - rubber gloves, floor cleaner, and something metallic that caught in the back of Sophia's throat. Wheels squeaked against linoleum as gurneys rolled past. A phone rang at the nurses' station, its electronic trill competing with the steady beep-beep-beep of heart monitors and the swish of automatic doors.

The vinyl chair beneath her stuck to her skin through her thin yoga pants, and the air conditioning raised goosebumps on her arms despite the summer heat outside. Someone's IV pump clicked rhythmically, marking time the way a metronome did. Down the hall, a baby's cry was quickly hushed, and the ice machine in the staff room clattered, dropping cubes into a metal bin.

"Mommy?" Emma's voice wavered beneath the chaos. "Can we go home now?" She clutched the stuffed dolphin her father had brought her home from his first business trip to Singapore.

Home. Such a simple word. Sophia had spent her childhood in six different homes across four continents, each one temporary, each one leaving its mark like rings in a tree trunk. Now home was a brownstone in Brooklyn, with Emma's art covering the refrigerator and her stuffed animals mounting a slow invasion of every available surface. Home was supposed to be safe.

"Soon, baby." Sophia tried to keep her voice steady. "The doctors just need to run some tests."

Tests. The word triggered another memory: antiseptic halls in another hospital, her father's hand squeezing hers too tight as the doctor used words she didn't understand. Congenital. Genetic predisposition. Her mother's absence already a physical thing, making her feel as though air had been sucked out of a room.

Somewhere down the hall, a woman was crying, her sobs punctuated by hiccupping breaths and someone's gentle murmurs. The

A Mother's Heart

wheels of a gurney squeaked past their curtained spot, accompanied by the rhythmic squeeze of a manual respirator.

"Ms. Greenwood?" The nurse's voice pulled Sophia back. "The doctor would like to run an EKG." She wheeled a portable machine next to Emma's bed.

"Thank you," she said, watching as a tech in blue scrubs attached electrodes to Emma's chest, each one a point of fear on her perfect skin. She was being so brave, this girl who cried over dead butterflies and insisted on holding funerals for fallen leaves. Emma smiled at her mother, and for a moment Sophia saw her own mother's smile in a faded photograph.

The machine beeped, numbers scrolling across its screen like secret messages Sophia couldn't decode. Behind its electronic pulse, she heard the hum of the overhead lights, the soft whoosh of the heating system, the squeak of rubber-soled shoes on freshly waxed floors. The beeping monitors echoed through time, each pulse carrying her back to another hospital, another bed, another set of worried eyes watching numbers scroll across screens.

Sophia didn't just see numbers - she saw her mother's last hospital stay captured in jagged green lines. Each peak and valley told a story: here was where Emma's heart worked too hard, as her grandmother's had and her own did. Here was where it struggled to maintain rhythm, echoing Sophia's own childhood battles.

The young doctor, barely out of medical school, frowned at the readout and something in his expression sent her hurtling back twenty-three years, to another doctor with another frown, looking at another heart that didn't work quite right.

"I need to get the cardiologist on duty to look at this," the present-day doctor said. He smiled at her, trying to be reassuring. "We want to be sure this young lady gets the best care possible."

Then he walked off, leaving Sophia with Emma and a deep, abiding fear. She pulled the hard plastic chair close to Emma's bed, sat, and took her hand. "What did you do in school today, sweetheart?"

"Why am I having trouble breathing?" Emma said, her breath catching.

"The doctors are going to figure that out," Sophia said. She squeezed Emma's hand. "On our way home, we can stop for ice cream. Would you like that?"

"Chocolate and pistachio," Emma said. She knew her mind, this little girl. Unlike Sophia at that age, when she'd been so lost.

They talked for a few minutes until the cardiologist arrived. He was older, with black hair streaked with gray. Sophia appreciated the way he spoke to Emma first, a smile in his voice. "I'm Doctor Gorbaty, but you can call me Dr. Vlad. I'm a special kind of doctor they call in when little girls have problems with their hearts."

Despite his foreign name, Dr. Vlad spoke perfect unaccented English. Probably the child or grandchild of immigrants, the way Sophia herself was.

Emma nodded, and coughed. "How's the rest of you?" he asked. "Anything else feel strange?"

"Mommy taught me to take my pulse by putting my finger on my wrist and counting," Emma said. "It feels way faster than normal."

"What a smart girl," he said. "Well, we'll look into that." Then he turned away with the ER doctor to look at the EKG results. They spoke so quietly that Sophia couldn't hear what they said.

Then Dr. Vlad turned to Sophia. "We'd like to admit Emma for observation," he said, and the walls started closing in. "There are some irregularities we need to monitor."

Irregularities. The word echoed in Sophia's head like a ball bouncing down an empty hallway. She heard Emma asking questions, heard herself answering, but it was as if she was listening to a conversation underwater.

The medical terminology Dr. Vlad used - "arrhythmia," "genetic markers," "preventive protocols" - each phrase carried the weight of inherited fear. But they also carried hope. When he explained a new medication they could try, Sophia remembered the heavy pills of her childhood, the ones that made her too tired to play. Emma's medicine would come in a tiny capsule, precisely calibrated to her body's needs, representing decades of medical progress paid for in heartbeats.

Dr. Vlad was still talking -- something about genetic testing, about family history. The PA system crackled again: "Respiratory therapy to Four West, respiratory therapy to Four West."

"I need some air," Sophia heard herself say. "Just... just for a minute."

She stumbled out of the curtained area, past the nurses' station where phones rang incessantly and computers chimed with incoming test results. She passed through automatic doors that whispered open like secrets being told. The Brooklyn night slammed into her – the air heavy with exhaust and humidity, car horns and subway rumbles and somewhere a car alarm creating an urban symphony of chaos that matched her internal rhythm.

"I can't do this," she whispered to no one. "I don't know how to do this."

Her reflection in the dark hospital window startled her - she hardly recognized the woman staring back. Her dark curls had frizzed in the late August dampness, strands escaping from the hasty ponytail she'd managed while calling 911. She wore one of Emma's paint-stained sweatshirts thrown over her yoga pants, and in her panic to get her to the hospital, she'd grabbed two different shoes - one running shoe and one of the ballet flats she'd worn that day as she worked at her computer.

Under the harsh outdoor lights, her olive skin looked sallow, and the shadows under her dark eyes betrayed too many sleepless nights even before this crisis. At thirty-four, Sophia was exactly the age her mother had been when she died. The significance of that number had been haunting her lately, each birthday a countdown she tried to ignore. Now, standing outside a hospital just like the one where her mother had spent her last days, the parallel felt too sharp to bear. But unlike her mother, who had faced her illness alone while Sophia's father buried himself in work, she would be here for Emma.

She would transform her inheritance of loss into a legacy of presence.

A gust of wind sent discarded fast-food wrappers skittering across the ambulance bay, and she wrapped her arms around herself, the sweatshirt too thin for the unexpected chill. Movement caught her eye - a shape emerging from the shadows between streetlights. At first it seemed like just another shadow, but as her eyes adjusted, she made out the solid form of a dog sitting perfectly still.

Its fur caught the harsh hospital lighting, glowing a rich red and white. An Irish Setter, she realized, with the breed's distinctive proud bearing and long, sinewy legs. But something was different about its silhouette - where four legs should have been, there were only three. Yet there was no sense of imbalance or imperfection in its pose.

The dog sat in the pool of light from a streetlamp, an Irish Setter with red and white fur. Its dark eyes fixed on her with a gaze that held serenity and peace. Something about those eyes reminded her of Keiko-san, her first caregiver after her mother died, who could silence a room with a single look.

The dog's gaze held hers, steady and knowing. She found herself matching her breathing to its calm presence - in for four counts, hold for four, out for four, just as Marie-Claude had taught her during thunderstorms in Paris. The panic began to recede, pulling back with the steady rhythm of retreating waves.

A siren wailed in the distance, making her turn instinctively toward the sound. When she looked back to where the dog had been sitting, the pool of light was empty. But somehow its brief presence had steadied her, reminded her that she wasn't that helpless nine-year-old anymore. Emma needed her to be stronger than her fear.

Chapter 2
Hidden Gardens

Before she went back into the hospital, Sophia pulled out her phone, checking the time. Ten PM in Brooklyn meant... what? She could never keep track of where Mark was now. Singapore? Hong Kong? Her finger hovered over his contact information. He should know about this - he was Emma's father, after all.

But if she called now, he would want every detail, would need to analyze each symptom and test result, would probably start researching specialists before she'd finished speaking.

She could hear his voice already: "What exactly did they say about her EKG? Have they run a genetic panel? What about that new cardiac monitoring system I read about?"

She didn't have those answers yet. Better to wait until morning, until after she'd spoken with Dr. Vlad, until she could present Mark with a complete picture he could organize into one of his comprehensive action plans.

She put the phone away without making the call and headed back inside. The fluorescent lights felt harsher after the darkness outside.

When she arrived at Emma's bed, her daughter was resting on

plumped-up pillows. "Dr. Vlad came in while you were gone. He says I have to stay here overnight."

"How about if I stay until you get settled, and then I'll go home and get your pajamas and your Little Mermaid toothbrush? We have to trust that Dr. Vlad knows what's best for you."

"I guess," Emma said.

A few minutes after she returned to Emma's bed in the ER, an orderly arrived to transfer her to the pediatric cardiac ward.

Emma got down from the bed herself and settled into the wheelchair. Sophia followed the orderly down the hall. As they waited for the elevator, a young boy in a wheelchair similar to Emma's rolled past, both parents hovering protectively at his sides. The father held an iPad displaying what looked like medical research, while the mother clutched a stuffed animal - both of them focused entirely on their son.

The elevator arrived, and they rose to the pediatric cardiac ward. There, the environment changed dramatically. Gone were the harsh emergency room lights and metallic surfaces. Here, the walls were painted with underwater scenes - dolphins leaping through waves, tropical fish darting between coral, sea turtles drifting lazily through painted currents. The nurses' station looked like a submarine's command center, and even the medical equipment was partially hidden behind wooden panels decorated to match the ocean theme.

The nurses wore scrubs decorated with bright patterns, and everything smelled of antibacterial soap and the vanilla-scented air freshener someone had plugged in at the nurses' station. Every few minutes, the PA system would chime softly before announcements, the sound gentler than the harsh emergency room alerts.

"You'll be in our Starfish Wing," the orderly told Emma, pushing her wheelchair past a series of rooms. "Each one has a special night light that makes patterns on the ceiling, like being under the sea."

Emma brightened at this, her earlier fear seeming to recede as she took in the whimsical surroundings. They stopped at a room with a starfish painted on the door, its five arms holding different medical instruments like treasures found on the ocean floor.

"Here we are," the orderly said cheerfully. "Let's get you settled in your new bed, and then a nurse will come in to set up your monitors. Your mom can stay right beside you the whole time."

A nurse arrived almost immediately, and Sophia watched with trepidation as her daughter was hooked up to a set of machines that would keep track of all her vital functions.

The machines spoke a language Sophia knew by heart. The pulse oximeter's steady beep brought back nights holding her mother's hand, counting spaces between sounds. But Emma's monitors sang a different song - one of prevention rather than crisis. Their quiet hums and gentle alerts promised early warning, time to act, a future where heart conditions meant management rather than mourning.

She arranged the few things she'd grabbed for Emma on the table beside the bed. "Go to sleep, butterfly," she said to her daughter. The endearment slipped out before Sophia could catch it -- her father's old name for her, now passing to her daughter like so many other inheritances.

Emma looked so small in the hospital bed when she finally fell asleep. Her dark curls spread across the institutional pillow, monitors standing sentinel over each heartbeat. The dolphin sat guard now too, keeping watch while Sophia and Mark couldn't.

Walking away tore at her, leaving half her heart behind in that sterile room. She touched her mother's locket, remembering suddenly how her father must have felt, leaving his wife in hospitals across continents, his helpless worry weighing him down with every step.

Leaving her there felt nothing like that first sleepover at her best friend Maya's house, when Emma had practically pushed Sophia out the door, eager for her adventure of pizza and movies and midnight secrets.

It felt nothing like that business trip to Montreal when Mark was still with them, when seven-year-old Emma had waved goodbye with such brave determination. Those separations had been wrapped in excitement, in growth, in the natural spreading of wings.

"I'll be back soon," she whispered to her sleeping daughter as she crept out of the room.

Outside, Brooklyn's night air carried the first hints of autumn. As Sophia began the walk home to get fresh clothes and Emma's favorite pajamas, she noticed the three-legged Irish Setter following at a respectful distance, its presence somehow reassuring. Under the streetlights, memories began to surface of another time when everything changed - a beach in the Hamptons, where she'd first met Mark.

Sophia had taken a few days off for a vacation, to escape her technical editing work by writing a short story that used details she recalled from her childhood. She sat cross-legged in the sand, notebook open, dark curls whipping in the wind as she wrote about a young girl discovering a hidden temple garden in Tokyo. The story was flowing from memories of her own childhood there. To help her with details, she'd sketched the temple in the margin, including the impossibly wide pine tree on the grounds.

"Is that Zen'yō-ji Temple?" Mark asked, noticing the sketch. He'd stopped to shake sand from his shoes after a run, but her absorbed expression and flying curls had caught his attention.

Sophia looked up, surprised. Most people assumed she was doing homework. "You know it?"

"I just finished an MBA case study on Japanese business culture, and one of the illustrations was that temple, and the immense tree." He sat down beside her, careful not to disturb the pages scattered around her like fallen leaves. "I'm Mark."

"Sophia. How did a Buddhist temple make its way into a business school case study?"

"We spent weeks studying Japan's corporate structure," he explained, "and none of my professors mentioned how the temple gardens affect business culture. One of my classmates argued that the Japanese work ethic comes purely from economic incentives, but I kept thinking there had to be more to it."

"Like what?" She was intrigued by how he leaned forward, hands gesturing as he worked through the idea.

"Like... how growing up seeing those gardens might shape someone's understanding of patience and attention to detail. In my case study, this CEO in Osaka took his whole management team to tend the company's rooftop garden before major decisions. The Harvard Business Review treated it as an inefficiency, but..."

"But maybe he knew that careful hands grow careful minds?" Sophia finished, remembering how Keiko-san had taught her to rake patterns in their tiny garden's gravel, each stroke a lesson in precision and peace.

"Exactly!" His eyes lit up with the excitement of connecting these dots. "That's the kind of insight I've been missing. The numbers tell one story, but there are always deeper stories underneath." He picked up a shell, turning it over in his hands with the same thoughtful attention he'd given her writing.

She found herself drawn to this unexpected blend of MBA practicality and genuine wonder, the way he could shift from market analysis to folklore without losing his enthusiasm for either. Here was someone who might help her bridge her own divided worlds - the practical editor and the secret storyteller, the responsible daughter and the dreamer.

"Would you like to hear about the time I tried to convince my housekeeper the temple cats were actually ancient spirits in disguise?"

"I would." He smiled, his analyst's precision softening into something warmer. "Maybe over tea? I know a place that serves great matcha, though probably not up to your standards."

That date stretched from matcha to dinner, her stories of growing up across continents weaving through his plans for international business. Where she saw cities as collections of memories and tales, he saw opportunities and connections - yet somehow these perspectives enriched rather than contradicted each other.

Their first real date was scheduled for a tiny Italian restaurant in

Brooklyn. Mark arrived with a folder of carefully researched reviews and a backup reservation in case the restaurant disappointed. Sophia laughed, not at him but with delight at finding someone who planned for contingencies the way she'd been taught by Marie-Claude.

But they discovered that a water main break had shut down the whole block. Mark started to pull out his contingency plans.

Sophia caught his hand. "Wait. Do you smell that?" A corner market a block away was still open, its door propped to let out the heat from their brick oven. The scent of fresh bread mingled with basil and olive oil.

Mark hesitated, and Sophia saw his carefully planned evening threatening to unravel. But he paused when she inhaled deeply, savoring the aroma. "We could…" He glanced around, getting his bearings. "Brooklyn Bridge Park is three blocks away."

They bought still-warm focaccia, local cheese, and wine the shopkeeper recommended. Mark arranged their impromptu feast on a park bench with the same careful attention he'd given to researching restaurants, making sure the sunset hit the bridge at the perfect angle.

"You plan everything so carefully," Sophia said, watching him transform their improvised picnic into something precise and orderly, "but you're willing to adapt when those plans change."

"I like having plans," he admitted, cutting the focaccia into equal portions. "But I'm learning that sometimes the best moments come from when those plans fall apart." He pulled a small notebook from his jacket. "Though I am making a note about checking with the power and water utilities before starting a date."

She laughed.

Over the next few months, they discovered how their differences complemented each other. Mark's methodical nature helped Sophia structure her freelance work life, while her creativity taught him to find joy in imperfection. What Keiko-san had called wabi-sabi, the profound beauty in things that bear the marks of time and wear, like a cracked teacup that tells stories of all the hands that held it.

He'd bring her detailed research about heart-healthy exercise programs; she'd teach him to dance in her kitchen to her mother's favorite Beatles songs.

The streetlights cast pools of light on the sidewalk as Sophia turned onto Atlantic Avenue. The Irish Setter's footfalls were nearly silent behind her. She passed the corner store where she and Emma bought ice cream every Friday after art class, and remembered another beginning.

When Mark proposed after a year of dating, it wasn't with the elaborate plan he'd originally made. Instead, seeing Sophia dozing on their couch after a long editing session, he knelt beside her with his grandmother's ring and a lifetime of promises: to protect but not confine, to plan but stay flexible, to face whatever came with equal measures of preparation and faith.

Thinking of Mark brought back the memory of their conversations about having children. After a year of dating, and two years of marriage, they sat in their Brooklyn brownstone with its extra bedroom ready to become a nursery. They were surrounded by takeout containers, in the middle of yet another discussion.

But this one was rooted in years of learning each other's rhythms - the way Mark researched medical studies to quiet his fears, the way Sophia processed emotion through stories. They weren't just two people debating parenthood; they were partners who'd learned to dance between certainty and chance.

"We would be amazing parents," Mark said. "Your creativity, my ability to manage problems as they come up. It's a great combination for parenting."

Sophia stared at the growing collection of medical literature Mark had gathered. Each article was highlighted, annotated, cross-referenced with others. He approached parenthood the way he approached his business deals - thoroughly researched, meticulously planned, every contingency considered.

"My heart condition," Sophia started.

"Is manageable," Mark finished. "Look at these studies from Mount Sinai Hospital. The cardiac care there is incredible. And with proper monitoring during pregnancy..." He pulled another journal article from his stack. "Women with cardiac myopathy are having healthy babies, Sophia. The risks are there, yes, but they're calculated risks."

Sophia touched her mother's locket, remembering hospital rooms, remembering fear. "Calculated risks are still risks, Mark."

He put down his papers then, really looking at her. "I know you're scared. But think about it - you've lived with this condition your whole life. You understand it better than anyone. What better mother could a child with the same genetic predisposition have?"

Mark had what someone had once told him were the Japanese characters that combined "danger" and "opportunity" in a small tattoo on his right shoulder. He said the image reminded him to find the advantage in disadvantage, the opportunity in obstacle. It was what made him brilliant at business, at solving problems. But this wasn't a business problem to be solved.

"And what if..." She swallowed hard. "What if I'm not around to be that mother?"

Mark's face softened. He gathered her into his arms, his usually crisp button-down wrinkling against her cheek. "Then I would make sure our child knows every story about you. How you learned to dance in Rio, to fold paper cranes in Tokyo, to find strength in every city where you made a home."

He kissed the top of her head. "But that's not going to happen. Because I've researched the best cardiac specialists, the best hospitals. I'll move heaven and earth to keep you both safe."

Nine months later, looking at their newborn daughter's dark curls and impossibly tiny fingers, Sophia understood. Some risks were worth taking, some fears worth facing. Mark had been right about that.

Chapter 3
Paper Butterflies

Now, so many years later, Sophia hurried through Brooklyn's darkened streets, the three-legged Irish Setter still her faithful companion as she made her way home to gather Emma's things for the hospital.

The wind picked up as she crossed Court Street, carrying the scent of bread from the bakery that was starting its overnight preparations. The dog waited patiently at each crossing, its steady presence reminding her of all the women who had guided her through difficult times. As she passed Emma's school playground, the sound of dripping from the recently rain-soaked swings triggered another memory - one of water and stories and different ways of handling crisis.

When Emma was four, a pipe burst in the middle of the night, sending a cascade of water through their kitchen ceiling. Sophia woke to the sound of crashing and found Emma standing in her doorway, clutching her favorite doll, eyes wide with fear.

Mark was immediately on his phone making calls, already building a spreadsheet to compare plumbers and restoration companies. Sophia gathered Emma into her arms and sat with her in the living room, making up stories about mermaids who had gotten lost and needed to find their way home. Later, reviewing the repair estimates, Mark couldn't understand why she'd "wasted time" with stories when there were decisions to be made.

"The water damage was getting worse every minute," he said, gesturing at his carefully researched options, color-coded by cost and availability. "We needed to act quickly."

"Emma was scared," Sophia replied. "She needed to feel safe more than she needed a perfect repair plan."

"And now the restoration will take longer because we didn't call immediately." He ran his hands through his hair, frustration evident. "I found a company that could have been here in twenty minutes if we'd contacted them right away."

"Sometimes," Sophia said quietly, remembering how Emma had finally fallen asleep mid-story, "taking care of the heart of a problem matters more than fixing its surface."

But Mark was already focused on his phone again, calculating overtime rates and insurance deductibles, missing the way Emma's drawings over the next few weeks filled with merpeople finding their way through storms to safety.

They'd weathered that storm, though Mark still felt it was better for Sophia to have handled the leak than kept Emma occupied with stories.

He wasn't all business, though. For Emma's fifth birthday, Mark and Sophia took her to Disney World - all three of them wearing matching Mickey ears, Mark surprising them with VIP passes he'd secretly arranged. Sophia delighted in how he joined Emma to celebrate at every opportunity.

Ten months later, Mark came home vibrating with excitement, his tie loosened, hair disheveled from running his hands through it. He found Sophia and Emma in the kitchen, making cookies from a recipe handed down from Sophia's grandmother.

"Regional Vice President for Asia," he announced, spreading printouts across their flour-dusted counter. "Singapore. Full expat package - housing allowance in one of those amazing high-rises with infinity pools, international schools, domestic help." His eyes shone as he pulled up photos on his phone. "Look at this apartment - forty stories up, view of the whole harbor. Emma will learn Mandarin. We'll travel all over the Far East - Tokyo, Bangkok, Sydney. Give her the kind of international childhood you had."

Sophia's hands stilled in the cookie dough. She looked at Emma's artwork covering their refrigerator, each drawing marking the passage of time in this place that had truly become home. The growth chart penciled on the doorframe. The window seat where they read stories every night, the same view of Brooklyn's lights making each book feel magical.

"Mark," she said carefully, "I didn't have an international childhood. I had a series of temporary homes. Different doctors, different schools, different languages. Every time I finally felt settled, made real friends, we'd pack up and leave."

"But that's what made you so adaptable, so worldly." He spread out more photos - gleaming shopping centers, botanical gardens, pristine beaches. "We could give Emma that same gift. Plus, the salary increase would mean private schools, music lessons, anything she wants."

"What she wants is stability. What she needs is roots." Sophia gestured at their kitchen, flour dusting her hands like memories. "She needs to know exactly which corner store sells her favorite ice cream, which swing at the playground flies highest, which neighbors will look out for her. The kind of stability I never had."

But Emma had already caught her father's excitement, bouncing on her toes as she looked at the pictures. "Can I really live in that tall building, Daddy? Like a princess in a tower?"

Mark's smile was triumphant. "See? She's ready for an adventure. We can try it for a year," he added, seeing Sophia's hesitation. "If it doesn't work out, I'll request a transfer back. I promise."

Sophia looked at her daughter's shining face, at Mark's eager plans spread across their kitchen counter like a map to a future she wasn't sure she wanted. She remembered all her own childhood moves - each one promised as temporary, then stretching into another and another until home became a concept rather than a place.

"Let me think about it," she said finally, turning back to their cookies. These, at least, were constant - her grandmother's recipe, made in her own kitchen, in the home she'd fought so hard to create.

Fortunately for Sophia, there was some disruption at Mark's office, and the option to transfer was postponed temporarily. But it still hung there over them, like a rain cloud that threatened to pour at any time.

Then came Emma's sixth birthday, and everything changed. That morning, Mark got the notice that his promotion had come through, and they were ready for him in Singapore.

He had spent the previous weekend transforming the backyard of their brownstone into what Emma called a "butterfly garden paradise," with tissue-paper flowers and fairy lights strung between the trees. The day of the party, a dozen little girls in pretty dresses twirled through the space, gossamer butterfly wings strapped to their backs catching the late afternoon light. The carefully curated playlist - a mix of Disney songs and kid-friendly pop - competed with high-pitched squeals of delight and parents' gentle reminders to "Walk, don't run."

Mark had outdone himself with the decorations, ordering custom butterfly-themed everything: from the lavender tablecloths to the delicate paper plates, from the hand-calligraphed place cards to the three-tiered cake covered in edible butterflies that looked almost too real to eat. The crafts table, where the girls had spent an hour making butterfly crowns, was still scattered with glitter and bright scraps of paper. Even the organic juice boxes had butterfly wings printed on them.

Now the party was reaching its crescendo with the piñata - a giant purple and silver butterfly that Mark had special-ordered from an artisan in Mexico. The girls took turns swinging at it, their wings fluttering with each attempt, while parents snapped photos and videos on their phones. When it was Emma's turn, she gripped the sparkly ribbon-wrapped stick with determination, her own wings slightly crooked from an afternoon of play.

The pinata burst open and Emma lunged for the scattered candy, her face flushed with excitement. Then she stumbled, pressing one small hand to her chest. "Mommy?" Her voice wavered, and Sophia's heart clenched with a recognition she'd spent years dreading. She knew that look, that gesture - had made it herself countless times as a child.

Mark reached Emma first, scooping her up with practiced calm while shooting Sophia a look that mirrored her own terror. But Emma recovered quickly, the way Sophia used to, already squirming to get down and rejoin her friends. They watched her race off, both of them trying to pretend this was normal childhood exertion, nothing more.

That night, they sat in Emma's bedroom, watching their daughter sleep. Paper plates with cake crumbs still littered the kitchen counter downstairs, forgotten in their preoccupation. Mark spread hospital brochures across Emma's desk, his hands trembling slightly.

"If you and Emma come with me to Singapore, we can get her excellent care there. The pediatric cardiac unit at Mount Elizabeth Hospital is world-class. The preventive care programs, the monitoring technology - they're years ahead of what we have here." He paused, touching Emma's completed homework on the desk. "If there's even a chance she inherited what your mother had, and what you have..."

"I want something different for her," Sophia said. "I want her to have one place that's completely hers. One neighborhood she knows by heart. Friends she grows up with, not just leaves behind."

Mark ran his hands through his hair. "But her heart..."

"Will need stability more than ever," Sophia said. "The kind that comes from having roots, from knowing her place, her connections. The kind of stability I never had."

He'd run his hands through his hair again, a gesture that reminded her of when they first met. That same look was in his eyes now - the one she now recognized that meant he'd already charted his course and was trying to navigate her toward accepting it.

"Let's put off moving the family for a while. I can set up a home office here for when I visit. Video calls every day while I'm in Singapore. Monthly visits. And the salary -- Sophia, I could make sure you never have to worry about medical bills. Never have to choose between treatments because of insurance limits."

"Like my father did with my mother?" The words came out sharper than she intended.

Mark had flinched. They both knew the story - how her father had worked endless hours to pay for experimental treatments that came too late to save her mother. How his absence then, and after her mother's death, had left Sophia with a rotating cast of caregivers instead of a parent's steady presence.

"It's different," Mark had insisted. "I'm not running away. I'm running toward something - toward giving both of you every possible advantage. Your father didn't know what was coming. We do. We can prepare."

The memory faded as Sophia reached her block, the familiar brownstones welcoming her home in the darkness. The Irish Setter still followed, its nails clicking softly against the concrete. The sound reminded her of how things had turned out - Mark in his sleek Singapore apartment, surrounded by spreadsheets and contingency plans, trying to father their daughter through carefully chosen gifts and scheduled video calls. For all his talk of being different from her father, he'd ended up just as distant, his love expressed through provision rather than presence.

Three months after Mark moved to Singapore, his face flickered on Emma's tablet screen, the pristine skyline visible through his office window. Behind him, a wall of screens displayed market data in red and green digits.

"Look, Daddy!" Emma held up her latest art project - a detailed drawing of their Brooklyn street, each brownstone carefully rendered with her growing skill. "Ms. DuVivier says I'm getting really good at perspective."

"That's nice, sweetheart." Mark glanced down, presumably at another screen. "Listen, I've been researching art programs. There's an excellent weekend workshop at the Met. Very selective, but one of the directors at the firm knows someone there. I could make a call—"

"But I already take art at the community center with Maya," Emma said, her excitement dimming. "We're learning about Frida Kahlo."

"The Met program would look better on school applications," Mark said. "Speaking of which, I've compiled data on the top prep schools. Their art programs are highly ranked." The sound of keyboard clicking carried through the connection. "I'll send you the spreadsheet, Sophia."

Sophia, folding laundry within earshot, watched Emma's shoulders drop. Their daughter had spent all morning practicing how to show her father the way she'd captured the morning light on their neighbor's windows.

"I don't want to change schools," Emma said quietly. "I like my friends here."

"Sometimes we have to think strategically about these things," Mark replied, his voice shifting into what Sophia thought of as his boardroom tone. "Now, about your piano lessons—"

"I have to go," Emma said suddenly. "Maya's mom is taking us for ice cream."

"It's a school night," Mark frowned. "Shouldn't you be focusing on—"

"It's to celebrate her losing her last baby tooth," Emma explained. "Like a rite of passage, her mom says."

"A what?" Mark's confusion was clear even through the slightly pixelated screen. "Never mind. We can discuss the Met program next call. I'll have the enrollment papers ready."

After Emma ended the call, she stayed at the kitchen table,

adding shadows to her drawing with careful strokes. "Daddy didn't even really look at it," she said finally.

Sophia sat beside her, studying the artwork. "Tell me about this window," she said, pointing to one Emma had drawn with particular care. "The way you caught the light - it reminds me of how the sun hits the café windows in Hopper paintings."

Emma's face brightened. "You noticed! Ms. DuVivier showed us his work last week. She says art isn't about being the best, it's about seeing the world your own way."

Sophia watched her daughter return to her drawing, adding details that would never show up on a school application but captured the heart of their Brooklyn home. In Singapore, Mark was probably already drafting emails about the Met program, missing the masterpiece taking shape right in front of him.

The custom dollhouse he sent for Emma's seventh birthday was exquisite - a perfect replica of their Brooklyn brownstone, each tiny room filled with handcrafted furniture. Yet Emma spent more time with the cardboard box it came in, drawing windows and doors until it became a home she could play in. She fell asleep clutching the tablet after their video call, her birthday cake half-eaten, waiting for a father who lived in her dollhouse but not in her daily life.

One year had become two, with the prospect of more. Video calls grew shorter as time zones and schedules collided. Monthly visits became quarterly, then "whenever I can get away." Mark sent packages of expensive toys, arranged for drawing, painting and pottery lessons, and made sure their health insurance was the best possible in case Emma's condition worsened.

Sophia climbed the steps to their building, fishing her keys from her pocket. The Irish Setter sat at the bottom of the stairs, watching as she unlocked the door. Inside, Emma's presence filled every room - half-finished drawings on the coffee table, her copy of "When You Trap a Tiger" splayed open on the window seat where she'd been reading about a girl finding magic and courage in family stories.

The book's placement felt meaningful now - Emma had been

reading about another girl facing family illness through stories and folklore, just as Sophia herself had learned to navigate her own mother's illness with the help of many maternal figures. She gathered fresh pajamas and Emma's special pillow, the one with constellations Mark had taught her to identify during their last family vacation.

Her phone felt heavy in her pocket. She should call him, tell him about Emma. He had a right to know. But she understood now -- his spreadsheets and specialists were his version of love, just as her steady presence beside Emma's bed was hers.

When she came back outside, the Irish Setter was waiting. Together, they began the walk back to the hospital, passing the landmarks of Emma's childhood - the park where she'd learned to ride a bike, the library where they spent rainy Saturdays, the deli where the owner always saved Emma's favorite cookies.

Mark would do what he always did - throw money at the problem, hire specialists, perhaps even fly in for a few days. But he wouldn't know how to hold Emma through her fears, wouldn't understand that what she needed wasn't just medical expertise but the kind of love Sophia was still learning how to give.

The hospital rose before them, its windows glowing like stars fallen to earth. At the entrance, the Irish Setter sat, its dark eyes meeting Sophia's with that ancient wisdom. She nodded in understanding - her daughter was waiting upstairs, needing not the perfect father Mark tried to be from across an ocean, but the imperfect mother who would sit beside her bed until morning.

The dog watched as Sophia entered the hospital. She gave it one last grateful look before heading inside. Whatever tomorrow might bring, tonight she knew exactly where she needed to be.

Chapter 4
The Art of Listening

Betty Martinez knew every kind of silence. After thirty years as a grief counselor, she'd learned to read the spaces between words as fluently as words themselves. There was the thick silence of fresh loss, dense as fog. The brittle silence of anger, sharp as broken glass. The heavy silence of depression, pressing down like stones. And sometimes, rarest of all, the healing silence that came when someone finally felt heard.

That last kind filled The Smiling Dog Café on quiet days, when sunlight painted patterns across the wooden floors and the gentle hum of the espresso machine provided a baseline for whispered confessions and tentative hopes.

She hadn't planned on becoming a café owner. The transition from counselor to barista might have seemed strange to her colleagues at the grief center, but to Betty, it made perfect sense. Both roles required the same skills: listening without judgment, creating safe spaces, knowing when to speak and when to let silence do its work.

Today, she watched Sarah -- one of her regulars -- grade papers in her usual corner. Three years ago, Duke, the German Shepherd, had led Betty to find Sarah sitting on a park bench during a rainstorm, clutching divorce papers and trying not to cry. Now she came most mornings, stronger but still healing, marking essays with the same red pen that had signed away her marriage.

Betty adjusted the coffee grinder, calibrating it with the precision she'd once used to measure her responses in therapy sessions. Too fine a grind would make the coffee bitter; too coarse and the flavor wouldn't develop properly. Like conversations about loss, brewing required balance.

The morning light caught the silver frames of the mirrors she'd salvaged from an old dance studio, transforming them into portals of reflection. She'd arranged them carefully behind the counter, understanding how important it was for people to see themselves clearly when they were ready.

A new customer entered -- a businessman in an expensive suit, his shoulders tight with exhaustion. Betty recognized the signs of someone running from grief. She'd seen it countless times in her counseling practice: the perfectly pressed clothes, the rigid posture, the careful control that suggested everything underneath was chaos.

"Welcome to The Smiling Dog," she said, keeping her voice gentle but matter-of-fact. No sympathy yet -- that would make him run. "What can I get you?"

He looked around, surprised to find himself in a café. "There was a dog," he said.

She nodded. "I know. There often is."

The man accepted that answer and ordered black coffee in the clipped tones of someone who hadn't slept properly in weeks. As she prepared his drink, Betty noticed how his gaze kept drifting to the wall of photographs -- faces of women throughout history who'd found their own ways to heal.

"Family photos?" he asked, trying for casual but betraying genuine curiosity.

"In a way," Betty replied, tamping the coffee grounds with practiced care. "Each one tells a story of healing. Like that one --" she nodded toward a black-and-white photo of a woman from the 1940s, "She lost everything in the war, then built a new life teaching others to dance."

The man's shoulders lowered slightly. Just a fraction, but Betty noticed. She'd spent decades noticing such things, reading bodies like books, understanding the subtle language of grief beginning to soften.

"My wife loved to dance," he said quietly, then looked startled, as if the words had escaped without permission.

Betty kept her movements steady, letting the confession settle into the café's warm air. She'd learned long ago that some truths needed space to unfold, the way coffee beans only released their full flavor under the right conditions.

The espresso machine's steam wand hissed -- a sound that had replaced the subtle white noise machine she'd used in her counseling office. Both served the same purpose: providing a gentle backdrop that made silence feel safer.

Sarah looked up from her grading, catching Betty's eye with understanding. She'd been where this man was, had spoken her own grief into an accepting silence. Now she came back not just for coffee, but to be part of the healing atmosphere she'd once needed so desperately.

Betty handed the businessman his coffee in one of the heavy ceramic mugs her late wife Maria had collected over the years -- each one chosen for the way it fit in shaking hands, cradling warmth with the intimacy of a secret. This one was deep blue, matching the stillness of twilight waters.

"Let me know if you need a refill," she said, not pushing, just offering. Like she used to do in her practice, leaving the door open for return without demanding it.

He nodded, wrapping his hands around the mug, anchoring himself. Betty turned to wipe down the already-clean counter, giving him space to either retreat or remain. Sometimes healing started with simply being allowed to exist in a space without expectations.

The morning continued its gentle rhythm -- regulars coming and going, new faces appearing with their hidden stories. Betty measured coffee beans and words with equal care, knowing both could be bitter or healing depending on how they were handled.

She'd replaced her counseling notebooks with coffee recipes, but they served the same purpose -- tracking what worked, what didn't, how to help each person find their way back to themselves. Some needed the bright clarity of lighter roasts, others the deep comfort of darker blends. Like grief itself, no two people's perfect cup was exactly the same.

The businessman stayed longer than she expected, something in his rigid posture gradually unwinding. When he finally left, he paused at the door. "Thank you," he said, not specifying for what. He didn't need to.

Betty smiled, remembering similar moments from her counseling days -- the first crack in the wall, the first step toward healing. She'd traded her office for a café, but the work remained the same: creating space where broken hearts could begin to mend.

Sarah packed up her graded papers, leaving a homemade chocolate chip cookie on the counter -- her ritual. "For the next person who needs sweetness," she said, the same words she repeated every week, remembering how Betty's cookies had helped her through those first bitter days.

Betty adjusted the coffee grinder again, preparing for the afternoon rush. Outside, Brooklyn continued its urban symphony, but in here, time moved differently. As her counseling office had been, the café was a pocket of peace in the chaos, a place where silence could speak and healing could begin with something as simple as a perfectly brewed cup of coffee.

She'd learned that some lessons translated perfectly from counseling to café-keeping: how to read people's needs in their posture, how to offer comfort without overwhelming, how to create an atmosphere where vulnerability felt safe. Most importantly, how to listen not just with her ears but with her whole being.

A Mother's Heart

The espresso machine hummed, grounding her in the present moment. Through the front windows, she saw people passing -- each carrying their own stories, their own griefs, their own hopes. Some would find their way in, when they were ready. Betty would be here, doing what she'd always done: listening, serving, helping hearts heal one cup at a time.

Chapter 5
Tokyo Tears

When Sophia woke Tuesday after Emma's night at the hospital, the house felt wrong without her daughter's morning chaos. No argument about five more minutes of sleep, no backpack to trip over by the door, no half-eaten toast abandoned on the kitchen counter. Sophia moved through their usual routine by muscle memory, then caught herself pouring two bowls of cereal instead of one.

When Mark had first taken the position in Singapore, Sophia had maintained their morning schedule rigidly, as if keeping Emma's routine would somehow make his absence less noticeable. But gradually they'd developed their own rhythms -- pizza picnics on the living room floor while reviewing Emma's math homework, Saturday morning pancake experiments that would have horrified Marie-Claude, midnight storytelling sessions when neither of them could sleep.

Now the silence pressed against her ears like deep water.

Sophia opened her laptop at the kitchen table, scanning through emails from clients whose technical manuals she edited. The flexibility of remote work had been a blessing when she became a single parent, though sometimes she missed the structure of office life.

Today's inbox held an urgent request for revisions on software documentation, two meeting invitations, and a reminder about quarterly deadlines.

She typed quick responses: "Family emergency. Will resume work remotely as situation stabilizes." Her fingers hesitated over the keys. How had her mother balanced it all? Or had she never had the chance, her illness consuming all other possibilities?

Memories surged as she grasped her cup of morning coffee. She thought not just of Emma's situation, but of her mother's story, the one that had started it all.

The diagnosis came too late for her mother - dilated cardiomyopathy, the doctors explained, a condition where the heart muscle weakens and can't pump blood effectively. By the time her symptoms became severe enough to investigate, the damage was extensive. The disease had likely been developing for years, masked by youth and determination until it couldn't be hidden anymore.

Nine-year-old Sophia endured weeks of medical tests while her mother was dying. Blood draws, ECGs, genetic testing - her father insisted on every available screening. The results confirmed their fears: she carried the same genetic mutation.

"But knowing early changes everything," her mother's cardiologist had said, his kind eyes meeting her father's worried gaze. "We can monitor, treat preventively, avoid the path your wife's condition is taking."

Then her mother died, and something changed in her father. One evening a few weeks after the funeral, he took her to the garden of their suburban New York house, the one her mother had planted, but then neglected as she got sick.

The stars spread out above them, and Sophia remembered her mother pointing out constellations. There was Orion with his belt and sword, the Big Dipper ready to pour light onto a darkened world. For a long while, he just held her hand, watching neighborhood lights blink on as dusk settled.

"Sophia," he said finally, his voice rough with emotion, "we need a fresh start. Away from all these memories." He gestured at the familiar skyline. "I've been offered a position in Tokyo. New office, new team to build." He squeezed her hand. "New doctors who can monitor your heart with the latest technology."

She looked up at him, seeing the shadows under his eyes, the way grief had carved new lines in his face. "But what about all our memories of Mom? Will we lose them if we move away?"

"We'll take photos, save some special things. But sweetheart, we can't live in a shrine to what we've lost." He knelt down to her level, the way her mother used to. "Sometimes the bravest thing we can do is begin again."

Two weeks later, they boarded a plane to Tokyo. Sophia clutched a small photo album and her mother's locket, leaving behind the garden where spring bulbs would bloom without them, the rooms still echoing with her mother's off-key Beatles songs. Their house had been packed up by professionals, everything either stored, shipped, or donated according to her father's efficient lists.

In Tokyo, their new apartment felt like a hotel at first - too clean, too precise, too devoid of history. That's where Keiko-san came in, recommended by her father's Japanese colleagues as someone who would help them adjust to their new life. But some adjustments proved harder than others.

"She'll teach you about Japanese culture," he'd said, as if that could make up for everything else Sophia was losing. As if learning a new way to live could help her forget the way life used to be.

The first time Keiko-san caught Sophia crying over her mother's photograph, she didn't offer comfort. Instead, she stood in the doorway of Sophia's bland new bedroom in a Tokyo high-rise, spine straight as a bamboo rod, and said in her careful English, "Time for folding. Come."

Sophia wanted to hate her for that, for the way she ignored tears as though they were merely raindrops on a window. But she followed her down the hall of the apartment, past walls so pristine they made their old home seem shabby in comparison. Her sock-clad feet whispered against the tatami mats, already trained to avoid the sharp crack of Keiko-san's disapproval that came with any careless stomping.

The laundry waited in precise stacks on the low table: sheets, towels, clothes sorted by color and size.

"Watch first," Keiko-san said, taking a crisp white sheet from the pile. Her movements were like a dance, each fold precise and purposeful. "Corner to corner, edge to edge. No wrinkles. No shortcuts." She gestured for Sophia to try with another sheet.

Sophia's first attempt was clumsy, the corners misaligned. Without a word, Keiko-san undid her work and guided her hands through the motions again. And again. And again. Until the muscle memory began to form, until the repetition became meditation, until the precise folds felt like creating order from chaos.

"Good," Keiko-san said finally, the single word carrying more weight than her father's elaborate praise ever had. "Now we do rest. Same way. Until perfect."

That same demand for perfection followed Sophia beyond their apartment. The private international school her father had chosen sat in an affluent Tokyo neighborhood, its Western-style buildings incongruous among the traditional Japanese houses. The weeping willow trees in the courtyard stood in military precision, another element of the school's rigid order.

Sophia was a misplaced brushstroke marring an otherwise perfect canvas, her grief smudging this ordered world. Each morning she would straighten her uniform tie, touch her mother's locket beneath her collar, and try to force herself into the same precision as everything around her.

Between classes, the other girls moved in tight clusters, their identical navy uniforms transforming them into schools of fish navigating the hallways. During lunch, they sat in the courtyard under bare cherry trees, their elaborate bento boxes arranged with ceremonial care.

"Mama made me tamagoyaki again," Lily Tanaka complained,

poking at the perfectly rolled omelet in her lunch. "She knows I'm tired of eggs every day." Lily's father was an industrialist, trained in the US, who preferred the American way of schooling to the strict Japanese one.

"At least your mom cooks," Katie Williams said. She was an Irish girl with red hair and freckles; her father worked at the British embassy. "Mine just throws money at the fancy bento shop near the station. Though I guess that's better than having to eat everything with seaweed like Anchali."

"My mom says seaweed is brain food!" Anchali Siriwong protested, but she was laughing. Her Thai food was always spicy, the curry powder staining her lips.

Sophia stared down at her own bento, arranged with Keiko-san's mathematical precision. The carrots cut into chrysanthemums, the rice shaped into a perfect half-sphere, the umeboshi centered like a red sun against white clouds. Beautiful, precise, and utterly loveless -- or so she thought then.

"What about your mom, Sophia?" Katie asked. "Does she make American-style lunch or Japanese?"

The question lingered, thickening the air between them. She could have said "My housekeeper makes my lunch" or "I prefer Japanese style" or any number of things that would have let the conversation flow on. Instead, she stood up so quickly her bento box crashed to the ground, its perfect arrangement shattering against the concrete. She ran, leaving behind the scattered remnants of Keiko-san's careful work and the echo of concerned voices calling her name.

That evening, her father came home for dinner, when he usually didn't arrive until she was in bed. He stood in the doorway of her room, his suit jacket draped over one arm, looking as lost as she felt.

"Keiko-san told me about the bento box," he said finally. "Get your coat. We're going out."

The Tokyo night embraced them with neon and noise. Her father hailed a taxi and gave the driver an address in Harajuku. As they approached their destination, Sophia pressed her face against the taxi window, at the streets which pulsed with color and life even on a weeknight.

They stepped out in front of a Sanrio store filled with images of the company's Hello Kitty logo. Katie carried a purse with the cat's face on it that Emma coveted, and she grabbed her father's hand and tugged him toward the store.

Everything in Harajuku seemed designed to be cute - even the street signs had cartoon characters, and the crepe stands displayed plastic food replicas decorated with hearts and stars.

She didn't see Katie's purse but she saw another that she fell in love with, hanging it over her arm and posing in the mirror, striking a fashion model pose. Her father laughed and bought it for her.

Outside, girls in platform shoes and pastel dresses floated past - exotic birds against the urban landscape. Their hair was dyed in impossibly bright colors - cotton candy pink, electric blue, lavender - and decorated with glittering clips and tiny bows. Some wore elaborate costumes that transformed them into dolls come to life, with petticoats and parasols, while others had become anime characters with wigs and carefully painted makeup.

Her father, who navigated boardrooms and international markets with ease, looked desperately out of place in his business suit, a crow wandering into an aviary of tropical birds. He kept checking his phone, as if seeking refuge in its familiar glow from this riot of kawaii culture that seemed to spill from every storefront and fill every inch of the narrow street with sugar-sweet excess.

"Here," he said finally, steering her into a toy store. The shelves were packed with dolls of every description -- anime characters, traditionally dressed apprentice geisha called maiko, cute mascots with impossibly large eyes. In one corner, a display of family sets caught Sophia's eye: mother, father, baby, all dressed in matching outfits.

"Choose whatever you like," her father said, his voice gentle in a way it rarely was anymore.

Sophia reached for one of the family sets, but then stopped, her hand hovering between two boxes. One contained a traditional

Japanese mother doll with a baby. The other held just the mother, her kimono patterned with cherry blossoms, her painted face serene and loving.

"Both," her father said, understanding something he rarely did. "You can have both."

After he paid, he said, "Now, let's have some dinner." On their way to a restaurant recommended by one of his co-workers, they passed a crowd of older girls who wore black and white Gothic Lolita dresses with intricate lace patterns, their movements graceful and precise as they posed for photos.

Sophia and her father sat crammed into a tiny table in a noodle shop, surrounded by salary men and teenagers with rainbow-colored hair. As they ate their ramen, he finally asked, "Do you want to talk about what happened at school today?"

Sophia stirred her noodles, watching the patterns the chopsticks made in the broth. "They were talking about their moms. About lunches and… and stuff." The steam from the ramen made her eyes water. At least, that's what she told herself.

Her father set down his chopsticks. "Your mother… she loved to make you lunches, and she used to sing to you while she packed your lunchbox. Do you remember that? She'd move around the kitchen and sing whatever came into her head -- usually old Beatles songs, completely off-key." He smiled, a rare expression these days. "The neighbors probably thought we were torturing cats."

Sophia tried to remember this, to conjure the sound of her mother's voice, but it slipped away like smoke. Instead, she remembered Keiko-san's words from that morning: "Structure gives grief a place to live."

"Keiko-san's lunches are pretty," she said finally. "Even if they're not… even if she's not…"

"She cares," her father said. "In her way. We both do, even if we're not very good at showing it."

When they returned home, she placed both dolls on her shelf -- the mother-and-baby set arranged in Keiko-san's precise style, the single mother doll slightly askew, caught in mid-dance. They watched over her as she slept, these silent guardians of her grief.

The next morning, Keiko-san was waiting with a new bento box, this one decorated with tiny cherry blossoms. "Today," she said, "I teach you to make tamagoyaki. Your mother cannot teach, so I teach. Different love, but still love."

Sophia was learning, slowly, that love wore strange disguises. Sometimes it looked like perfectly folded sheets and precisely arranged vegetables. Or it looked like discipline and structure and hours of patient instruction. Sometimes it looked like a father trying his best in a toy store, or a housekeeper teaching what a mother no longer could.

Every other Thursday, Keiko-san would accompany her to Tokyo American Clinic, where Dr. Watanabe tracked her heart's rhythm with quiet precision. Keiko-san never commented on these appointments, simply adjusting their schedule around them as naturally as she adjusted the flowers in their entryway.

One afternoon, racing up the apartment building's stairs because the elevator was too slow, Sophia felt her heart flutter strangely. She sat down hard on the landing, more scared than out of breath. Keiko-san, who had been following with the groceries, set down her bags without a word and sat beside her until the moment passed.

"Come," Keiko-san said finally. "Time to learn something new."

That afternoon, while they waited for her father to come home from the office, Keiko-san taught Sophia to fold her first crane.

Her fingers fumbled with the delicate paper, its whisper against her skin so different from the clean snap of Keiko-san's precise folds. The paper had a faint floral scent, like tea ceremonies and temple incense. But Keiko-san didn't scold, didn't undo her work. Instead, she placed her hands over Sophia's, her skin cool and dry, her touch as steady as her footsteps on the tatami mats.

Outside, Tokyo's evening traffic created a distant hum, while inside their apartment, small sounds took on heightened meaning - the soft tick of the kitchen clock, the rustle of Keiko-san's cotton dress as she leaned forward, the gentle purr of the air conditioning that never quite conquered the humidity.

The metal tools and counters of their kitchen caught the fading sunlight, transforming the familiar space into something sacred - a place where guidance came not through words but through the silent language of patience, through hands learning to create beauty from imperfection.

"Remember," she said, as the paper slowly took shape beneath their joint efforts. "Crane is symbol of hope, of wishes carried to heaven. Each fold is prayer, each crease is path forward."

The finished crane was far from perfect, its wings slightly uneven, its head tilted at an awkward angle. But when Sophia placed it beside her mother's photograph that night, it seemed to glow in the moonlight, carrying her wishes upward into the star-scattered Tokyo sky.

Chapter 6
Complicated Gifts

It was still too early to return to the hospital when Sophia finished her morning emails and her first cup of coffee. Emma wouldn't be awake yet. But she couldn't stay in that empty house any longer.

The three-legged Irish Setter waited outside like a guide from another world. As she approached, it met her eyes with that same emotion she'd seen the night before. Without a sound, it turned and began limping down the street, its parti-colored fur catching the early morning light. Sophia's feet moved of their own accord, drawn by some instinct she didn't understand but trusted completely.

At each corner, the dog would pause and look back, its dark eyes holding hers until she caught up. Her fingers tingled with an odd mixture of fear and anticipation as they moved deeper into Brooklyn's maze of streets. The buildings grew older, their weathered bricks telling stories of generations past. Salt air from the river made her skin prickle, carrying memories of other waters that had marked her journey - the Seine's romantic flow, the Sumida's careful precision, the Ganges' sacred rhythms.

The Irish Setter's three-legged gait never faltered as it led her down an alley. Sophia's heart quickened as the passage opened into a small courtyard. There, golden light spilled from café windows, warming her face like a mother's touch. The sign read "The Smiling Dog," and there in the window - her breath caught - was the Irish Setter's portrait, those same knowing eyes captured in oils.

The café door was open, the sound of gentle Brazilian jazz flowing out. It made her remember Isabella and how she danced to that music, how she had taught Sophia the six basic steps. Without thinking, she was moving her feet to the rhythm of the music.

Following her guide inside, Sophia's boots sank slightly into worn wooden floors that held the memory of countless footsteps. Her fingers trailed along a mahogany counter polished to a honeyed gleam. Every surface she touched seemed to hold its own story. The mirrors behind the counter caught and multiplied the warm light, making her feel wrapped in a gentle glow.

The Irish Setter had vanished, but Sophia still felt its presence, like a thread pulling her forward. Behind the counter stood an elderly woman with silver braids caught up in a neat crown, her brown face lined with the kind of insight that comes from watching others heal. She smiled as if she'd been expecting Sophia.

"Welcome to the Smiling Dog," she said. "I'm Betty. And you look like you could use a cup of coffee."

Something about her reminded Sophia of all of them -- Keiko-san's dignity, Isabella's warmth, Lakshmi's knowing smile. She thought of Emma in her hospital bed, of all the things mothers passed down, intentionally or not.

"Yes," Sophia said, and her voice was steady despite the tears threatening to fall. "Yes, I think I could." She took a seat at the counter. There were several other customers at tables by the side walls, beneath paintings of many different dogs.

As Sophia sat, she caught a glimpse of movement in the vintage mirror behind Betty's head. For a moment, she could have sworn she saw Lakshmi's purple sari swishing past, could almost smell cardamom and rain. But when she looked again, there was only Betty, methodically wiping down the copper espresso machine.

"I'll prepare you a special cup," Betty said, reaching for a jar of beans to grind. "Sometimes the brew tells us what we need to remember."

The mirrors lining the café's back wall were old, their silvering softened by time, creating depths that seemed to shift in the warm lighting. As Betty worked, Sophia saw another shadow move across their surface -- was that Keiko-san's straight spine, her precise movements as she folded invisible cloth?

"They do that sometimes," Betty said quietly, noting Sophia's transfixed gaze. "The mirrors. They've been here since the café opened, and they've caught a lot of memories. Like the ones you hold of your mother."

Sophia turned to face Betty, trying to escape the ghost-images in the mirrors. "I'm not sure I know how to mother," she admitted. "Everyone who taught me after my mother died -- they all had such different ways. Keiko-san with her precision, Lakshmi with her spices and superstitions, Isabella in Rio who taught through music and movement..."

"And you think you have to choose?" Betty's voice held a gentle challenge. "Who says mothering comes in only one flavor?"

Betty didn't ask why Sophia was out so early, didn't comment on the hospital visitor's badge she'd forgotten to remove from her windbreaker. Instead, she moved with practiced grace behind the counter, her hands dancing over various canisters and jars. "I think," she said, measuring fragrant beans into a grinder, "you need a very special blend this morning."

As Betty worked, Sophia found herself drawn to the painting of the three-legged Irish Setter. In the warm light of the café, its eyes seemed to follow her, holding the same knowing look they'd had on the street.

"Her name is Kiyomi," Betty said, following Sophia's gaze. "It's a Japanese name that means pure truth. She's a purebred, and had several litters, watching each puppy go off to their own homes, until she lost her leg, and she wasn't any use to the breeder anymore."

She smiled. "She had a nose for those who needed a cup of comfort, that one."

The rich aroma of coffee filled the air as Betty worked, but underneath it Sophia caught other scents -- cardamom like Lakshmi's kitchen, green tea like Keiko-san's morning ritual, vanilla like the cookies her own mother used to bake on good days. Her throat tightened at the memories.

"Your daughter," Betty said quietly, setting a steaming mug before Sophia, "she's in good hands at Langone."

Sophia's head snapped up. "How did you--"

Betty's smile held generations of understanding. "Kiyomi never brings anyone here by accident, dear. And mothers..." she paused, her hands busy with wiping down the already spotless counter, "mothers always know when another mother's heart is hurting."

She wrapped her hands around the warm cup, realizing as she did so that she was mimicking the way her mother used to hold her tea - both hands cradling the warmth, protecting something precious. She'd seen Emma do the same thing with her hot chocolate, these unconscious gestures passing down through generations like secret messages.

"They're running tests," she found herself saying. "Her heart... they think it might be the same thing that..."

She couldn't finish, but Betty nodded as if she'd heard the complete sentence. "Sometimes," she said, "the things our mothers give us are more complicated than we'd like them to be." She gestured to the wall behind the counter, where photographs of women of all ages smiled down at them. "But sometimes, they give us exactly what we need to face those complications."

The coffee tasted like nothing Sophia had ever had before -- rich and complex, with notes of something she couldn't quite identify. As she sipped, the knot of fear in her chest began to loosen. Outside, the Brooklyn morning continued its urban symphony, but here in the Smiling Dog, time seemed to move at a different pace.

The steam from Betty's coffee machine curled into the hospital corridors of her memory, each wisp carrying her back to those sterile halls where she'd first learned about inheritance.

Betty settled on a stool behind the counter, her own cup steaming before her. "Tell me about your mother," she said softly. And somehow, in this warm space watched over by a three-legged dog's painted eyes, Sophia found herself ready to begin.

The words came slowly at first, like water from a long-unused tap. "She loved to sing," Sophia said, surprising herself. It wasn't the usual beginning of her mother's story -- not the illness, not the hospitals, not the ending everyone always seemed to expect. "She was terrible at it, completely tone-deaf, but she didn't care. She'd sing Beatles songs while we baked together."

Betty nodded, her hands wrapped around her own coffee cup. The steam rose between them like memories taking shape.

"I was nine when she died," Sophia continued. "The same age Emma is now." The parallel hit her fresh, making her hands shake around her cup. "They said it was genetic -- her heart condition. And now Emma..."

"Ah," Betty said, and that single syllable held volumes of understanding. She pulled a tin of cookies from beneath the counter. "These need eating," she said, setting them between them. They were simple ones that smelled of cornstarch and sweetened condensed milk, the kind Isabella made in Rio.

"The doctor said they need to run more tests," Sophia said, picking up a cookie but not eating it. "But I saw the way they looked at her EKG. The same way they used to look at my mother's." The cookie crumbled in her trembling fingers.

"Medical knowledge has come a long way," Betty observed, brushing crumbs into her palm. "What was a sentence then might be just a chapter now."

"I don't know how to do this," Sophia admitted. "How to be strong for her when I'm terrified. How to be the mother she needs when I barely remember what that looks like."

Betty refilled their cups without asking. The coffee's aroma enveloped them, a cocoon of warmth. "Tell me," she said, "about the women who taught you after your mother was gone."

Sophia's mind went to Keiko-san, to her precise movements and carefully measured love. To Isabella in Rio, who'd taught her to dance away her sorrows. To Lakshmi in Mumbai, who'd shown her how spices could be prayers. "There were many," she said slowly. "Each one gave me something different."

"Mm," Betty hummed, a sound of deep understanding. "And what did your mother give you, in the time she had?"

The question hung in the air between them, heavy with possibility. Outside, a siren wailed in the distance, reminding Sophia of the hospital, of Emma sleeping in her too-big bed, of all the fears waiting to be faced. But here in the warm light of the Smiling Dog, watched over by the three-legged guardian's painted eyes, she found herself ready to remember.

Sophia traced the rim of her coffee cup with one finger, remembering. "She gave me stories," she said finally. "Even when she was too tired to get out of bed, she'd make up these elaborate tales about ordinary things -- how the neighbor's cat was really a princess in disguise, how the mailman had a secret life as a dragon tamer."

Betty smiled, an expression that transformed her entire face. "Ah, a storyteller. Those gifts echo through generations."

"Emma does the same thing," Sophia realized aloud. "She makes up stories about everything -- why the subway is late, why her lunch sandwich is triangle-shaped instead of square. I never made the connection before."

"The things we inherit aren't always written in medical charts," Betty said softly.

Betty wore an apron in brilliant tie-dyed swirls over a crisp white blouse, her silver braids caught up in a neat crown. She moved with quick, precise gestures, muttering to herself as she reorganized already-perfect canisters on the shelves behind her. Despite her brisk efficiency, warmth radiated from her smile as her hands moved with practiced grace.

She moved to adjust one of the photographs on the wall -- a young woman with a baby, both laughing at something beyond the camera's frame. "Sometimes they're in the way we see the world, the way we choose to tell its story."

The coffee in Sophia's cup had cooled to drinking temperature, and as she sipped it, unexpected flavors bloomed -- chocolate, yes, but also something else, something that reminded her of the tea Keiko-san used to make on difficult mornings.

"I've been so focused on what else Emma might have inherited," Sophia admitted. "The heart condition, the genetic predisposition to..." She stopped, unable to finish the thought.

"To ending a story too soon?" Betty suggested gently. She sat back down, her movements carrying the fluid grace of someone completely at home in their space. "But that's not the only story being told here, is it?"

Through the window, the city lights blurred, and for a moment Sophia saw her own reflection overlaid with the Irish Setter's painted portrait -- both of them watching, both waiting for something she couldn't quite name.

"Tell me about Emma," Betty said, her voice carrying the same gentle authority Keiko-san's had held. "Not about her medical charts or her test results. Tell me about her stories."

And somehow, in that warm space that smelled of coffee and memories, Sophia found herself talking about her daughter -- not as a patient, not as a potential heir to a genetic legacy of loss, but as the bright, creative spirit who filled their Brooklyn brownstone with imagination and life. As she spoke, something began to shift in her chest, like light breaking through clouds.

The three-legged dog in the painting seemed to watch with approval, its eyes holding all the knowledge of guardians who understand that sometimes the path forward requires a slight limp, a certain asymmetry, a willingness to find balance in imperfection.

After her second cup of Betty's memory-laden coffee, Sophia's phone felt heavy in her pocket. She had actual test results now, concrete information Mark would want. Her finger hovered over his contact information for the second time in two days. But the words still wouldn't come - how could she tell him their daughter had inherited not just her dark curls, but the shadow in her heart as well? No. Better to wait until she had Dr. Vlad's complete assessment, until she could present Mark with both the problem and the solution. She tucked the phone away, but its weight stayed with her all the way home.

Chapter 7
Mumbai Spices

As she walked to the brownstone, that second cup of coffee's spicy aroma with hints of citrus, a slightly peppery quality, and a touch of mint filled her senses, Sophia found herself transported to another time, another place where spices had taught her about love. Her first morning in the new house in Mumbai had begun with the sound of bells and the scent of cardamom. She lay in her new bed, watching dust motes dance in the slanted sunlight, listening to someone singing in a language she didn't yet understand. The air felt different here -- thicker, warmer, alive with spices and possibilities.

Downstairs, something clattered in the kitchen, followed by a woman's voice speaking rapid Hindi. Sophia pulled her pillow over her head, trying to block out this new reality. She missed the precise silence of Tokyo mornings, the careful routine of breakfast with Keiko-san, the predictable rhythm of their days together.

"Miss Sophia!" The voice floated up the stairs, musical despite its insistence. "Time for breakfast! Mars is favorable today -- very good day to start new things!"

That was Lakshmi, the housekeeper her father had hired before they arrived. She'd greeted them at the airport with a garland of marigolds and immediately begun explaining about the positions of various planets and their influence on daily life -- something Keiko-san would have dismissed with a single raised eyebrow.

Sophia dragged herself out of bed, the cotton nightgown already sticking to her skin in the morning heat. The wooden floors of the colonial-era house creaked under her feet as she made her way downstairs, following the scent of whatever was cooking in the kitchen.

She found Lakshmi at the stove, her gray-streaked hair tied back in a long braid, her sari a swirl of purple and gold as she moved between pots and pans. The kitchen counter held an array of small metal bowls filled with colorful powders and seeds -- Sophia would later learn these were the masalas, the spice blends that Lakshmi treated with the same reverence Keiko-san had shown to her tea ceremony implements.

"Ah, good morning, good morning!" Lakshmi beamed at her. "Sit, sit! I make proper Indian breakfast today. No more cornflakes -- growing girl needs strong food! Besides," she added, tapping her nose knowingly, "Jupiter is aligned with your third house. Very good for trying new things."

Sophia slid onto a kitchen chair, watching as Lakshmi poured something golden and steaming into a metal cup. The woman moved differently than Keiko-san had -- all flowing motion and energetic gestures, a dance set to music only she could hear.

"First, masala chai," Lakshmi announced, setting the cup before Sophia. "Good for digestion, good for mind, very good for homesick heart." She tapped her chest meaningfully. "I put extra cardamom today. It opens the heart chakra, you know? Very important for new beginnings."

The tea was nothing like the careful green tea used in ceremonies Sophia had learned in Tokyo. It was bold and sweet, warming her from the inside out. Lakshmi watched her first sip with eager eyes, hands clasped together in anticipation.

"It's... different," Sophia said carefully, the way she'd been taught to be polite about new things.

"Different is good!" Lakshmi clapped her hands. "Different means we are learning. Now, breakfast."

She set a plate before Sophia -- something that resembled crepes but wasn't quite, served with a small bowl of spiced potatoes and another of coconut chutney. "Dosa," Lakshmi explained. "Very lucky food. See how it spirals? Life is spiral, always turning but moving forward. My grandmother taught me this. Her grandmother taught her. Now I teach you."

Sophia stared at the spiral pattern in the dosa, remembering how Keiko-san had arranged her rice in perfect geometric shapes. Here, everything seemed to curve and flow, refusing to be contained in straight lines.

"My mother--" Sophia started, then stopped, surprised by the words that had risen unbidden to her lips.

"Yes?" Lakshmi paused in her cooking, giving Sophia her full attention. "Tell about your mother. Is good to speak of those we miss. Keeps them close to heart."

Sophia traced the spiral pattern on her plate with one finger. "My mother used to make pancakes on Sundays. They were always burned on one side and raw in the middle. But she'd make faces on them with chocolate chips, and she'd sing while she cooked."

"Ah!" Lakshmi's face lit up. "She knew important thing -- food made with singing has more love. In my village, women always sing while cooking. Different songs for different spices." She turned back to the stove, her voice lifting in a melody that seemed to dance with the steam rising from the pans. "This song is for turmeric. Very good for health. Also makes everything yellow -- sunshine in the stomach!"

Despite herself, Sophia smiled. The kitchen was so different from Keiko-san's precise domain, where everything had its place and silence was a virtue. Here, spices dusted the counters like fallen stars, pots clattered their own rhythm section to Lakshmi's singing, and the morning light painted everything in shades of gold.

"Your father says you don't eat much breakfast anymore," Lakshmi said, setting another dosa on Sophia's plate. "Not good.

Breakfast is breaking the fast -- breaking silence between night and day. Must be done with joy, with spice, with song!" She sprinkled something green over the potatoes. "Coriander -- for making new friends. You start new school today, yes?"

Sophia's stomach tightened at the reminder. Another new school, another set of uniforms, another group of girls to try to understand. In Tokyo, she'd finally learned the rhythms of friendship, the careful dance of belonging. Now she would have to start all over again.

"Venus is in your house of friendship. Very auspicious," Lakshmi said firmly, anticipating her fears. She placed a small cloth-wrapped package beside Sophia's plate. "For lunch. I make special tiffin for you. Food that carries blessings travels with love."

Sophia unwrapped the package to find a stainless-steel tiffin carrier, its stacked containers clicking together with a musical sound. Inside, each level held something different -- rice decorated with bright yellow turmeric, tiny cauliflower florets stained orange with spices, triangle-shaped flatbreads wrapped in foil.

"Each spice has purpose," Lakshmi explained, pointing to the containers. "Turmeric for protection. Cumin for mental strength. Cardamom to help words flow smooth as honey when meeting new friends." She winked. "Also mango lassi in thermos. Sweet things make bitter things easier to swallow."

It was nothing approaching Keiko-san's precise bento boxes with their architectural arrangements. This was food that refused to stay in neat compartments, flavors bleeding into each other with the soft blend of watercolors.

"But what if the other girls think it's weird?" Sophia asked, remembering the careful neutrality of her Tokyo school lunches, how she'd learned to make her food appear exactly the same as everyone else's.

Lakshmi's laugh filled the kitchen, resonant as music. "Weird? No, no. Different. Special. Your food carries stories. Stories of your mother's pancakes, Keiko-san's bentos, my masalas. All part of who you are." She adjusted her sari, the purple silk catching the morning light. "Besides, a stomach that knows only one kind of food is akin to a heart that knows only one kind of love -- very boring!"

A horn honked outside -- Sophia's father, waiting in the car to drive her to her new school. Lakshmi quickly wrapped a red thread around Sophia's wrist. "For protection," she said. "And to remind you -- life is like my spice box. Many different flavors, all needed for the perfect taste."

As Sophia stood to leave, Lakshmi pressed something into her hand -- a small packet wrapped in wax paper. "Special chocolate barfi," she whispered. "If day becomes too spicy, a little sweetness helps. Just like your mother's chocolate chip pancakes, yes?"

The car ride to school was silent, her father focused on navigating the chaotic Mumbai traffic. Sophia watched the city wake up through the window -- women in bright saris sweeping their doorsteps, vendors setting up carts of fruit arranged in geometric patterns, crows swooping between buildings that mixed colonial architecture with modern glass and steel.

"Lakshmi seems to be nice," her father said finally, breaking the silence. "She came highly recommended. Very experienced with expat families." He paused at a traffic light, fingers drumming on the steering wheel. "Different from Keiko-san, of course, but..."

"She sings while she cooks," Sophia said quietly. "Like Mom used to."

The light turned green, but her father didn't move immediately. A chorus of horns erupted behind them, and he startled back into motion. "Yes," he said, his voice rough. "Yes, she does."

At the school gates, he handed her a new phone. "Latest model. It has all the emergency numbers programmed in. And you can call me anytime." He hesitated, then added, "Your mother would have been better at this part. The new schools, the transitions. She always knew what to say."

Sophia clutched her tiffin carrier, feeling the warmth of the containers through the metal. "Lakshmi says different spices have different powers. She claims cardamom brings friendship."

Her father's laugh sounded surprised, rusty with disuse. "Well, that's one approach, I suppose. Better than my 'excel at everything' strategy." He looked at her then, really looked at her, something soft breaking through his usual businesslike expression. "You know, your mother believed in magic too. Not through spices and planets as Lakshmi does, but... she had her own special way."

The school bell rang, its sound so different from the crisp chime of her Tokyo school. This one resonated deep and rich.

That afternoon, when Sophia returned home, she found Lakshmi in the kitchen garden, picking mint leaves while having an animated conversation with a crow perched on the fence. The air was thick with humidity, promising one of Mumbai's sudden monsoon showers.

"Ah, you're home!" Lakshmi brightened at the sight of her. "Come, come. Tell how the tiffin magic worked while I make afternoon chai." She shooed the crow away with a friendly wave. "He brings news of rain coming. Very clever birds, crows. In Hindi we call them kaaga -- messengers between worlds."

Sophia followed her into the kitchen, where the counters now held different spices than the morning's array. She put down her school bag and carefully unpacked the tiffin carrier, now empty except for a note written on yellow paper.

"A girl named Priya wrote 'Please bring more tomorrow' in English," Sophia said, holding out the note. "She shared her mother's samosas with me after I let her try the cauliflower."

Lakshmi's smile rivaled the afternoon sun streaming through the windows. "Ah! Food shared is friendship begun. Your mother knows this -- see how she guides you still? Making friends over burned pancakes, now her daughter makes friends with spiced cauliflower." She began measuring tea leaves into cups. "In India, we say the first sharing of food is like planting a seed. With proper care, it grows into strong tree of friendship."

Thunder rolled in the distance as Lakshmi prepared the chai, adding extra cardamom "for the heart" and ginger "for courage." The kitchen filled with steam and spices, and Sophia found herself relaxing into its warmth, so different from Keiko-san's precise domain but comforting in its own way.

Lakshmi held up a small cardamom pod. "This is special medicine for heart. My grandmother taught me - cardamom and cinnamon, *haritaki* and *arjuna* bark. All good for keeping heart strong." She smiled knowingly. "Doctor at Apollo Hospital says same thing, yes? Modern medicine, ancient wisdom - both want same thing. Strong heart, long life."

Sophia touched the medical alert bracelet hidden beneath her school uniform sleeve. Lakshmi pretended not to notice, but that evening's dinner featured all the heart-strengthening foods her research had uncovered.

"You know," Lakshmi said, setting a cup before her, "there is old saying: we carry our mothers in our hands when we cook, in our voices when we sing, in our hearts when we love. Different mothers, different ways, but all same love." She tapped her chest. "Your mother, she lives here still. In pancake memories, in friendship-making heart, in stories you will tell your own children someday."

The rain began then, a sudden symphony on the tin roof, and Lakshmi smiled at the sound. "Perfect timing! Rain washes away old worries, makes space for new joy. Now, you help me make pakoras? Is best food for rainy day, and I teach you proper spice-choosing prayer. Very useful skill, choosing spices. Like choosing right words, right friends, right ways to keep memories alive."

And as the rain painted patterns on the windows, Sophia learned another way to remember her mother -- not in silence and precision as in Tokyo, but in the chaotic dance of spices and rain and love that spoke in many languages.

Chapter 8
Drawings

The physical therapist came to take Emma for her cardiac rehabilitation assessment late on Tuesday afternoon. "This will take about two hours," the therapist said. "Why don't you take a break? Emma will be in good hands."

"I could use some coffee," Sophia admitted. Sophia kissed her daughter's forehead. She knew exactly where she would go.

She found herself retracing her steps from that morning, drawn back to The Smiling Dog in the glow of the afternoon. Betty looked up from polishing glasses. The painted Irish Setter's eyes seemed to follow Sophia as she sank into what was already becoming her usual seat at the counter.

The afternoon crowd had their own rhythm - different from the morning visitors but just as much a part of the café's fabric. A teacher sat in the corner grading papers. A man doing the Times crossword puzzle had claimed a window seat, occasionally muttering over particularly challenging clues. The scent of coffee mingled with butter and vanilla from the day's last batch of baking, while the sun painted long shadows across the mahogany counter.

"Time for your next cup," Betty said, reaching for a different canister than she'd used that morning. "This blend is special. Has a bit of cardamom in it -- good for healing hearts, or so a wise woman from Mumbai once told me."

Sophia's head snapped up. "You couldn't have known Lakshmi..."

Betty's smile contained secrets, spiced with knowing. "Didn't have to. Some insight finds its way around the world, passed through generations with cherished recipes." She began preparing the coffee with movements that somehow reminded Sophia of both Keiko-san's precision and Lakshmi's flow. "Tell me about the hospital."

"More tests," Sophia said, watching the steam rise from Betty's copper coffee machine. "They're being careful, thorough. Emma's scared, but she's trying not to show it. Just like..." She stopped.

"Just like you did?" Betty asked softly. "Or just like your mother did?"

The coffee, when it came, smelled of cardamom and something deeper -- cinnamon maybe, or memories. Betty added a splash of warm milk, creating a spiral pattern that reminded Sophia of Lakshmi's dosas.

"The hardest part of being a mother," Betty said, beginning to polish another glass, "is watching your child face the same fears you once faced yourself."

"Did you..." Sophia wrapped her hands around the warm cup. "Did you lose someone too?"

Betty set down her polishing cloth, her movements deliberate as temple bells. "My wife. Different illness, same fear." She reached up to touch one of the photographs on the wall -- a young woman with a beautiful smile, caught mid-laugh. "Cancer, not heart problems." She shook her head. "Sometimes love feels like a curse we pass on without meaning to."

The coffee tasted different from the morning's brew -- warmer somehow, with notes of spice that opened like flowers on Sophia's tongue. Through the café's windows, she saw puffy clouds float across the Brooklyn sky, reminding her of the night Lakshmi had taught her to make chai under a monsoon moon.

"But here's what I learned," Betty continued, pulling another cup for herself. "The love we share gives us strength. Resilience. The ability to face fear with grace." She gestured to the wall of photographs. "Every mother here passed down both shadows and light to their children. The trick is learning to see both."

When she returned to Emma's hospital room, her daughter was back from her assessment, but ready for more tests. During the echocardiogram, Sophia watched her daughter's heart dance on the screen - so much smaller than her own, but already so much stronger. The sonographer pointed out chambers and valves, using clinical terms that once frightened a nine-year-old Sophia.

During the genetic counseling sessions, Emma traced their family tree with her finger, pausing at her grandmother's name, then at her mother's, then at her own - three generations of hearts beating in different rhythms.

In Emma's physical therapy session, each exercise carried echoes. When the therapist guided Emma through gentle stretches, Sophia remembered her own childhood therapy - the fear of pushing too hard warring with the need to build strength. But Emma's face showed determination rather than dread, her movements confident under the watchful eye of sensors that could detect the slightest strain.

Even the pills had changed - no more bitter adult tablets broken into child-sized pieces. Emma's medication came in small, colorful capsules, their very design speaking of childhood rather than hospitals. When Emma swallowed them, she called them her "superhero pills" - medicine transformed into magic, treatment into triumph.

Sophia found herself touching the old scar from her childhood IV ports while watching Emma's blood draws done with tiny butterfly needles, so different from the large gauges she remembered. The nurse used a vein visualization light that made Emma giggle about having "glowing superhero veins," transforming a moment of fear into one of wonder.

Sophia spent the evening in Emma's hospital room, her laptop balanced on her knees as she tried to focus on technical specifications for banking software while her daughter wrote an elaborate story about the three-legged dog's secret life as a superhero. The nurses came and went, checking vitals, adjusting medications, their efficient movements reminding Sophia of Keiko-san.

"We'd like to keep her one more night," Dr. Vlad said during evening rounds. "Just to monitor how she responds to the first dose of medication. You should go home, get some real rest. She's in good hands."

Emma, who had been so brave all day, finally showed a crack in her armor. "Do you have to go?"

"I do. But I'll be back tomorrow."

Emma clutched her stuffed dolphin. "Promise?"

"Of course." Sophia tucked the hospital blanket around her daughter, making sure the heart monitor wires weren't tangled. "Try to get some sleep, butterfly. Dr. Vlad says rest is the best medicine right now."

She kissed Emma's forehead, lingering a moment to breathe in the familiar scent of her daughter's hair, now mingled with hospital antiseptic. The monitors beeped steadily, their rhythm almost like a lullaby. Emma's eyes were already growing heavy, the day's tests and treatments taking their toll.

"Love you, Mom," Emma murmured, her voice trailing off as sleep began to claim her.

"Love you too, sweetheart." Sophia waited until Emma's breathing evened out before gathering her things. At the door, she paused for one last look, remembering all the times she had done the same for her own mother - watching her sleep in hospital beds, counting breaths, measuring love in heartbeats.

The night nurse smiled reassuringly as Sophia passed the station. "We'll take good care of her," she promised. "Get some rest yourself - you look exhausted."

But Sophia knew rest wouldn't come easily tonight.

Chapter 9
Shadows in the Mirror

As she expected, sleep eluded Sophia Tuesday night. The hospital's stark fluorescent lighting had burned afterimages on her retinas - ghostly shapes that danced behind her closed eyelids. In the darkness, her phone glowed accusingly from the bedside table, Mark's contact information still open on the screen. Three times she'd picked it up that night, three times she'd started to type a message: "Emma's tests show..." but each attempt remained unfinished.

A text would be easier than a call. Less immediate. Less real. But what could she possibly write that would convey everything? "Our daughter has our hearts - both the strength and the weakness of them." Delete. "Remember how we used to joke that she got my curls and your business sense? She got something else from me too." Delete. "She needs you. Not your research, not your plans, just you." Delete.

Dawn on Wednesday found Sophia sitting at her desk, surrounded by Emma's drawings. She'd given up on sleep hours ago and had been sorting through her daughter's artwork - sketches of their Brooklyn neighborhood, portraits of friends and teachers, imaginative scenes from the books they read together. Each page captured Emma's view of the world, full of color and possibility despite the shadows that lurked in her genes.

It was still too early to return to the hospital - Emma wouldn't be awake yet. But the silent apartment pressed against her ears like deep water. The three-legged Irish Setter waited outside like a guide from another world, and Sophia found herself following without hesitation. Under the early morning light, memories began to surface - not just of Emma, but of all the mornings she'd spent in foreign kitchens, learning different ways to begin each day.

When she reached The Smiling Dog, the café's golden light spilled from the windows, warming her face like a mother's touch. Betty looked up as she entered, as if she'd been expecting her.

"The early morning blend isn't quite ready," Betty said, her hands already moving among her collection of canisters. "But I think you need something different today anyway." She selected a ceramic jar painted with flowers. "This was Maria's favorite."

"Maria?"

Betty's movements slowed, becoming deliberate. "My wife. She loved watching the sunrise from our bedroom window while I got ready for work. Said morning light made everything look like a watercolor painting." She measured beans into the grinder with careful precision. "Even when she was in the hospital, she insisted I bring her coffee from home instead of drinking that institutional brew."

"What did she do?"

"She was a cop," Betty said. "Walked a beat in Bay Ridge for years, then got her detective shield just as they found the cancer."

Betty's hands never stopped moving as she worked, but her voice carried the weight of memory. "She taught me that sometimes the bravest thing is just being present. Not fixing, not planning, just... being there."

The morning light caught the silver frames of the mirrors, and for a moment Sophia thought she saw a woman's reflection among the

A Mother's Heart

shadows – a woman in a police uniform, with a smile that could warm the coldest morning.

Customers came and went in the café, some settling into chairs, others taking their brews to go, but Betty had a kind word for each one, commenting on a beautiful scarf, wishing a student luck on an exam, adding ice to a runner's cup.

Sophia loved the atmosphere and the sense of connection among all the patrons. This was no commercial coffee shop, where the customers came and went quickly. Even those on their way to work stopped for an extra minute to chat.

Sophia's phone buzzed and the hospital's number lit up the screen. Her hands trembled as she answered the call. Betty moved away discreetly, but stayed within sight, her presence steady as a lighthouse beam.

"Ms. Greenwood?" Dr. Vlad's voice sounded tinny through the phone. "We have some preliminary results from Emma's tests." A pause that stretched like taffy. "There are some concerning patterns in her EKG that I want to discuss. Can you check in with me when you come to the hospital?"

The words "concerning patterns" echoed in Sophia's head, bringing back another hospital, another doctor's voice using careful terms like "genetic predisposition" and "inherited condition." In the mirror behind the counter, she caught a glimpse of her mother's face -- not the smiling one from photographs, but the tired one from hospital beds, trying to be brave.

"I'll be there soon," Sophia managed to say, her voice sounding distant to her own ears.

As she ended the call, Betty handed her a to-go cup, and a box wrapped in brown paper. "For later," she said, placing the package in Sophia's hands. "Butter cookies. Sometimes sweet things make bitter news easier to bear. Your mother knew that, didn't she? With her chocolate chip pancakes?"

Sophia stared at the package, remembering suddenly how she

would sneak chocolates into her mother's hospital room, handing them over away from the prying eyes of nurses like secret messages of love. "How did you--?"

"The mirrors remember," Betty said simply. She gestured to the wall of photographs behind her. "Each of these women found their own way. Some baked, some sang, some folded perfect corners, some made spice magic. But they all loved."

In the mirrors, shadows seemed to dance -- Keiko-san's straight posture, Lakshmi's flowing sari, Isabella's graceful movements. Each woman who had taught Sophia a different way to care, to love, to mother. Their reflections merged into a story written across time, one she was only now beginning to read.

"Before you go," Betty said, reaching beneath the counter, "take this." She pulled out a small tin, its lid painted with cherry blossoms. "For Emma. Hospital tea. Not as strong as coffee, but it carries its own magic."

The tin felt warm in Sophia's hands, and when she opened it, the scent brought tears to her eyes -- green tea, layered with subtle notes of cardamom and vanilla. "This smells..."

"Just as Keiko-san's morning ritual did," Betty nodded. "And your mother's cookies. And Lakshmi's chai. Memories blend in remarkable ways, don't they?"

Some inheritances came through blood, Sophia thought, but others flowed through love - wisdom from Lakshmi's spices, strength from Keiko-san's careful rituals, courage from Isabella's defiant joy. She'd gathered different kinds of strength from each of them, gifts she could now pass to Emma along with the DNA she'd inherited.

Through the café window, Sophia saw the sky lightening. The hours since the Irish Setter led her to the café had melted into sweetness, dissolving with her memories.

"I don't know how to protect her," Sophia whispered, clutching the tin. "My mother couldn't protect me from inheriting her heart condition. What if I can't protect Emma either?"

A Mother's Heart

Betty's reflection in the mirror seemed to overlap with all the other women for a moment -- straight spine, flowing movements, gentle hands. "Perhaps," she said softly, "protection isn't always about preventing pain. Sometimes it's about teaching our children how to be strong through it. Your mother did that for you, didn't she? And all these other women showed you different ways to be strong."

Sophia's phone buzzed again -- a text from the nurse saying Emma was asking for her. In the mirror, she caught one last glimpse of her mother's face, not the sick one this time, but the one who used to sing off-key while making imperfect pancakes. The one who had taught her that love didn't have to be perfect to be strong.

She brushed away that memory and walked back to Langone Medical Center, the three-legged Irish Setter padding silently beside her through Brooklyn's busy streets. The sky held that peculiar shade of blue that comes just before sunrise, the same color she'd watched from hospital windows in Tokyo, Mumbai, Paris, Rio, Singapore - all the places she'd learned different languages of love.

The dog stopped at the hospital entrance, its fur ghostly in the early light. It sat, watching her with those knowing eyes that reminded her of every woman who had helped raise her.

"Thank you," she whispered to the dog, understanding now why it had led her to Betty's café, why the timing of everything had been so precise. Her mother's final gift was not the genetic inheritance of a failing heart, but the legacy of all these women who had taught her how to be strong.

Emma was asleep, but she found Dr. Vlad by the nurse's station.

As he explained Emma's genetic test results, each scientific term felt like a stone in Sophia's pocket. But then he showed her Emma's treatment plan on his tablet, and the weights transformed into stepping-stones - each medical advance a path forward through fear.

She carried the tin of Betty's special tea back to her daughter's room with the starfish on the door. Emma was awake again, propped up against her pillows, doodling in her sketchbook with one of the pencils from the box Sophia had brought with them when they left for the hospital.

Her daughter was restless, her dark curls wild against the white pillowcase. "Mom!" Emma's face lit up. "The nurse let me pick what I want for breakfast but I know their pancakes won't taste like yours." She looked up. "You're wearing different shoes today," she noticed with a grin. "And what's in the container you're carrying?"

Sophia hesitated, the memory of The Smiling Dog feeling almost dreamy in the harsh hospital lighting. "I found this café. Or maybe it found me. There was this dog, an Irish Setter with three legs, who led me there. It sounds crazy, doesn't it?"

Emma's eyes lit up with interest, her pencil pausing mid-stroke. "A three-legged dog? Like in the story about the Japanese temple guardian?"

"Yes, exactly. And the café..." Sophia smiled, remembering the warm glow, the walls of dog portraits, the mysterious mirrors. "It's the most amazing place. The owner, Betty, makes these special coffee blends that somehow taste like memories."

Sophia smiled, remembering how the Irish Setter had appeared exactly when she needed guidance, as if it knew precisely when to lead her toward healing. She'd seen it three times now - outside the hospital, leading her to the café, and guiding her back to Emma - each appearance marking a moment when she most needed direction.

"Tell me about the café, Mom," Emma said, sitting up straighter in her hospital bed. Her sketchbook lay open on the rolling table, colored pencils tumbled across its surface in cheerful disarray. "I want to draw it."

Sophia settled into the chair beside the bed, remembering the warm glow that had welcomed her. "It's in this old brick building, with big windows that catch the morning light. The door has a bell that echoes temple chimes when you enter. And everywhere you look, there are dogs."

"Dogs?" Emma's pencil moved across the page, rough shapes beginning to take form.

A Mother's Heart

"Paintings of them, all kinds. But they're not ordinary portraits. Each dog has a story in its eyes. Some are missing legs, or ears, or eyes, but they all look... wise. Like they've seen into people's hearts and understood what they found there." She watched Emma sketch the outline of windows, adding the soft glow of early morning. "The counter is old wood, polished by thousands of hands until it gleams. Behind it, there are mirrors with silver frames that catch memories in their depths."

"What about Betty?"

"She has silver braids and eyes that seem to know exactly what kind of comfort you need. She moves like she's dancing to music only she can hear, between her copper coffee machine and all these mysterious canisters of coffee beans."

Emma added details to her drawing – the coffee machine with its gleaming pipes, the rows of canisters labeled in Betty's flowing script. "And the three-legged dog? The one that led you there?"

"His portrait hung in the window – an Irish Setter with a noble bearing and gentle eyes. Even in the painting, his gaze holds such understanding." Sophia touched her daughter's hand, stilling its movement for a moment. "Just like you captured in your drawing."

Somewhere down the hall, a child was watching cartoons, the familiar voices of SpongeBob characters mixing with the quiet conversations of doctors doing their rounds. A young patient walked slowly past Emma's door, pulling his IV pole that squeaked slightly with each step, his mother's hand steady on his back. The floor's tile pattern made a hopscotch grid that some kids used for physical therapy, counting their steps as they grew stronger.

Dr. Vlad found them as Emma added the final touches to her artwork while Sophia described the way morning light painted patterns across the café's wooden floors. He smiled at the drawing before pulling up a chair.

"That's beautiful, Emma. You've captured something special there." He turned to Sophia, his expression growing more serious but maintaining its gentleness. "I've been reviewing your mother's medical records from twenty-five years ago. The same condition, but the landscape of treatment was very different then."

Sophia nodded, remembering the heavy restrictions of her childhood. "I had to wear a heart monitor that almost weighed more than my schoolbooks. Every activity was a calculation of risk versus reward."

"The technology has come so far," Dr. Vlad said, pulling up charts on his tablet. "The monitor we're giving Emma is smaller than a watch, and it's smarter too. It doesn't just track her heart rate – it learns her patterns, predicts potential issues before they become problems." He showed them a graph of Emma's readings from the past day. "See these algorithms? They're like having a team of cardiologists watching 24/7."

"I remember being scared to run during recess," Sophia said softly. "My guardian in Paris, Marie-Claude, she'd count my steps, time my activities down to the second."

Emma squeezed her mother's hand. "But I can still dance, right? You promised."

Dr. Vlad smiled. "With proper monitoring and medication, yes. The drugs we have now are more targeted, more effective. They work with your body instead of just restricting it." He turned to Sophia. "Your mother's generation helped us understand this condition better. Every case, every response to treatment, became part of the knowledge that's helping us treat Emma today."

Sophia thought of her mother's last days, how even then she'd insisted on dancing to Beatles songs in her hospital room. "She would have loved knowing that her experience helped make things better for her granddaughter."

"Science advances one heartbeat at a time," Dr. Vlad said, his accent wrapping the words in extra warmth. "Emma won't need the same restrictions you had. We'll teach her to listen to her body, yes, but also to trust in her strength."

Emma held up her drawing of The Smiling Dog. "Can I put this on a wall when I come back for checkups? So other kids know there's a magical café where dogs lead you to healing?"

Dr. Vlad looked at the drawing for a long moment, taking in the three-legged Irish Setter's knowing eyes, the warm glow of Betty's coffee machine, the mirrors that caught memories in their depths. "I think that would be perfect," he said. "Sometimes the best medicine is knowing you're not alone on the journey."

Chapter 10
Paris Afternoons

Outside the hospital window, rain began to fall, a gentle patter against the glass that reminded Sophia of other rains, other protections. Paris had greeted her with rain and Marie-Claude's umbrella, held at precisely the right angle to prevent a single drop from touching her charge.

"Non, non," Marie-Claude clucked as Sophia tried to step out from under its protective cover. "You will catch your death, and then what would your father say?"

After the warm chaos of Mumbai, the precise concern in Marie-Claude's voice felt like a steel band around Sophia's chest. Every movement, every decision, every breath seemed to be monitored, measured, protected. Marie-Claude had come with impeccable references -- she'd cared for diplomats' children, celebrities' offspring, young aristocrats who needed the perfect blend of education and etiquette.

"I have researched your medical history," Marie-Claude had announced on her first day, brandishing a leather-bound notebook. "Every hospital within ten kilometers has been notified of your condition. I have mapped the fastest routes, learned the names of all emergency personnel, and created a comprehensive crisis protocol."

Now, three months into their time together, Sophia watched raindrops race down the windows of their apartment in the 16th arrondissement, while Marie-Claude prepared her afternoon snack -- organic fruits cut into precise portions, arranged like flowers on Limoges porcelain.

"Did you remember to take your vitamins this morning?" Marie-Claude asked, though she knew the answer. She monitored every pill, every supplement, recording them in her notebook. "And your heart rate during physical education? I've told your teacher you must not exceed one hundred and thirty beats per minute."

Sophia stared at the perfectly cut apple slices, remembering Lakshmi's messy, joyful kitchen, the way spices would dust every surface like colorful snow. Here, everything was antiseptic, controlled, measured to the millimeter.

"I want to go to Amélie's birthday party on Saturday," Sophia said, the words bursting out before she could stop them. She'd been carrying the invitation in her school bag for three days, afraid to mention it.

Marie-Claude's spine stiffened. "The party at the roller rink? Absolutely not. Too much excitement, too many possibilities for injury. We cannot risk it with your condition."

"But I'm not sick!" Sophia pushed her plate away, the careful arrangement of fruit disrupted. "I just have to be careful sometimes. Lakshmi let me dance in the rain. Keiko-san taught me to ride a bicycle."

"And that was very irresponsible of them," Marie-Claude sniffed, already pulling out her notebook. "Here, look at the statistics for childhood accidents at roller rinks. The potential for elevated heart rate alone--"

"I hate you!" The words exploded from Sophia like a thunderclap. "You're not my mother! You can't keep me in a bubble forever!"

The silence that followed was absolute. Even the rain seemed to pause. Marie-Claude stood very still, her face doing something

A Mother's Heart

complicated behind her perfect makeup. Then, to Sophia's shock, she sat down heavily in one of the delicate dining room chairs.

"*Non*," she said quietly. "I am not your mother. But I made a promise, you see. Not to your father -- to your mother."

Sophia stared at her guardian, all the angry words dying in her throat. "What? But... my mother died years before you..."

"I knew her," Marie-Claude said, her perfect posture softening slightly. "I was a nurse at the American Hospital in Paris when she was here for treatments. Before you were born." She opened her leather notebook, and for the first time, Sophia saw that its precision came not from rigidity, but from fear wrapped in love.

"She was so young, your mother. So afraid of what her heart condition might mean for her future children." Marie-Claude's French accent grew stronger with emotion. "We would talk during her treatments. She made me promise -- if I ever had the chance -- to protect any child she might have. 'Not just from danger,' she said, 'but from the fear of living.'"

The rain resumed its rhythm against the windows. On the table, the displaced apple slices lay like scattered puzzle pieces.

"I have not kept that promise well," Marie-Claude continued, touching her notebook. "I protected you from danger, yes. But I have also protected you from living. Your mother... she used to talk about dancing in thunderstorms. About how the best parts of life sometimes come with risk."

She stood abruptly, smoothing her skirt with trembling hands. "We will need proper safety equipment, of course. And I must speak with the roller rink staff about their emergency protocols. But perhaps... perhaps we can find a way to let you attend this party."

Saturday arrived under clear skies, Marie-Claude having consulted three different weather services to be sure of optimal conditions. The roller rink was in a converted warehouse near the Seine, its windows casting rainbow patterns across the wooden floor.

Sophia's French, polished in Mumbai at the Alliance Française her father had insisted on, flowed more easily now after three months in Paris. Still, she felt the slight hesitation before each word, the way Amélie and her friends would sometimes exchange glances when she used the wrong tense.

"Sophia! *Tu es venue!*" Amélie glided toward her, already on wheels, her dark curls bouncing. She kissed the air beside both of Sophia's cheeks, grown-up and graceful in the way of Parisian girls. "I didn't think Madame Marie-Claude would let you come!"

Behind them, Marie-Claude was deep in conversation with the rink's safety officer, her notebook open, probably documenting the location of every first aid kit and emergency exit.

"Your skates," the attendant said in careful English, noting Sophia's hesitation. "Have you used them before?"

"In Mumbai," Sophia said, remembering how Lakshmi had blessed her first pair of roller skates with a red thread and a prayer to Ganesha, remover of obstacles. "But not much."

The French girls flowed across the rink in elegant patterns. They'd all taken lessons since they were small, their mothers watching from the café area, sipping espresso and sharing knowing looks.

"Don't worry," Amélie said, taking Sophia's hand. "We'll teach you. Claire's mother is a dance instructor - she says everyone falls before they can fly."

The first fall came quickly, Sophia's feet sliding out from under her like untethered birds. She landed hard, the impact shooting through her tailbone, and heard Marie-Claude's sharp intake of breath from across the rink.

But before her guardian could rush over with ice packs and incident reports, Amélie and Claire were already helping her up, their laughter kind rather than mocking. "*Parfait!*" Claire declared. "Now you are truly skating. The first fall is a baptism, *non?*"

"*Ma mère* says you lived in Japan?" Amélie asked as they guided Sophia along the rink's edge. "And India? Were there skating rinks there?"

"Not really," Sophia said, concentrating on staying upright. "In

Tokyo, I learned tea ceremony. In Mumbai, I learned to make spicy snacks for the rain." She wobbled, clutched the rail. "My mother... she used to ice skate. Before she got sick. I saw pictures."

The French girls exchanged glances, but not the usual ones of linguistic judgment. Something softer passed between them. "My aunt died," Claire offered quietly. "When I was small. Sometimes I wear her old necklaces, and Maman says it's like having her with me."

"Like spirits," agreed Amélie, "but the good kind. The protecting kind."

Sophia thought of her mother's photo album, full of ice-skating pictures. Young, healthy, spinning on a frozen pond somewhere in America. She'd never tried ice skating -- it wasn't the kind of risk Marie-Claude would approve of. But here she was, on wheels instead of blades, trying to find her balance.

The DJ switched to a French pop song, and Amélie's face lit up. "Ah! This is perfect for learning! Count with the beat - *un, deux, trois*, glide. *Un, deux, trois*, glide."

The rhythm swept her forward -- *un, deux, trois*, glide. Lakshmi's voice echoed in her head, singing her spice-choosing songs. Keiko-san's lessons about balance and precision surfaced in her movements. The wheels beneath her feet transformed from chaos into possibility.

"*Voilà!*" Claire clapped as Sophia completed her first solo circle of the rink. "You have a dancer's posture."

Marie-Claude had migrated to the café area, her notebook closed for once. She sat with the mothers, who had somehow coaxed her into accepting a small cup of espresso. Sophia caught her guardian's eye, saw the moment when protection wavered and pride slipped through.

When the birthday cake appeared -- a towering *création* from Amélie's favorite pâtisserie -- Marie-Claude didn't even check her notebook for Sophia's sugar allowance. Instead, she watched as her charge sat among the French girls, all of them talking at once, their words flowing together like the Seine after rain.

"Your French is getting better," Amélie said, passing Sophia an extra strawberry from her cake slice. "But you still say *'merci'* like you're singing it."

"That's how we said it in Mumbai," Sophia explained. "Everything there was musical."

"And in Tokyo?" Claire wanted to know. "How did they say thank you there?"

Sophia demonstrated the proper bow, nearly toppling forward on her skates, and the girls caught her, laughing. Their hands were sticky with cake frosting, their cheeks flushed from skating. In that moment, Sophia felt her mother's joy from those old ice-skating photos -- the freedom of movement, the trust in gravity, the sweet taste of risk.

Later, as they unlaced their skates, Amélie asked, "Will you come to my ballet recital next month? It's at the little theater near Luxembourg Gardens."

Sophia glanced at Marie-Claude, who was pretending not to listen while methodically sanitizing their rental skates. Her guardian's notebook remained closed, tucked into her pristine handbag.

"Theater seats are very stable," Marie-Claude said quietly, surprising them both. "And the Gardens are lovely in spring. Perhaps... perhaps we will have lunch at that little crêperie afterward?" She smoothed her skirt, a nervous gesture Sophia had never seen before. "Your mother loved the Luxembourg Gardens. She used to write there during her treatments."

The drive home was different from their usual careful journeys. Marie-Claude took the long way, along the Seine where the early evening light painted the water gold. She rolled down the windows -- just a crack, but enough to let in the scent of spring and fresh baguettes from the boulangeries they passed.

"I have been thinking," Marie-Claude said as they waited at a traffic light. "Perhaps we can look into beginning ballet lessons. Very gentle ones, of course. With proper medical supervision and emergency protocols in place." She gripped the steering wheel tighter.

"Your mother loved to dance, you know. Even in the hospital, she would sway to the music from the nurses' station."

Sophia watched Paris rush past the window, all the opportunities and adventures that awaited her.

"I know," Marie-Claude continued, her voice catching slightly, "that sometimes I forgot the second part of my promise to your mother. About not protecting you from living." She pulled into their usual parking spot, but didn't turn off the engine immediately. "She would have wanted you to dance, to skate, to fall sometimes. She knew... she knew that love without freedom is like a bird in too small a cage."

Chapter 11
Patterns of Healing

Betty had seen many kinds of pain walk through her café door, but generational grief carried its own particular weight. She recognized it in Sophia's posture that first morning -- the way her body curved protectively when she spoke of Emma, as if love could be a shield against inherited heartache. Betty had seen that same protective curve in countless mothers during her counseling years, each trying to guard their children from wounds they themselves still carried.

The morning light painted patterns across the café's wooden floors as Betty prepared for opening. She moved through her routine with practiced efficiency, each action weighted with purpose. The coffee beans needed to be ground, the machines cleaned and primed, the pastry case arranged. Simple tasks that created order in a chaotic world -- something she'd learned was as necessary for healing as any words of comfort.

While she worked, her mind kept returning to Sophia and her daughter in the hospital. In her thirty years as a grief counselor, she'd learned that trauma echoed through generations like ripples in still water. But so did healing.

Sarah arrived with her usual stack of papers to grade, settling into her corner spot. She'd been there when Sophia came in, and now she looked up as Betty adjusted the thermostat.

"That mother yesterday," Sarah said, "reminded me of myself after the divorce. So determined to be strong for my daughter."

Betty nodded, understanding what Sarah saw. Parents facing their children's fears often developed that particular kind of courage -- both fragile and indomitable.

The morning regulars began filtering in, each carrying their own stories. The businessman who'd finally started talking about his wife's death. The retired teacher working on her memoir. The medical student who came to study, dark circles under her eyes betraying more than just academic stress. Betty served each one their usual orders, remembering how she used to keep careful notes about her therapy clients' preferences and progress.

Now she tracked healing in different ways: how the businessman's shoulders gradually loosened, how the teacher's writing grew more confident, how the medical student's smile began reaching her eyes. Small victories, measured in sips and sentences.

The café's phone rang -- a doctor's office confirming their regular monthly order of coffee and pastries for their staff meeting. Betty smiled, remembering how that connection had started. One of the hospital rheumatologists had wandered in during a difficult shift, drawn by the scent of fresh coffee. Now his entire unit knew about The Smiling Dog, some sending their patients here when they needed more than just medical care.

She'd learned that healing happened in layers. First the urgent medical needs, then the emotional wounds, then the deeper work of understanding. Like preparing the perfect cup of coffee, each step had to happen in its own time -- you couldn't rush the bloom any more than you could rush grief.

Sarah's quiet voice interrupted her thoughts. "You're thinking about them, aren't you? That mother and her daughter in the hospital?"

Betty began preparing Sarah's second cup of coffee, the movements automatic after years of practice. "Watching Sophia reminds me of sessions I used to have -- mothers and daughters dealing with inherited conditions. The fears pass down alongside the genes."

"But so does strength," Sarah noted, accepting the fresh cup. "I see it in my classroom all the time. Young people carrying their parents' burdens, but also their resilience."

The morning light shifted, catching the silver frames of the mirrors behind the counter. Betty adjusted a fresh vase of flowers -- nothing fancy, just simple daisies, but their cheerful faces brightened the space. In her counseling office, she'd kept plants for the same reason: life continuing despite everything, beauty persisting through all seasons.

A young woman came in, one Betty hadn't seen before. She moved with the hesitant steps of someone carrying fresh grief, her hands playing nervously with a hospital visitor's pass. Betty recognized the logo -- the same hospital where Emma stayed.

Without being asked, Betty began preparing a cup of her special blend -- the one she'd served Sophia. Some wounds needed more than just coffee, but having something warm to hold was always a good start.

The woman sat at the counter, her posture reminding Betty of countless therapy clients perched on the edge of sharing their stories. The three-legged Irish Setter's portrait seemed to watch over her with particular attention.

"I saw you talking to another mother last night," the woman said softly. "The one with the little girl in cardiac care. I... I'm in the same unit with my son."

Betty placed the coffee in front of her, noting how the woman's hands trembled slightly as she reached for it. "Happiness and hardship often walk together," she said, the words coming naturally, shaped by years of practice. "One doesn't cancel out the other."

The woman's tears started then, quiet but steady. Betty pulled out a clean napkin, setting it beside the coffee cup without comment. Sometimes silence was the best invitation to speak.

"My son," the woman began, and Betty settled in to listen, doing what she'd always done -- whether in a counselor's office or behind a café counter.

Morning sunlight painted Brooklyn's streets with possibility. Inside, the café held its own gentle rhythm -- coffee brewing, hearts mending, hope rising like steam from perfectly warmed cups. Betty knew that somewhere in the hospital, Sophia sat beside Emma's bed, both carrying their shared condition not as a burden but as part of their story -- mother and daughter facing forward together, each heartbeat a tiny victory over fear.

Betty turned back to the woman at the counter, ready to bear witness to another story of love and loss and healing. This was what The Smiling Dog did best -- create space where pain could be spoken, where healing could begin, where hope could rise like steam from a perfectly warmed cup.

Chapter 12
Rio Rhythms

Wednesday evening, the steady beep of Emma's heart monitor took on a different rhythm in Sophia's tired mind - not the harsh electronic pulse of medical equipment, but something warmer, more alive. Like drums echoing through Rio's streets, like Isabella teaching her that even mechanical sounds could dance if you let them.

Sophia shifted in the hospital chair, automatically straightening her spine the way Keiko-san had taught her, and caught a whiff of coffee from the nurses' station. Not the usual institutional brew, but something richer, spiced with cardamom and memory. It reminded her of Lakshmi's kitchen, of Marie-Claude's careful measurements, of all the ways she'd learned to move through the world.

After the careful constraints of Paris, Rio de Janeiro exploded around Sophia like fireworks. Isabella arrived on their first morning, bringing not a leather notebook of protocols the way Marie-Claude did, but a portable radio and a bag of ripe mangoes.

"Too thin!" she declared, looking Sophia up and down. "Too careful! In Rio, we cure sadness with samba and sunshine." She threw open all the windows of their Ipanema apartment, letting in the sounds of the beach, the street vendors, the endless music that seemed to pulse through the city like a heartbeat.

At fourteen, Sophia had mastered the art of being careful. She took her medications exactly on schedule, monitored her heart rate religiously, and never exceeded Marie-Claude's carefully calculated safety margins. But Isabella operated on a different frequency.

"Your heart is not just a muscle to be managed," Isabella told her that first morning, slicing mangoes with casual grace. "It is an instrument in the orchestra of your body. It needs to sing, to dance, to remember it is alive!"

Sophia watched juice drip from the knife onto the counter, remembering how Marie-Claude would have immediately wiped away such disorder. "My doctor says I need to be careful about overexertion."

Isabella's laugh was musical. "Careful, yes. Dead, no. There is a difference, *menina*." She turned up the radio, bossa nova floating through the apartment like a warm breeze. "Watch. Dancing is just a conversation between your body and gravity."

Isabella moved through the kitchen with fluid grace, her feet tracing patterns on the tile floor. Not the precise movements of ballet that Marie-Claude had eventually permitted, but something organic, natural as breathing. "See? Start with the feet. They are your roots. Like trees in the rainforest, you must be both strong and flexible."

Sophia's father, when he came home that evening, found them in the kitchen -- mangoes forgotten, dishes undone, Isabella teaching his daughter how to feel the rhythm of samba in her bones.

"This is not what we discussed," he said stiffly, his tie still perfectly knotted despite Rio's humid heat. "The agency assured me you were qualified to handle her medical needs."

Isabella met his gaze steadily. "I am qualified, Senhor. Twenty years of caring for children with chronic conditions. But I treat the whole child, not just the diagnosis." She gestured to Sophia, who had instinctively stilled at her father's arrival. "Look at her color -- better already. The heart needs joy to be healthy, no?"

Later that night, Sophia overheard them talking on the balcony, their voices carrying on the warm air.

"Her mother was like you," her father was saying. "Always dancing, always pushing the boundaries of what the doctors said was safe. And look where--" He stopped abruptly.

"Where it got her?" Isabella's voice was gentle but firm. "It got her a daughter who remembers her dancing. Better than a daughter who only remembers her being afraid, no?"

The next morning, Isabella arrived with a heart rate monitor strapped to her own wrist. "See? We can be careful and free at the same time." She showed Sophia how she'd programmed it with the doctor's recommended limits. "When it beeps, we rest. When it's quiet, we dance. Simple."

Life with Isabella developed its own rhythm, as different from Marie-Claude's rigid schedule as samba was from ballet. They did their marketing in the local *feira*, where vendors called out in musical Portuguese and Isabella taught her to choose fruit by scent and feel rather than appearance. They took afternoon walks on the beach, where the sound of waves created its own kind of music.

"Your mother," Isabella said one afternoon as they watched surfers ride the waves at Ipanema, "what kind of music did she love?"

Sophia dug her toes into the warm sand. "Beatles songs. But she sang them wrong. Off-key."

"Ah!" Isabella's face lit up. "Then she understood the most important thing -- that music isn't about perfection. It's about joy." She pulled her ever-present radio from her bag, tuning it until she found a scratchy Beatles station. "Come. Show me how she sang them."

Right there on the beach, Isabella taught Sophia to sing "Here Comes the Sun" as badly as possible, both of them laughing until they had to sit down. The heart monitor remained silent, but Sophia's chest felt full of something that might have been happiness.

"My mother died because her heart was weak," Sophia said

suddenly. "Everyone since then has tried to protect me from the same thing. Except you. Why?"

Isabella was quiet for a moment, watching the waves. When she spoke, her voice had lost its usual musical lilt. "I had a sister. Laura. Beautiful girl, born with a weak heart like you. The doctors, our parents, everyone wrapped her in cotton wool. No running, no dancing, no living." She traced patterns in the sand with her fingers. "She died anyway, at sixteen. In her bed, reading a book. Safe. Protected. And do you know what she said to me, the night before?"

Sophia shook her head, feeling the weight of Isabella's words heavy in her chest.

"She said, 'Bella, I never felt the rain on my face. Never danced until I couldn't breathe. Never knew if my heart was racing from fear or joy or love.' That's when I knew -- sometimes protection can be its own kind of disease."

The waves crashed against the shore, a rhythm as old as time. On the radio, "Here Comes the Sun" faded into "Let It Be."

"So yes," Isabella continued, her smile returning like sun through clouds, "we monitor your heart. We respect its limits. But we also let it feel joy, let it dance, let it live. Because a caged heart can be just as dangerous as a racing one."

That evening, when Sophia's father came home, he found them in the kitchen again. But this time, Isabella had drawn a chart on the whiteboard -- heart rate readings throughout the day, plotted against activities. Dancing, walking, singing, resting. A scientific record of joy, measured in beats per minute.

"See?" Isabella pointed to the data. "Her numbers are more stable than when she was in Paris. The body knows how to balance itself, if we trust it."

Rio bloomed around them in explosions of color and sound -- the bright umbrellas dotting Copacabana beach, the rainbow-painted steps of Selarón's staircase, the endless parade of fruit vendors with their carts piled high with mangoes, papayas, and passion fruit.

Isabella taught Sophia to navigate it all with a dancer's awareness, finding pockets of rest within the motion.

"Listen," Isabella would say, as they sat at a corner juice bar, acai bowls melting in the afternoon heat. "Every city has its own heartbeat. Paris marches to a metronome's strict time. Tokyo flows with the precision of a careful stream. Mumbai moves to the wild syncopation of autorickshaws and bicycles, street vendors and sacred cows, temple bells and taxi horns all weaving together in glorious chaos. But Rio?"

She gestured to the street around them, where businessmen in suits dodged soccer-playing kids, where music spilled from every doorway, where elderly couples danced impromptu samba on street corners. "Rio pulses with the rhythm of a heart in love -- sometimes fast, sometimes slow, but always with passion."

On Sundays, they would join the crowds at the Hippie Fair in Ipanema, where artists spread their wares under flowering trees. Isabella bought Sophia a bracelet made of wooden beads, each one painted with a different pattern. "For counting blessings," she explained, "not heartbeats."

One day they took the cable car up to Cristo Redentore. It swayed gently as it lifted them from the station, drawing gasps from other passengers. Sophia gripped the metal handrail, her heart pounding against her ribs. Through the windows, Rio receded beneath them, the city's craziness transforming into orderly patterns. Palm trees shrank to dots of green, streets narrowed to ribbons, and the endless stream of traffic became mere threads of movement woven through the urban fabric.

"Now," Isabella said, her hand steady on Sophia's shoulder, "pay attention to your heart. Feel how it races?"

Sophia nodded, unable to look away from the ascending view. The bay spread out before them, sunlight dancing on the water, while Sugar Loaf Mountain emerged from the morning haze. Her pulse thundered in her ears.

"That first racing - that's fear." Isabella's voice carried the same steady rhythm as the cable car's movement. "Notice how it makes everything tighten, makes you want to hold your breath?"

As they rose higher, the city's noise fell away. Even the other tourists' chatter seemed distant, muffled by the altitude and anticipation. A fresh breeze carried the scent of the ocean mixed with the green perfume of the rainforest clinging to the mountainside.

"But now," Isabella continued as they cleared the last outcropping of rocks, "watch what happens."

Cristo Redentore appeared suddenly, impossibly massive against the sky. Sophia's heart leaped again, but differently - this time her chest felt open, expanding. Her grip on the handrail loosened. Each breath came deeper, fuller.

"That's wonder," Isabella said softly. "See? Your body knows. Fear closes us in. Awe breaks us open."

The cable car slowed as it approached the final station, but Sophia barely noticed. Her racing heart now felt like wings unfurling in her chest, lifting her even higher than the machinery that had carried them into the clouds.

One evening, as the sun painted Guanabara Bay in shades of gold and pink, Isabella convinced Sophia's father to join them for dinner at a small restaurant in Lapa. The owner, Dona Clara, was an elderly woman with salt-and-pepper hair and dancing eyes.

Dona Clara embraced their caregiver like a long-lost daughter. "And this must be your Sophia, the one you say needs to remember how to dance!" She turned to Sophia's father, who sat stiffly in his business suit, looking out of place among the restaurant's cheerful chaos. "And you, *senhor*, you also look like someone who has forgotten how to dance."

She brought them *feijoada* and fresh *pão de queijo*, while her grandson played guitar in the corner. Sophia watched her father attempt to maintain his usual corporate dignity while Dona Clara piled their table with food -- not just the *feijoada*, rich and steaming, but crispy *pasteis*, grilled chicken fragrant with garlic and herbs. The grandson's guitar was joined by other instruments as more musicians arrived, gathering in the corner like birds coming home to roost.

"Your mother," her father said unexpectedly, his voice nearly lost under the music, "would have loved this place." He picked up a *pão de queijo*, examining it for secrets. "She always said I was too serious. That I needed to learn to love the mess of life."

Isabella, for once, stayed quiet, letting the moment unspool.

"One day after I met her," he continued, "she was dancing in the rain outside the library. Just... spinning in circles, laughing, waiting for me. I thought she was crazy." He smiled, a real smile that made him look years younger. "I was studying for my economics final, and she made me come outside and dance with her. Said some things were more important than perfect grades."

The guitarist started playing "Girl from Ipanema," and Dona Clara appeared at their table again, clapping her hands. "Ah! Perfect! Everyone must dance now. Doctor's orders!" She winked at Sophia. "The best medicine for a healing heart is to remember it can still feel joy."

Sophia watched in amazement as Dona Clara coaxed her father onto his feet, showing him the basic samba step. He moved awkwardly at first, his tie swaying out of rhythm, but gradually something softened in his shoulders. Isabella was right -- dancing was just a conversation with gravity, and slowly, her father was remembering how to speak that language.

"Sophia," he called, his face flushed with either embarrassment or joy, maybe both. "Come show your old father how it's done. Isabella says you're getting quite good."

The heart monitor on her wrist maintained its steady green rhythm as Sophia joined them, moving to the music the way Isabella had taught her -- from the feet up, letting her body find its own path through the melody. The monitor's gentle blinking matched her movements, showing her heart was strong enough for joy.

Around them, other diners were dancing too, the whole restaurant becoming a celebration of nothing more special than a Tuesday evening in Rio.

Dona Clara's grandson switched to a Beatles song -- "Here Comes the Sun" -- played bossa nova style. Sophia's father stopped dancing abruptly, but then he laughed, a sound she hadn't heard in years.

"Your mother used to massacre this song," he said, shaking his head. "Absolutely destroy it. Couldn't carry a tune in a bucket." He looked at Sophia, really looked at her. "But she never let that stop her from singing."

Isabella appeared with three glasses of passion fruit juice, beaded with condensation in the warm evening air. "A toast," she declared. "To those who teach us to sing off-key, to dance out of step, to love without fear."

And there in that tiny Rio restaurant, watched over by Dona Clara's knowing smile and wrapped in the warmth of a Brazilian night, Sophia felt her heart beating strong and steady -- not just surviving, but dancing.

Chapter 13
Calling Mark

"You're doing very well," Dr. Vlad said to Emma when he came by during evening rounds on Wednesday. "But how about you stay with us for one more night? Just to make sure we have everything perfect?"

Emma, who had been so brave all day, finally showed a crack in her armor. "Do I have to?"

Sophia took her hand and squeezed. "If Dr. Vlad thinks you should, then we have to listen to him."

"I guess so," Emma said.

Emma's face took on the considering look that Sophia recognized - the one that meant her daughter was about to drive a bargain. "Okay, but if I stay tonight and all my numbers are good, can we finally get that digital drawing tablet? The one that connects to the computer?" She turned to Dr. Vlad. "Drawing is very relaxing. It would probably be good for my heart."

Dr. Vlad tried to hide his smile. "She makes an excellent point about stress reduction."

"You've been asking for that tablet for months," Sophia said, but she was already weakening. After all Emma had been through, and how brave she'd been about it all...

"And I've been saving my allowance," Emma pressed her advantage. "I can pay for half. Plus, I promise to do all my cardiac exercises without complaining. For a whole week."

"Make it a month," Sophia countered.

"Two weeks, and I'll clean my room every Saturday without being reminded."

"Deal." Sophia couldn't help smiling. Trust Emma to turn even a hospital stay into a negotiation opportunity. "But Dr. Vlad has to confirm your numbers are good first."

"They will be," Emma said with complete confidence. "I'm going to be the best cardiac patient ever."

Dr. Vlad smiled and turned to Sophia. "Time for you to go home and get some real rest. Emma's stable, and we'll call if anything changes."

Sophia kissed her daughter's forehead, adjusting the blanket one last time. She waited until Emma had drifted off to sleep, then walked back to the brownstone surrounded by people on their way home from dinners out and those going to work on late shifts. She had so much work to do, and as soon as she settled down she pulled out her laptop and began answering emails and working on edits.

Being busy helped, because the house felt wrong without Emma's steady breathing in the background. The apartment didn't need cleaning - it had already been sanitized by her nervous energy the night before. But still she moved through the rooms, adjusting picture frames, realigning books, trying to impose order on a situation that defied control. If Lakshmi were here, she'd be burning healing incense and saying prayers. If Isabella were here, she'd insist they dance away their fears. Instead, Sophia folded another towel, then another, until exhaustion finally drove her toward sleep.

Her phone sat heavy on the kitchen counter. She should call Mark, tell him about Emma. Her fingers hovered over his contact information. She remembered their scheduled video call earlier the past week, when Mark had surprised them both. Instead of his usual office backdrop, he was in his apartment, and instead of launching into updates about educational opportunities or investment accounts, he'd asked Emma about her drawings.

"I was walking through Gardens by the Bay," he said, "and saw these little girls feeding koi. One of them was sketching the fish. Made me think of you." He shifted his phone camera to show a small bag from a local art store. "I found this place that sells those special pens you mentioned last time. They're coming your way."

Emma's face lit up. "The watercolor ones? Like Ms. DuVivier uses?"

"Yes, I remembered your telling me about them. I thought..." He cleared his throat. "Maybe next call you could show me how they work. If you want."

It wasn't quite the same as being there, but it was something new - attention without agenda, interest without investment strategies.

Before she could put it off any longer, she pressed the button to dial his number.

"Sophia?" Mark's voice came through, surprised. With the time difference, he was probably already at his desk in Singapore. "Is everything all right?"

"Emma's in the hospital." Sophia curled her fingers around a clay heart Emma had made in ceramics class, then painted with a face that was supposed to resemble Sophia's. "She's stable, but they found the same heart condition. My condition. My mom's condition."

Papers shuffled on his end. "Which hospital? I'll have my assistant book the first flight—"

"No." The word came out sharper than she intended. She softened her tone. "No, Mark. She's getting excellent care here at Langone. Dr. Gorbaty is one of the best pediatric cardiologists in New York."

"But surely the specialists in Singapore—"

"She needs stability right now, not a fifteen-hour flight." Sophia straightened a row of Emma's drawings on the refrigerator. "Medical science has advanced so much since my mother's diagnosis, and mine.

Dr. Gorbaty says with proper monitoring and medication, she can live a completely normal life."

"I should be there. I'm her father."

"Yes, you should be here. But not just for medical emergencies." She touched one of Emma's sketches - a family portrait from happier times. "She needs you present in her daily life, not swooping in to take control when things go wrong."

Mark was silent, and Sophia worried she had gone too far. She continued, softening her tone.

"The doctors are being careful, thorough. Emma's scared, but she's trying not to show it." Sophia paused, then added, "I found this café nearby - The Smiling Dog. It's... it's helping me cope. The owner used to be a grief counselor. She seems to understand exactly what we need."

The silence stretched between them, heavy with unspoken words.

"When can she come home?" he finally asked, his voice smaller.

"Tomorrow, probably. We'll set up a regular monitoring schedule, adjust her activities as needed." She moved to the window, watching Brooklyn's lights flicker. "I'll send you her test results and Dr. Gorbaty's reports. But Mark? She's going to be okay. Different from Mom's time. Different from my childhood. I promise."

Another silence, then: "I see you've got this. I'm impressed."

"I learned from the best." She smiled, thinking of all her mothers. "Each one of the women who took care of me taught me something different about being strong."

"Each one?" His voice carried a hint of confusion, then understanding. "Ah. Keiko-san and the others. You never talk about them anymore."

"I think about them all the time lately. Especially now." Sophia touched her mother's locket. "They all helped raise me after Mom died. Now they're helping me raise Emma, in a way. Through everything they taught me."

"I remember when you first told me about them. That day at the beach, sketching the Japanese temple garden." A pause, then, "I was so caught up in the business aspects of different cultures, and you understood the heart of them."

"That's what Emma needs now. Not just the best medical care, but the heart of things. Understanding. Presence."

"I've been trying to protect her future," Mark said quietly. "Like your father did. Working harder, earning more, researching better doctors. But maybe..."

"Maybe she needs what I needed back then. Someone to just be there. To help her find joy even in hard times."

"Like your Isabella in Rio. Teaching you to dance despite everything."

The fact that he remembered that detail, after all these years, made something shift in Sophia's chest. "I'll have Emma call you tomorrow when we get home," she said, her voice gentler now. "Maybe you could tell her some of your own stories. Help her understand she comes from a long line of strong hearts."

"I'd like that," Mark said. "And Sophia? Thank you. For being the kind of mother she needs. The kind who knows how to dance with fear instead of running from it."

With the call finished, Sophia finally slept. Dawn was breaking over Brooklyn when she returned to The Smiling Dog after Emma's third night in the hospital. The city wore that peculiar hush that comes just before the morning rush, when even the pigeons seem to be gathering their thoughts.

Today the café held layered scents -- her mother's Sunday morning kitchen mingled with Lakshmi's spice-blessed breakfasts and Isabella's mango-sweet afternoons. The three-legged dog in the painting watched with knowing eyes as she took her now-familiar seat at the counter.

"This blend is for remembering," Betty said, already reaching for yet another canister, this one ceramic and painted with dancing figures.

"How do you do that?" Sophia asked, watching Betty's hands

move among her coffee supplies. "Make each cup carry memories in its scent?"

Betty smiled, her silver braids catching the early light. "Coffee mirrors love -- it changes depending on what you need from it. First cup shows you what you've forgotten. Second cup helps you understand why you forgot. This cup..." She paused, measuring beans into the grinder. "This cup shows you how to remember without pain."

If everything went according to plan, she would be able to take Emma home that morning, with her heart monitor and her pill routine. Mother and daughter, sharing the same path.

"Tell me," Betty said, her movements precise as she prepared the coffee, "what have all these mothers taught you about being one?"

Sophia watched the steam rise from Betty's copper coffee machine, curling like the questions in her mind. Through the mirrors behind the counter, she caught glimpses of shadows dancing -- or were those memories? Keiko-san folding hospital corners into crisp perfection. Lakshmi blessing every doorway with vermillion powder. Marie-Claude with her leather notebook of safety protocols. Isabella teaching the difference between a racing heart and a dancing one.

"They each gave me something different," Sophia said slowly. "Keiko-san taught me that structure can hold grief. Lakshmi showed me how love speaks in spices and prayers. Marie-Claude..." She paused, remembering the roller rink, the moment protection had softened into possibility. "She taught me that sometimes love means being afraid but letting go anyway."

"And Isabella?" Betty's hands never stopped moving as she worked, but her attention remained focused on Sophia.

"Joy as defiance. Dancing even when -- especially when -- the world tells you to be still." The words caught in her throat. "But my own mother... I have so few memories. Burned pancakes. Off-key Beatles songs. Hospital rooms."

Betty set a cup before Sophia, the coffee in it darker than the previous brews, its aroma bringing unexpected tears to her eyes. The

A Mother's Heart

scent carried Sunday mornings and midnight stories, wrapping her in memories of laughter and possibility.

"Sometimes," Betty said softly, "the shortest lessons are the ones that echo longest. Your mother taught you that love doesn't have to be perfect to be true."

The café's early morning silence enveloped them in its warmth. Outside, the city was waking up, but in here, time flowed golden and slow, honey-thick in the sunlight.

Sophia opened her laptop, the familiar glow of her work screen grounding her in the present. The technical manual she was editing was for medical monitoring software, a curious coincidence to Emma's illness. Or was it? Sophia was learning that coincidence mattered.

Today's document detailed heart monitoring algorithms, the cold precision of machine learning applied to the rhythm of human hearts. "'The system analyzes patterns to predict potential cardiac events,'" she read aloud, then frowned at the sterile language. Her cursor hovered over the text as she considered the revision. "How about: 'The software learns to recognize each heart's unique rhythm, helping doctors understand its story'?"

Betty, wiping down the counter nearby, nodded. "Makes it sound more human. After all, hearts are more than just muscles sending electrical signals."

"That's what Isabella used to say." Sophia took another sip of the coffee, which somehow managed to taste like every kitchen she'd ever called home. "She'd hate this manual -- all these charts and graphs trying to contain something as wild as a heartbeat."

She scrolled through pages of technical specifications, thinking of Marie-Claude's notebooks full of similar measurements. But between the lines of code and medical terminology, she began to see something else -- a mother's love translated into algorithms, someone's attempt to protect other people's children through technology.

As Sophia finished her coffee, Betty wrapped a second package of butter cookies, tucking it into a paper bag with the tea tin. "For Emma," she said. "Sweet things make medicine easier to swallow."

Sophia gathered her belongings, taking one last look at the mirrors where memories seemed to dance in the early morning light. The three-legged Irish Setter was waiting outside, its breath visible in the dawn chill. Together, they walked through Brooklyn's awakening streets, the dog matching its pace to hers as if it had all the time in the world.

At the hospital entrance, the Irish Setter sat, its dark eyes meeting hers with that deep connection. Sophia understood now - its work was done. She had found what she needed at The Smiling Dog. Now it was time to face what waited ahead.

The pediatric cardiac unit was quiet at this early hour, just the soft squeak of nurses' shoes and the steady beep of monitors. Dr. Vlad was already there, reviewing charts at the nurses' station. He looked up as she approached, his face holding both concern and something that might have been hope.

"Ms. Greenwood," he said, rising to meet her. "I was hoping to catch you early. I have Emma's complete results here."

Sophia's hands trembled as she waited to hear from him. It was a skill learned from watching her father handle business calls through multiple crises. "The genetic markers we identified indicate the same condition your mother had, and that you inherited from her."

Sophia closed her eyes, generations of heartache condensing within her chest, heavy and inevitable.

"But," the doctor continued, "we've made remarkable advances in treatment since your mother's time, and even since your childhood. The medication Emma started yesterday is part of a new class of drugs that wasn't available twenty-five years ago. And the monitoring systems -- actually, I believe you're familiar with CardioTrack's software?"

Sophia's eyes flew open, landing on her laptop screen where the manual she'd been editing glowed. "Yes, I'm editing a new edition of their documentation right now."

A Mother's Heart

"Perfect! Then you understand how sophisticated the tracking algorithms have become. We can adjust Emma's medication in real time, predict and prevent episodes before they happen. This isn't the same journey you or your mother faced."

"So Emma can still..." she started.

"Dance? Play? Live fully? Yes, absolutely. With proper monitoring and some reasonable precautions. In fact, regular exercise will help strengthen her heart. We just need to be smart about it."

They walked down the hall to Emma's room, Dr. Vlad carrying the new monitor, which resembled a slim watch with a soft band. "This is your new heart monitor, Emma," he said. "Much nicer than the bulky ones your mom had to wear when she was young."

Emma sat up straighter in her hospital bed. "I get to wear it on my wrist?"

"The sensor part goes here," he demonstrated, touching two small patches to his own chest. "These stick on and connect wirelessly to the wrist display. You can check your heart rate anytime, just like your mom does."

Emma beamed. "Mom always lets me take her pulse the old-fashioned way - with fingers on the wrist while counting. She says that's how Grandma taught her."

"And now you'll have your own monitor," Dr. Vlad smiled, helping Emma position the patches. "The wrist display shows your heart rate, and it can alert us if anything needs attention. It's like having a tiny doctor watching over you all the time."

"Just like Mom's!" Emma exclaimed, admiring the sleek device. "Does it come in different colors?"

"We have blue, pink, or purple. And you can customize the display screen."

"Purple please," Emma said. "Mom, look - we match now!"

Sophia felt tears prick her eyes as she watched Emma trace the monitor's screen with her finger, transforming what could have been scary medical equipment into something special - a connection between mother and daughter, a shared experience that spanned generations.

Dr. Vlad's hands were gentle as he adjusted the device, his accent softening with memory. "I was twelve when my sister was diagnosed with a congenital heart condition in Romania. Back then, in the 1980s, our doctors could diagnose but couldn't do much else. My parents sold everything to take her to Vienna for treatment."

Emma watched him curiously as he checked her readings. "Did she get better?"

"She did. But I never forgot how it felt, being the healthy sibling, watching my sister struggle. I promised myself I would become the doctor I wished we'd had - one who understood not just the medical side, but the family side too."

He smiled at Sophia. "When your mother was being treated, the technology was somewhere between my sister's time and now. Each generation of patients has taught us something new. Your mother's generation helped us understand genetic patterns. My sister's doctors learned what to look for. And when you were a patient, you taught us about preventive care." He gestured at Emma's tiny monitor. "And now, Emma's generation is teaching us how to help children live normal lives despite these conditions."

He stood back. "That's why I chose pediatric cardiology. Because every advance in treatment, every new piece of technology, every refined technique - they're all building blocks. Each patient's story helps us write a better ending for the next one."

Dr. Vlad left them, and she sat next to Emma, as the morning light grew stronger, painting the room in shades of hope. Sophia watched her daughter trying out the monitor, which showed strong, steady rhythms. Something was tugging at her consciousness - a realization she hadn't quite grasped until now.

The same condition that had taken her mother had lived in her own heart all these years, carefully monitored, treated, understood. And she was still here, strong enough to sit vigil by her daughter's bedside, strong enough to carry both their fears.

A Mother's Heart

The memory came then, clear as Betty's mirrors - her mother in the hospital, thin and tired but still somehow radiant. It was one of her last good days, when the pain medication was working but hadn't pulled her too far under. She'd asked the nurses to help her sit up, to fix her hair, to make her "presentable for my daughter."

"Come here, butterfly," she'd said, patting the edge of her bed. Nine-year-old Sophia had climbed up carefully, mindful of the tubes and wires. Her mother had taken her hand, studying her face and memorizing every detail.

"I need you to remember something," she'd said, her voice hoarse but determined. "Your heart - it's not just the one the doctors measure. It's not just the muscle that might sometimes give you trouble. Your heart is also the part of you that loves, that creates, that finds joy even in dark places." She'd squeezed Sophia's hand. "Promise me you won't let fear make your world small."

Sophia hadn't understood then. But now, watching Emma draw, she finally grasped what her mother had been trying to tell her. She'd lived past thirty-four not just because of medical advances, but because she'd learned to live fully despite her fears. Keiko-san's discipline, Lakshmi's joy, Marie-Claude's careful protection, Isabella's defiant dance steps – they had all taught her different ways to keep her heart strong.

"She's going to be okay," Sophia whispered to her mother's memory. "Better than okay. She has all of us watching over her - you, me, all the mothers who helped raise me. And medicine that you couldn't even dream of back then." She touched her own heart, feeling its steady rhythm. "You were right, Mom. Fear didn't make my world small. And it won't make Emma's small either."

Through the hospital window, she caught a glimpse of something moving - a flash of fur, a three-legged shadow disappearing around a corner. The morning sun caught the edge of Emma's heart monitor, making it gleam like Sophia's mother's last gift: the understanding that hearts could be both fragile and fierce, both careful and courageous, both protected and free.

Chapter 14
Singapore Silence

The hospital air conditioning hummed with mechanical precision, its steady drone reminding Sophia of Singapore's endless climate-controlled spaces. Even the antiseptic smell carried echoes of that other time and place - the same industrial cleaners used in high-rise lobbies across Asia, their sharp efficiency masking the tropical heat outside.

The phone call with Mark had already transported her mind halfway across the world. Now, watching Emma doze in the carefully regulated hospital room, Sophia remembered another kind of controlled environment, another time when silence had spoken louder than words.

The last place Sophia had lived with her father, before returning to the United States for college, was Singapore. She recalled how the air there was wet silk against her skin as she stood on the balcony of their high-rise apartment, watching lightning dance between skyscrapers. At sixteen, she'd learned to read weather patterns in four different languages - Tokyo's gentle rains, Mumbai's dramatic monsoons, Paris's persistent spring drizzle, Rio's tropical storms. But Singapore weather had its own vocabulary, one that their new housekeeper Mrs. Tan seemed to translate with a glance.

"Storm coming. Better close windows." Mrs. Tan's English was perfect, her tone clipped to bonsai precision. She moved through the apartment with quiet efficiency, her black pants and white blouse retaining their crisp perfection from dawn until midnight. Where Lakshmi had worn flowing saris and Isabella had danced through rooms, Mrs. Tan operated in straight lines and right angles.

The apartment gleamed with matching precision, every surface polished to mirror brightness. Even the air seemed filtered, purified, controlled by systems that hummed behind pristine walls. Such perfection made Sophia afraid to leave fingerprints.

"Your father called," Mrs. Tan said, methodically closing each window. "Late meeting. Again." She didn't sigh, didn't ramble with Lakshmi's commentary or resort to Marie-Claude's disapproving sniffs. She simply stated facts, dropping them into the silence where they sank deep and still.

Sophia nodded, used to these abbreviated conversations. In the three months since they'd moved to Singapore, she'd learned to parse Mrs. Tan's minimal communications like a new programming language. A cup of honey-lemon tea appearing on her desk meant Mrs. Tan had heard her coughing. A meal in the fridge ready to be warmed meant she'd noticed Sophia skipping lunch. An umbrella by the door meant rain in the forecast.

The storm broke over the city, rain painting patterns on the windows like calligraphy. Mrs. Tan moved through her evening routine - checking locks, adjusting thermostats, laying out tomorrow's necessities with mechanical precision. But as she passed Sophia's spot on the balcony, she paused. "Your mother liked storms too."

Sophia turned sharply, but Mrs. Tan was already moving away, her soft shoes silent on the marble floors. It was the first time she'd mentioned knowing anything about Sophia's mother.

Later that night, unable to sleep, Sophia found Mrs. Tan in the kitchen, methodically preparing something that filled the sterile space with an unexpected fragrance - ginger, star anise, something deeper and more complex.

"Cannot sleep?" Mrs. Tan didn't look up from her work. "Sit."

A bowl appeared in front of Sophia - congee, but not the plain rice porridge served in hotel breakfast buffets. This was something else entirely, each spoonful revealing new layers of flavor. As the woman who made it, its complexity was hidden beneath a simple surface.

Something about Mrs. Tan's quiet efficiency had always reminded Sophia of a hospital - the same precise movements, the same attention to detail, the same careful monitoring. At first, Sophia thought it was just Mrs. Tan's way. But small things began to accumulate, like evidence in one of her father's business reports.

The honey-lemon tea that appeared whenever Sophia's throat felt scratchy - the exact same blend her mother had sworn by. The Beatles songs playing softly on the kitchen radio, though Mrs. Tan usually preferred classical music. The way Mrs. Tan's eyes lingered on Sophia's locket.

In between eating the congee, Sophia wrote notes in her journal - something she'd started doing after finding her mother's old notebooks.

"Your mother loved words too," Mrs. Tan said quietly.

The pen slipped from Sophia's fingers. "You knew my mother?"

"No, but your father has told me about her. How she wrote in the hospital gardens between treatments. That she said putting fears on paper made them smaller." Mrs. Tan adjusted a vase of orchids with mathematical precision. "Your father says she had great hope for you."

The spoon froze halfway to Sophia's mouth. Mrs. Tan continued her methodical cleaning, but her words fell into the midnight quiet like rare pearls.

"He says she was a very brave lady. Always smiling, even on bad days."

Thunder rolled across the city, and Mrs. Tan glanced at the windows, checking their seals.

Mrs. Tan nodded toward the congee, precise as a metronome.

"Good for healing. Good for heart. Malay people say its taste is love without words."

The storm spent itself against Singapore's steel and glass walls, but inside the apartment, something had shifted. Mrs. Tan's silence was like the potent pause between musical notes. It was full of meaning for those who knew how to listen.

In the following weeks, Sophia began to notice more - how Mrs. Tan left art supplies on the table when she was struggling with homework, just as her mother used to encourage creative breaks. How she stocked the kitchen with the same brand of chocolate her mother had favored. How she kept a small radio in the kitchen, tuned to the classical station, playing so softly you had to be still to hear it.

Love, Sophia was learning, didn't always announce itself with Lakshmi's songs or Isabella's dances. Sometimes it spoke in congee at midnight, in umbrellas appearing before rain, in silence that wrapped around you like a blanket, protecting you from the storm.

At Singapore American School, Sophia found herself drawn to the newspaper room, where the chaos of journalism provided counterpoint to her ordered home life. The click of keyboards and shuffle of paper reminded her of all her past homes - Tokyo's precision, Mumbai's energy, Rio's rhythm - but transformed into something new.

"Your edits are always perfect," Tiara Megat said one afternoon, as Sophia marked up another article with her red pen. She was a Singaporean native, with a long Malay ancestry behind her. Sophia envied her connection to the place where they lived. "How do you make everything sound so... clean?"

Sophia smiled, thinking of Mrs. Tan's methodical housekeeping. "It's like tidying up. You keep what matters and arrange it beautifully." She'd learned this language of precision from Keiko-san, this attention to the weight of words from Lakshmi's spice-measuring songs, this flow of narrative from Isabella's dance lessons.

The newspaper advisor, Ms. Munsi, began giving Sophia the most challenging pieces to edit. "You have a gift," she said, watching

A Mother's Heart

Sophia transform a tangled feature article about the school's new environmental initiative into something clear and compelling. "You don't just correct grammar - you find the heart of the story."

At home, Mrs. Tan would sometimes pause in her cleaning to read Sophia's latest editorials, her face impassive but her attention complete. One evening, she placed a book on Sophia's desk - *The Elements of Style* by Strunk and White. Inside the cover, in her precise handwriting: "Your mother loved words too."

The revelation hit Sophia like a Singapore thunderclap - her mother had been a writer. She found herself studying the hospital waiting room during her monthly checkups, imagining her mother in the same space years ago, perhaps with a notebook, perhaps capturing stories between treatments.

Mrs. Tan began leaving other books - style guides, literary journals, collections of essays. They appeared silently, the way the honey-lemon tea and bamboo-ribbed hand fans did, each one a wordless message of support. When Sophia won the school's newspaper prize, Mrs. Tan's only comment was "Mother would be proud." But that night, dinner included all of Sophia's favorite dishes.

"Language is like architecture," Mrs. Tan said one evening, watching Sophia struggle with a particularly difficult article about quantum computing. "Must have strong foundation, clean lines, clear purpose." She adjusted a vase of orchids with minute precision. "But also must have heart. Like Singapore - all steel and glass outside, but temples and gardens inside."

Sophia began to see her mother's influence in her own writing - the way she sought stories beneath surfaces, the way she transformed technical jargon into accessible narrative. Even her father noticed, reading her editorial about the school's new cardiac emergency response system with unusual attention.

"You've made it... human," he said, surprised. "All the medical details are there, but it reads like a story about people, not just procedures."

"That's what Mom did, didn't she?" Sophia asked. "Made complicated things make sense?"

Her father's silence held volumes. Finally, he reached into his briefcase and pulled out a worn notebook. "She was working on a book when... when she got sick. About living with heart conditions. Not the medical part - the human part." He handed it to Sophia. " Mrs. Tan found it when she was cleaning out some boxes we've been carrying around forever. She thought you should have it."

That night, Sophia sat on her balcony, reading her mother's words as lightning painted the Singapore sky. Mrs. Tan appeared silently with two cups of late-night congee. They ate together without speaking, the sound of rain and distant thunder filling the space where words weren't needed.

In her mother's notebook, between medical observations and appointment notes, Sophia found stories - about the way sunrise looked through hospital windows, about nurses who sang while changing IV bags, about the hope that lived in the space between heartbeats. Her mother's voice, preserved in ink, spoke of fear transformed into courage, turning clinical procedures into moments of connection.

Sophia brought the notebook to school the next day, placing it beside her computer in the newspaper room. As she edited articles about pep rallies and physics competitions, she found herself channeling her mother's gift for finding humanity in technical details, for making complicated things comprehensible, for telling stories that helped people feel less alone.

Mrs. Tan, reading the next issue of the school paper, traced her finger along Sophia's editorial about living with chronic conditions. She didn't speak, but her nod held all the approval of Keiko-san's precise gestures, all the blessing of Lakshmi's spice prayers, all the joy of Isabella's silent dances.

That evening, a new notebook appeared on Sophia's desk - leather-bound, with crisp pages waiting to be filled. Inside the cover,

Mrs. Tan's neat script: "For your own stories. Strong foundations, clear purpose, open heart."

Chapter 15
The Grandmothers

They took a cab from the hospital back home, and Emma was delighted to reunite with all her stuffed animals. She was still tired, so Sophia tucked her into bed with the dolphin she'd taken to the hospital beside her.

The heart monitor on Emma's wrist wasn't just measuring vital signs - it was counting moments of freedom. Unlike the bulky device Sophia had worn, which had announced every dangerous moment with harsh beeping, Emma's monitor silently watched over her, sending data to doctors to prevent problems before they started. Each technological advance measured the distance between a mother who died too young and a daughter who could dance without fear.

Emma's sketchbook sat on the bedside table, open to a drawing of a three-legged dog with knowing eyes, leading a line of women through a door marked "The Smiling Dog."

Sophia picked up the book, recognizing each figure Emma had captured: her mother with her bright smile and off-key Beatles songs, Keiko-san's straight spine, Lakshmi's flowing sari, Marie-Claude's elegance, Isabella's dancing feet, Mrs. Tan's quiet dignity. And at the end, two figures walking hand in hand - mother and daughter, their curly hair haloed by the rising sun.

Emma opened her eyes, smiling at her mother. "I drew them all," she said sleepily. "Your mommy, and all the grandmothers you told me about. I think they're all still watching over us."

Sophia sat on the edge of the bed, gathering her daughter close. Through the window, she caught a glimpse of parti-colored fur disappearing around a corner - the guardian keeping watch, still leading hearts home.

"They are," she said, her voice steady with the strength of all she had learned. "And your grandmother, my mother - she gave us something more precious than time. She showed us how to find joy even in fear, how to sing even when off-key, how to love completely even when time is short. And all these other mothers taught me how to pass that gift on to you."

She stood for a moment watching her daughter drift peacefully into sleep, the new heart monitor on her wrist glowing softly. Dr. Vlad had discharged her that afternoon with strict instructions about rest and activity levels, but Emma had been more excited about customizing her monitor's display screen than listening to medical advice.

The afternoon light filled the room like a blessing, and somewhere in the distance, Sophia could have sworn she heard the echo of Beatles songs, sung gloriously, perfectly off-key.

Now, watching her daughter's steady breathing, Sophia felt the exhaustion of the past few days settle into her bones. She lay down next to her daughter, curling the small body into hers, and slept.

When they woke, Sophia dug out some chicken stock from her cabinet and poured it into a pot of boiling water on the stove. She stirred it, adding a pinch of cardamom just as Lakshmi had taught her.

Then she opened the freezer and removed a bag of frozen matzoh balls, which she had made a few weeks before according to one of the few recipes she had of her mother's, written in faded pencil on the back of an electric bill. Her mother had made this soup whenever Sophia was sick, and now she made it for Emma, the recipe evolving through the years with additions from all her surrogate mothers.

The spice's warmth would blend with the soup. A dash of ginger went in next - Mrs. Tan's influence, good for circulation. The matzo balls were lighter than her mother's, thanks to Marie-Claude's insistence on properly beaten eggs, and she'd added fresh dill the way Keiko-san had shown her, believing that even simple foods deserved careful attention to detail. Isabella's contribution was the way Sophia hummed while she cooked, knowing that love made any dish taste better.

"Is that Grandma's soup?" Emma asked from her perch at the kitchen counter, her new heart monitor catching the light as she sketched in her notebook. "The one that makes everything better?"

"With a few special additions," Sophia said, ladling the golden broth into bowls. "Every good recipe grows with time."

They ate at the small kitchen table, steam rising from their bowls like prayers. Emma dunked pieces of challah bread into her soup - another of her grandmother's recipes, though Sophia had never managed to make it quite the same. But maybe that was okay. Maybe recipes, like love, weren't meant to stay unchanged but to evolve, gathering new flavors while keeping their essence intact.

That night, reviewing Emma's cardiac data on their linked tablets, Sophia saw more than just numbers. Each graph told a story: here was where Emma chased butterflies in the park, her heart strong enough for joy. Here was where she danced in her room, the monitors showing a heart keeping perfect time with happiness instead of fear. Here was where she fell asleep reading, her rhythms steady and sure in ways Sophia's mother's never had the chance to be.

Emma went back to sleep. Confident that her daughter would be all right on her own for an hour or two, and that the alarm would sound if there was a problem, Emma packed up her laptop and the folder that contained the book her mother had been writing, and walked outside.

Kiyomi the Irish Setter was there, but this time, instead of leading

Sophia, she settled on the ground, a watchful eye toward the brownstone where Emma slept.

Sophia found her way easily to the Smiling Dog Café on her own. When she reached it, she told Betty the news. "I'm so glad," Betty said. "You'll always worry—that's a mother's life. But you have a technology backup."

The coffee Betty served seemed to sharpen Sophia's editorial focus, a blend that smelled of purpose and possibility. She opened her laptop bag and showed Betty the pages her mother had written.

"Mom never finished it," she said. "She was writing a guide for other parents with heart conditions. Not the medical part - the human part. How to let your children live fully despite fear."

Betty watched as Sophia opened her editing software. "And now you have the skills to finish what she started."

Sophia began marking up the manuscript with the same precision she used for technical manuals, but this was different. Each chapter needed bridging - her mother's experience in the 1980s, Sophia's childhood in the 1990s, and Emma's story now. Three generations of medical advancement, three ways of facing the same fears.

"I can update the medical information," she said, already making notes. "Add current research, new treatments. But keep her voice - her hope, her determination to find joy despite everything."

She would weave in her own story too - all the mothers who had taught her different ways to be strong. And Emma's journey, showing how far treatment had come, how children with heart conditions could now dance, play, live without constant fear.

"A book that begins with one mother's voice," Betty said, "and ends with three generations of insight."

Sophia worked steadily for two hours, then closed the laptop and walked home in the dark, her way guided by lampposts. As she approached the apartment building, she saw the three-legged dog sitting on her haunches. Sophia caught her eye and smiled, and the dog stood and trotted off into the darkness.

When she stepped inside, the brownstone was quiet, but a moment later she heard Emma's voice. "Mom? is that you?"

Sophia found Emma curled up on the window seat, sketchbook in her lap. "You should be in bed, butterfly."

"I was drawing the café again. For Betty." Emma yawned, letting Sophia guide her back to her room. "Did you finish working on Grandma's book?"

"Not yet. But I'm getting there." Sophia led Emma to her bed and tucked the blanket around her daughter, checking the heart monitor's steady green glow. "Sweet dreams."

She sat at Emma's desk for a while, watching her daughter's peaceful breathing, thinking about all the mothers who had taught her different ways to keep vigil. When she was certain Emma was asleep, she returned to the kitchen where her laptop waited.

It was well past midnight, but once again Sophia couldn't sleep. This time, though, restlessness transformed into purpose. Her mother's manuscript lay open beside her laptop, the pages worn soft with time and handling. Each scene she edited wove together three generations of experience - her mother's courage, her own journey, and now Emma's story, stronger than both of them.

Her phone sat within reach, and for once, the sight didn't fill her with complicated emotions. When Mark's voice came through, clear despite the time difference, she heard in it the same determination she felt. "I've been thinking," he said, skipping their usual careful greetings. "About what you said regarding being present versus just providing."

Through the phone, she heard the familiar sounds of his Singapore office – keyboards clicking, muted conversations in multiple languages, the subtle whir of high-powered air conditioning.

"Mount Elizabeth Hospital is excellent," he continued. "State-of-the-art everything. But when Emma was in Langone, all that technology didn't matter as much as having you there, holding her hand."

Sophia touched the worn manuscript pages. "Sometimes the best medicine isn't medicine at all."

"I've requested a transfer back to New York." The words came out in a rush. "It might take six months to arrange, and I'll still have to travel sometimes, but... I miss her, Sophia. I miss the little things. The way she hums while she draws. How she always wants one more story at bedtime."

"She misses you too." Sophia looked at Emma's latest drawing, pinned to the refrigerator – a family portrait where Mark's figure wasn't reduced to a face on a tablet screen.

"I've been trying to protect her future so hard, I forgot to be part of her present." The background noise in his office had faded, suggesting he'd moved somewhere private. "When I heard she was in the hospital... all I could think about was your mother, and how your father buried himself in work instead of being there."

"It's not too late," Sophia said softly. "Emma's condition is manageable. We have time – time my mother didn't have, time to get things right."

"I'll come next week," Mark said. "Not just for a flying visit. I've cleared my schedule for two weeks. Maybe... maybe we could take her to The Smiling Dog Café you told me about? I'd like to see this magical place that helped you both heal."

Sophia smiled, remembering Betty's knowing eyes. "I think that's exactly where we need to go."

After they hung up, Sophia went to check on Emma. Her daughter slept peacefully, the heart monitor glowing softly on her wrist. Through the window, she caught a glimpse of parti-colored fur – Kiyomi making one last round, ensuring all was well.

Tomorrow, they would begin writing a new chapter – not just in her mother's book, but in their own story. A story about hearts that heal in more ways than one, about fathers learning to be present, about families finding their way back to each other.

Some healing happened in hospitals, with monitors and medications. Some happened in magical cafés, guided by three-legged dogs. And some, Sophia was learning, happened in the quiet moments of forgiveness, in the space between what was broken and what could still be mended.

Each day for the rest of the week, while Emma was in school, Sophia worked on the manuscript in between her editing jobs. She was happy with the way the book was evolving, bringing together everything she had learned from all the women who had raised her.

When Saturday arrived, Emma demanded to see the Smiling Dog Café herself. The morning was crisp, the streets full of fallen autumn leaves and the breath of winter in the air. Emma's cheeks held the flush of health, her curls bouncing as she practically danced in place. She was carrying her sketchbook, eager to show it off to Betty, whom she felt she already knew.

"Can I have hot chocolate?" she asked, touching the heart monitor on her wrist - sleeker than Sophia's childhood models, almost like jewelry. "My numbers have been perfect since I came home."

"We'll ask Betty to make it with extra milk," Sophia said. "You know there's only a little bit of caffeine in hot chocolate but…"

Emma interrupted her. "But Dr. Vlad says there's a stimulant in it called theobromine, and I have to be careful not to have too much of that."

"You are correct," Sophia said. "Maybe we'll make a cardiologist out of you someday."

The café's warm light spilled onto the sidewalk, but something was different. The frame where the three-legged Irish Setter's portrait had hung was empty.

Inside, Betty was helping a woman who sat where Sophia had sat that first night. The woman's hands trembled around her coffee cup, her face bearing the hollow look Sophia recognized from her own mirror during Emma's hospital stay.

A different dog sat beside the woman's chair - a Border Collie with graying muzzle, its attention focused on its charge with the same steady wisdom Kiyomi had shown.

Emma ripped out a page from her sketchbook and walked over to the woman, her steps careful but confident. "I was in the hospital," she said. "I made this drawing of the nurses because they were so good to me. They helped me feel better." She handed the page to the woman. "I think they will do the same thing for your son."

The heart monitor on her wrist blinked steadily, tracking the rhythm of a life no longer limited by fear. The woman took the page and said, "Thank you. I'll show this to my son."

Betty looked up. "Ah," she said. "I was hoping to meet Emma." She was already reaching for the hot chocolate supplies, her movements precise as a ceremony. "Emma, would you like to help me make this? Your mother tells me you're learning your way around a kitchen."

"Yes, please! With extra milk to minimize the effect of the theobromine."

"Of course," Betty said. "I was going to suggest that myself. You're an awfully smart young lady. I can see you're going to take very good care of yourself."

As Emma bounced behind the counter, Sophia studied the empty space where Kiyomi's portrait had hung. "Did something happen to..."

"She is out on the streets," Betty said simply. "Looking for someone who needs the help she can provide." She gestured to a photo album on the counter. "Each dog finds the ones who need them, leads them here, stays until the healing begins. Then they move on, making room for the next."

Sophia studied the empty frame again, understanding now. Like her mother's unfinished manuscript, it wasn't about absence but about possibility. The blank space waited not just for Kiyomi's return, but for all the stories yet to be told, all the healing yet to happen. Each guardian spirit moved through that frame like generations through time – present when needed, then stepping aside to make room for the next. Just as her mother's legacy lived on through her, and would live on through Emma, transformed but unbroken.

Betty caught her looking and smiled. "Some frames need to stay empty," she said softly, "so new healing can find its way in." She gestured to the woman holding Emma's drawing, whose tears had finally stopped. "Just as some stories need space to grow beyond their beginnings."

Sophia watched the Border Collie rest its head on the crying woman's knee, offering silent comfort. Emma was carefully sprinkling cinnamon on her hot chocolate, her movements precise as Keiko-san's tea ceremony, joyful as Isabella's samba lessons.

"Sometimes," Betty said, sliding a coffee toward Sophia - the same blend from that first night, somehow holding all the memories of her journey - "the best way to heal is to help others find their way. Your mother knew that. It's why she was writing her book, wasn't it?"

Sophia touched the laptop in her bag, where her mother's unfinished manuscript sat beside her own growing collection of stories. Tales of women who mothered with precision and spices, with protection and dance, with silence and strength. Stories of hearts that learned to beat in time with joy instead of fear.

The woman with the Border Collie was pulling out her phone, showing Betty pictures of her son in a hospital bed.

Outside, Brooklyn was busy, the autumn sun painting everything in shades of possibility. Through the café window, Sophia caught a glimpse of a white tail disappearing around a corner – Kiyomi making her rounds, finding others who needed guidance to this place of healing.

Emma settled beside her mother. "Tell me again about all my grandmothers. The ones who taught you how to be my mom."

Sophia wrapped her hands around her coffee cup, feeling the warmth of all those lessons learned across continents and years. Through the window, she watched another mother being led toward healing, another story beginning to unfold.

"Well," she began, "it started with my mother and her off-key Beatles songs..."

Author's Note

I am indebted to Alexandra Alter's *New York Times* article about healing fiction, which introduced me to this genre and inspired me to write these two novellas. My own heart resonated with this idea, as I realized it reminded me of the gentler stories I read as a kid, including the village stories of Miss Read.

As a judge for the Lilian Jackson Braun awards for Mystery Writers of America, I read over 80 cozy mysteries, and gained a clear understanding of the structure of both the cozy mystery and the romance, including a third-act crisis. Now, many times as I read, I'm dreading that big crisis—I just want to get to the happy ending.

The romances of Cat Sebastian, including *You Should Be So Lucky*, taught me that I can enjoy a story without that big crisis—a gentler story about human beings and their emotions. I hope my readers will, too, as I have ideas for many more! The next in the series is *The Bridge Between Us*, a full-length novel about the reconciliation between a brother and sister. Follow me on Facebook at https://www.facebook.com/neil.plakcy for news of new books

About the Author

After retiring from a twenty-year college teaching career, Neil Plakcy now writes full-time, kept company by his husband and their two rambunctious golden retrievers. He is fortunate to live in South Florida, where he walks the dogs under palm trees and picks sand from their toes, and he couldn't be happier about it. He has published over 70 novels in mystery, romance and adventure, and loves exploring new technologies. His website is www.mahubooks.com.

He was the kind of kid who always had a book with him, reading even when trailing behind his parents in stores. He got into e-books because it meant that if he had his phone with him, he always had something to read. His favorite genres are MM romance and cozy mysteries, with a dollop of fantasy and science fiction. He collects Starbucks bearista bears and rubber ducks, and anything to do with dogs!

Acknowledgments

Once again, Randall Klein provided outstanding editorial services, and Kelly Nichols created an adorable cover that reflects the book.

Thank you, dear readers, for your support of my books. I hope you will enjoy this new direction in my dog-centric writing. It has been inspired, as always, by the many dogs who have shared my life. And of course, what I know of love I have learned from my parents, my family, and my husband, Marc, whose care inspires me every day.

If you're so inclined, I'd love a review of this book at Amazon or wherever you get your books. It helps new readers discover the series.

And if you haven't already, please sign up for my newsletter, where I sent out regular missives about what I'm writing.

www.ingramcontent.com/pod-product-compliance
Lightning Source LLC
LaVergne TN
LVHW011949060526
838201LV00061B/4268